THE LEGACY SERIES

Praise for

Jamie Lyn Smith

Supple, deeply rooted in place, and astonishing in their bite and wit, the stories in *Township* reveal Jamie Lyn Smith's mastery of the form. The scenes and characters are searingly local, yet burst with significance onto the national literary scene, reminding us of Flannery O'Connor, Jayne Anne Phillips, and Lorrie Moore, but with an incisive presence all Smith's own. They are a cause for joy.

—David Lynn, Editor Emeritus of the *Kenyon Review*

Jamie Lyn Smith's voice rings with the authenticity of hard-won wisdom. The stories in her debut collection, *Township*, open the hearts of the broken and put-upon and finds the underside of the overlooked, the ignored, the tossed-away, the miscreant, the wild, the wandering. Despite their missteps and follies, her characters hold faith in second-chances, grace, redemption. They long to be loved and to love in return. I admire the clear-eyed portrayals of lives lived on the edge—lives that are sometimes comic, sometimes tragic, sometimes a bit of both, but always glorious in the very human tale they have to tell.

—Lee Martin, Pulitzer Prize Finalist
author of *The Bright Forever*

Township

Stories by

Jamie Lyn Smith

Cornerstone Press
Stevens Point, Wisconsin

Cornerstone Press, Stevens Point, Wisconsin 54481

www.uwsp.edu/cornerstone

Printed in the United States of America.

Library of Congress Control Number: 2021944095
ISBN: 978-1-7333086-7-0

This is a work of fiction. Names, characters, businesses, places, events, and incidents are either the products of the author's imagination or used in a fictitious manner. Any resemblance to actual persons, living or dead, or actual events is purely coincidental.

Cornerstone Press titles are produced in courses and internships offered by the Department of English at the University of Wisconsin–Stevens Point.

Director & Publisher
Dr. Ross K. Tangedal

Executive Editor
Jeff Snowbarger

Senior Editors
Lexie Neeley & Monica Swinick

Senior Press Assistants
Claire Hoenecke & Gavrielle McClung

Press Staff
Rosie Acker, CeeJay Auman, Shelby Ballweg, Kala Buttke, Caleb Feakes, Emma Fisher, Camila Freund, Kyra Goedken, Brett Hill, Adam King, Pachia Moua, Annika Rice, Alexander Soukup, Bethany Webb

For Brett Fletcher

Contents

Lake
Owl Creek
Cavalt
BORRON
Laurelton
swamp/
wetlands
River
Buckton
The Ride
Mountains
Cleveland
100
Columbus
60

Nature Preserve

There were three spots on the parks commission in the South County township election; no one ran for the third, so Ross joked that he and Cecil both won by a landslide. The job was just a trusteeship overseeing the nature sanctuary, a 100-acre forested wetland that an elderly recluse deeded the county in her will. Cecil had just retired from the department of natural resources when he first ran for the office and now, after a decade toiling at trail maintenance and policing the deer dump, along came Ross Berger. As far as Cecil knew, Ross was the same sanctimonious punk he had been in high school. Now here they stood, forty years later, toe to toe in the township hall. Colleagues.

Ross's forty-something girlfriend lurked nearby, wearing a long fuzzy sweater that appeared to be held together out of fitful chunks of gray wool. In a heathered voice, she introduced herself as "Skye, with an e" and frowned when Cecil asked if that was her given name or an assumed one. When the trustees convened, Cecil noted that Ross's jaw slacked while oathing "So help me God" and that his hand floated somewhat north of the Bible while swearing in.

Ross was a notorious local eccentric, semi-retired "environmental attorney, activist, and rabble-rouser"—Or so read his business card. It was printed on thick, handmade paper flecked with leaves and what looked like lumpy varicose veins.

"Skye makes these if you ever want some done up," Ross said.

Cecil glanced at Ross's calf-high moccasins and wanted to ask if she also chewed the leather for those moccasins; instead, he smiled politely and tucked the card into his billfold. Ross jawed on about collaborating as friends as well as colleagues and burying the hatchet.

"After all them years lawyering," Cecil said, "You wouldn't know a hatchet if it slit you sideways across the hind end."

"I guess I'll just have to learn what I don't know by watching you," Ross replied. "Especially when it comes to public relations."

Cecil's teeth locked. Ross had been breakfasting at AmVets a couple weeks back when Cecil strode in, all knuckles and pique. Cecil dropped a plastic grocery sack on Sheriff Hallinan's table, scolding him that he had some nerve littering when he was a sworn lawman. TC sifted through the contents—food cartons, mail, cigarette butts—with the end of his fork, then stood. The bassoon growl of his chair scraping against the linoleum broke the quiet.

"I appreciate your enthusiastic approach to law enforcement," TC said, "But I'm afraid you've collared the wrong perp. My mail was stole this week."

Ross saw Cecil's face redden when TC pressed the bag into Cecil's hand. "Now take this rubbish on outta here and mind your manners with a *sworn lawman.*"

Cecil stammered an apology over the hum of the onlookers' suppressed laughter then slunk out shamed as a kicked dog. Ross hadn't seen him there since. So, he said, "Let's meet down at AmVets tomorrow and come up with a plan."

"All right," Cecil replied. "I'll buy."

Skye sidled up next to Ross. He put his arm around her small waist, looping one thumb through the belt tab of her wretched sweater. She leaned in conspiratorially towards Cecil and said, "Ross is so excited about this. Really looking forward to sharing all his experience in activism and community organizing."

"The campaign is over, ma'am," Cecil replied.

Skye's smile tightened, "That must be a relief to you."

She whispered to Ross that Cecil was an asshole, just like he said. Cecil almost liked her, then. They took leave of each other in the parking lot: Cecil squeezed Skye's hand farewell, then gave her a wink when Ross closed the passenger door and made his way around to the driver's side.

Ross adjusted his mirror several times on the drive home. That had to be Cecil behind him, tailgating as usual. The men lived on opposite ends of Church Road—a two-mile long stretch of gravel that ran from their respective properties and bordered the nature preserve.

"The closer you get, the slower we go," Ross muttered, tapping the brake a few times.

They were approaching the Laurelton limits, where a park of double-wides called Country Court housed folks that Skye referred to as "the working poor." Across the road, the Pentecostal church sign proclaimed, "*This is God's Country*!" in red, pulsing light.

Ross swerved when a ball of mud and gravel skittered across the windshield and Skye cried out. He hit the brakes and glanced in the rearview mirror just in time to see a shadowy figure in a red hoodie run towards the woods.

Cecil's tires squealed and he veered into the ditch just behind them. He threw open his door and gave chase, with

Ross and Skye trailing him. The grass was wet and the turf was uneven, peppered with groundhog holes eager to wrench Cecil's knees right out of their sockets. He could hear Ross's footfalls squelching and sucking in the mud several yards back. Cecil glanced behind him, saw Skye on his heels, and stumbled. Clearing a fence, the kid melted into the woods. Cecil was bent over, hands on his knees, breathing heavily when Ross caught up to them.

"You ok?" Ross asked.

"That little sonofabitch sure can run," Cecil said.

"Get a look at him?"

"I did," Skye said. "He—"

Cecil interrupted her. "Looked like Lon Vance's boy, or one of them."

"Brandie's or Marla's?"

"Your guess as good as mine."

"Should we call the police?" Skye asked.

Cecil snickered.

"They won't come for this kind of thing, honey," Ross said. Skye frowned. Cecil asked Ross how his moccasins held up in water. Ross flipped him off. Skye whistled the theme from *The Good, The Bad, and The Ugly.*

Cecil joined her. She stopped.

Cecil shined a flashlight on the truck. "Ditch put a dent in my fender."

"Should we go talk to him?" Ross asked.

"It's been tried."

"A little compassion can go a long way," Skye said.

"So will a little putty and paint," Cecil said. "I'm getting on to supper."

He got in the truck and started the engine. Ross waved him ahead, then bright beamed him all the way to Church Road. Sonofabitch.

The next morning, Cecil and Ross hammered out an agreement to split the workload at the preserve. As they made rounds of the property and inspected equipment, Cecil cautioned Ross about the kids who snuck back there to party, ride quads, and park. The occasional reports of drug transactions in the parking lot. The elderly couple regularly spotted getting frisky in the upper reaches of the observatory deck intended for birdwatching. Despite himself, Ross shook with laughter as Cecil recounted the dialogue he'd had with an old boy he caught prying 2x6's off a footbridge, to rehab a porch.

Then there was the deer dump at the far end of the property. For as long as anyone could remember, poachers unloaded between five and fifteen carcasses during gun season alone. Dusk was falling by the time they made their way to it.

"This is our main job in the winter," Cecil said. "Look."

He pointed down into a shallow ravine just off the roadside where a tangle of bones lay whitening. A jawbone missing all but a few molars. Several femur, a shoulder, a vertebrae. A few bones bobbed in the algae-clogged water near the edge of the creek, scattered by coyotes and with deep golden blades of foxtail grass peeking up between them. The swollen and distended innards of a recent kill lay splayed out a few yards away, its ribs still magenta with meat. Flies gathered in small, blotched huddles. Two crows circled above them, cawing outrage.

"I've got me an idea about this," Ross said.

"Well goody," Cecil replied. "I'm plumb out."

After Ross left to meet Cecil, Skye rose early and painted all morning. After lunch, she started some bread and left it to rise before heading out to the preserve for a run. She jogged slowly. The woods trail was thick with the pungent smell of swamp ground, walnut hulls, and crisp leaves. or a run at the preserve.

A branch snapped and Skye stopped short. She laughed at herself and glanced around, abashed at her own edginess in the woods. Ross grew up here, but country life was an adjustment for her despite its appreciable charms. Wild apple trees. Blackberries that grew along the fencerow between fields. A red-tail hawk once flew over her with a baby rabbit in his beak, the rabbit releasing a stream of shit and a distress cry that sent her inside, shrieking for Ross. He gently reminded her that this was nature: cruel, cutthroat, survival of the fittest.

She heard a strange, whimpering bleat and stopped in her tracks. That's when she saw the boy and the deer. The fawn still had traces of its spots. It strained against a rope braided from baling twine, a ring of red flesh worn raw around its neck. The end of the rope was knotted and stuck between two limbs fallen across a downed birch. The boy tugged at the rope.

"Easy there!" she said. "I'll help you."

"Don't need no help."

"She sounds hurt."

"It's not she."

Skye stepped closer.

"Watch out, he kicks like hell. Hooves will cut you good," the boy said. He rolled his shirt sleeve up and showed her a deep purple quarter-moon bruise. "And he bites."

"Is the mother near?"

"There ain't no mother. He's mine."

He was, she would guess, maybe fifteen years old. Dark hair in a buzz cut. His face showed a bit of peach fuzz, the skin still soft and child-like around his full cheeks.

Skye took a step towards them. "You shouldn't put a rope on a deer."

"I had to. My uncles was going to kill it."

"His neck looks awfully sore."

"He run off last night and got hung up. I been looking for him all morning."

"If you hold him, I can cut him loose. I have a knife."

Skye held it out to the boy, her hand flat.

"That's a nice one," he said.

"My partner got it for me."

The boy nodded. Skye took another slow step forward, the loose earth, leaves, and twigs crunching under her running shoes. The deer raised its head up and stomped its back leg again, snorting. "Ok, get closer . . ." he urged. "Deer's like horses. If you're close, the kick idn't as strong."

Skye closed in, reaching to pet the deer's flank. She cut the rope loose in one fell. When the rope went slack, the fawn collapsed, flattening himself into the briars and fall nettles.

"They do that to hide," he said. "It's a defense mechanism."

Skye pointed to a handful of round sores on the deer's leg. "What is this?"

"My damn uncles burnt him with cigarettes. That's why I brung him."

Skye tried to relax the tension in her face. "That was really good of you to do."

"There's a old house fell in, just a basement. I been keeping him in it."

"Won't your uncles know to look there?"

"They ain't looking," he said. The boy smiled and spit on the ground. "They was going to kill him. So, I shot a different fawn, and told 'em it was him."

Skye felt nauseous.

The boy frowned. "I had to."

"See if he can walk," Skye said. The boy slid his hand underneath its body. The fawn buckled to its feet, legs trembling.

"I'd like to take him home if you'll let me," she said.

"It's my deer."

The boy pulled on the fawn's rope. It locked its knees, resisting.

"We've got a barn to keep him in. You could keep him there."

"Where do you live?"

"About a mile down the road. Out at the old Berger place."

"You his wife?"

"Ross is my life-partner."

"What the heck does that mean?"

"It means we love each other," she replied.

The boy stared at her, his jaw moving slowly, reading. Skye felt exposed by the way his eyes traveled from her face to her watch, to her dirty running shoes and mud-splattered leggings. She crossed her arms.

"Please," she said. "You could come see him anytime you want."

"If I bring him, you can't change your mind. He's still my deer."

"I promise."

The boy shifted his weight from one leg to another. The fawn used its hoof to crack open a walnut, which he ate part and parcel, with a mighty gnashing chomp.

"My car is here. Let's get him loaded up before anybody sees us, especially Cecil."

"My uncle says that guy's a prick."

"He is. Deal or not?"

She folded her knife closed and held it out to him.

"Go ahead," she said, "It's yours. My part of the bargain."

The boy took the knife, passing it between their palms when they shook hands.

Skye smiled at the boy. "I'm Skye. With an 'e.'"

"Billy. With a 'b.' This here's Buck Owens."

Skye laughed. "Like the guy from *Hee Haw*?"

"You know *Hee Haw*?"

"Ross loves that show. I used to pick on him for it, but now I'm hooked."

"It's a good show."

The deal struck, Skye jogged ahead to make sure no one was around. Billy followed, baiting Buck with sassafras leaves. She spread an old horse blanket in the hatch and Billy coaxed Buck inside, then half swaddled him.

"Keep an eye out," Billy said as he climbed in. "Buck gets loose in this car, he'll kick me half to death."

But the deer curled up next to Billy, wrapped regally in the blanket and curving his body around the boy for warmth. Skye drove home slowly, hoping and praying they wouldn't pass anyone before she had a chance to explain it all to Ross. She knew there'd be hell to pay; they'd had bad luck before with her rescue missions. The wounded squirrel that later attacked them. A crow that Skye fed kitchen scraps until it began knocking itself concussive against the picture window, went mad and sat on the porch plucking out its own feathers. Any number of stray dogs and cats that left Skye weeping and exhausted when she and Ross took them to the Laurelton shelter. How this would turn out, she didn't dare to wonder.

At the barn, they set up a stall for Buck to sleep in, with a warming lamp pressed into service from the henhouse. Billy held Buck while Skye dubbed salve on the deer's wounds. Skye invited Billy to supper, asking him if he needed to call his mother and tell her where he was. Billy responded by asking if she needed him to carry in a few pieces of wood for the fire. She nodded, washed her hands, and started dinner.

Billy was sitting at the kitchen table carving a piece of wood and Skye was putting the bread in the oven when Ross appeared in the doorway, Cecil behind him, both of them shouting "Hello . . ." The men froze when they saw Billy.

"Well, well, well," Ross said, kissing her on the cheek. "What have we here?"

"Good lord," Cecil said. He turned to Skye. "Do you know who this is?"

Billy's shoulders jerked, reflexively.

"Yes," she said, not turning around from the sink. She put her elbow into scrubbing at a stubborn bit of grease stuck to a pot. "Cecil, this is Billy Vance."

Cecil said, "Little sonofabitch that threw rocks at the car last night."

Billy's face tightened.

"What's going on here?" Ross asked.

"Billy," she said. "Go ahead and tell them what you want to say."

Billy cleared his throat. He had been in trouble enough to know what was expected of him. "I'm sorry about the vehicles."

Skye beamed at him. Ross looked at Skye, then Billy.

Cecil frowned at the boy. "You came here to apologize?"

"Hell no," The boy shook his head no. "She invited me."

"That isn't the half of it," Skye said, opening the oven door. The kitchen filled with the scent of fresh-baked bread. "Care to join us?"

Later, when Cecil would recall the evening—and he had a great deal of trouble doing so, as did Ross, for they drank a lot that night—he would see how much he underestimated Skye-with-an-e. She charmed Ross with the tale of how Billy rescued the fawn. She shot down Cecil's objections about imprinting, nanny states, and feral-versus-domestic animals with a request for his considerable expertise in recuperating Buck. Ross jumped in with a mini-lecture on the appropriate mix of goat and sweet milk. Soon the two men were in lively debate about how to teach foraging, the importance of mimicking animal play, and various methods of repatriating deer to the wild. Billy reminded them that it was his deer.

At the table, Skye kept refilling their wine glasses. Talk shifted from Buck to Billy when Cecil pointed out that the deer indicated the boy had some sense. But did Billy plan to remedy Cecil's misconception that he was an irredeemable delinquent, or just sit around sucking down quarts of chili that didn't even have meat in it?

"I'll fix the cars," Billy said.

"No thanks," Cecil replied, at the same time Ross said, "You don't say?"

"My uncles taught me." Billy sat a little straighter in his chair. "I been tinkering since I could barely see over a beer."

"What a ringing endorsement," Cecil said.

But Ross urged the boy on, and Billy rattled off a list of things he could fix: dirt bikes, lawn mowers, chainsaws, weed whackers, and all things 2-cycle. Cecil noticed that Skye's eyes smiled approvingly at Ross over the rim of her teacup. It wasn't long before Ross and Cecil were in a heated exchange over just who would supervise the boy, while Skye opened another bottle of wine.

After dessert, Skye helped Billy write out an agreement to work off the damages. The boy would work ten hours a week at the nature preserve for the next two months. Billy was responsible for Buck's care and eventual repatriation to the wild. Cecil was at least of wit enough to insist that if Billy missed an hour of work for any reason, including sickness, he must work two to make it up.

"Hardass." Skye said. Cecil shrugged. The men signed. Skye witnessed.

By ten o'clock, Cecil's brain was swelling. He walked home, enjoying the half hour of crisp air between his door and Ross's. He glanced up at the stars and saw a lone apple, still good enough for eating, hanging from a branch. He bit into it, the cold fruit rough against his tongue. He turned his neck to wipe his chin on his shirt collar, the green twill rustling against his corduroy coat. He slept well that night, better than he had in a long while.

Mondays, Wednesdays, and Fridays, Billy roared and backfired into the nature preserve on a little dirt bike his uncles procured for him. He was quite adequate at the work they gave him, showing up when he was supposed to. He sweated alongside them: fixing the footbridges, spreading wood chips to fill marsh trail, and hauling brush. Cecil was pleased to see how much the boy already knew—he could sling a wrench, change oil on the Gator, replace belts and tires and the like. Billy even helped with the slow and stinking work at the deer dump, tossing bones into the fire, ripping up hides fused to the grass. They wore bandanas over their faces as they burnt the remains, tears leaving streaks of soot in the creases of their eyes from the thick, white smoke of burning bone.

When Ross's camera arrived, they all agreed it was a beauty. The scope on it would pan nearly 180 degrees, texting both Ross and Cecil an alarm when its digital beam captured movement by anything larger than sixty pounds. It operated flash-free, offering no warning to vandals or signal where they might shoot out its lens. Photos would be delivered directly to Ross's email, and the live-feed option let him project the surveillance in real time and zoom in if he saw something. Billy himself pegged his way up the poplar tree, wired it and wrapped it in camo tape, patting it like a baby before descending to high-five Ross and Cecil.

As the fall turned down into winter and the first snow fell, Buck improved. By Thanksgiving, his spots disappeared, his coat turned a rich, field-mouse brown. He gained weight, abandoned the goat's milk for forage. Buck became a fixture on Church Road, bounding alongside Skye when she went jogging, greeting vehicles at the mailbox, startling the FedEx delivery man and charming neighbors into leaving treats out for him—a few apples, some oatmeal, a pile of hickory nuts.

Billy was changing, too. He rushed home from school to romp with Buck, the two of them sparring, charging, feinting, and butting heads. Buck learned to jump in and out of Cecil's truck bed and the cargo hold of the Gator, turning his nose to the wind as they cruised around on work calls. Buck sent a thrill through the lunchtime crowd at AmVets, standing patiently by the deck waiting for Billy to feed him applesauce from a Styrofoam dish.

Cecil struggled to rid himself of a lingering unease. He tested the boy, leaving loose change—just a dollar or two—sitting around, to see if the kid would swipe it. He sent him on errands and counted the change carefully when Billy returned. It was always exact, always honest. There were many days when Billy was extraordinarily preoccupied or sullen. Ross attributed it to adolescent temperament, Skye fretted, and Cecil suggested shiftiness.

Skye struck her own deal with the boy: he could stay for dinner any night he wanted, so long as he did his homework first and carried in firewood. Ross half-grumbled that he had to take a number to make time with her anymore. Cecil frequently joined them, handing Skye a bag of collard greens as his contribution to the meal. Cecil caught himself wishing he'd grown a better stand of them, covering the plot with straw when the mercury dipped to keep the plants going. All because Skye smiled and sometimes touched his shoulder to thank him. And because her gesture made Ross bare his teeth at Cecil from across the room.

And that is how they wound up a motley crew: Skye with her turquoise jewelry and artist's soul, Ross and his love of a worthy cause, the Boy, as Cecil came to think of him, who loved that deer, and Cecil—an old turkey, the lonely widower.

It doesn't change a damn thing, Cecil thought.

Just for show, once a week or so he would decline Skye's invitation, swinging his front door open to reveal the dark and hollow home he used to share with Angie. But over the weeks and months, fewer evenings groaned under the weight of his contemplative silence. His plates saw less of the standard bachelor's rotation of Dinty Moore canned stew, frozen corn, and game meat. Soon, he was at the Bergers as often as Billy was, and the four of them—five, if you counted Buck—settled into a routine.

The men worked all through October, into November's first hard frosts. Billy's indenture, as they jokingly came to call it, had been over for a few weeks when Cecil and Ross decided to pool their salaries and pay the boy for staying on. Billy took the money quietly each week, two crisp $20 bills in an envelope, with a nod of acknowledgement. At Thanksgiving, Ross and Skye traveled to see her family in Rye. Cecil dined with his mother at the nursing home, reminding her of his name every few minutes and supping on turkey the consistency of damp cardboard. Billy didn't mention much about his holiday, only that they got their box from the Baptist church, and his mother cooked it while his uncles sat in the garage. For Christmas, Skye would have none of this "diaspora" as she called it.

"Whatever the hell that is," Cecil groused.

"It means you need to be here at six on Christmas Eve," she said. "And bring up some collard greens the day before."

Cecil pulled into the drive at five past the hour. Ross met him with a beer, and Skye called hello from the kitchen. The men ate squares of cheese and good deer sausage off a gruesome aqua-and-orange star-shaped ceramic plate—handcrafted by Skye, of course. He made a point of complimenting her on it, while they all made small talk and wondered what the hell was keeping Billy.

Ross was about to start the Gator and go looking for him when they heard his footsteps on the porch. Nearly ashen with cold, Billy went directly to the fire, the pouch of his red sweatshirt bulging with odd-shaped lumps.

"I can't stay," Billy said. "Mom said I had to just run up to drop off presents."

"That's no way to act . . ." Cecil began.

"Oh Billy, that's too bad," Skye said. "We were expecting you."

"She wants me home," he said. "All my uncles are getting into it."

Skye looked confusedly at Ross. He tipped a glass to his lips. Ross gestured Billy over to the tree to open his gifts.

"Don't be shy, Billy," Ross said, "Tear in."

The boy opened Ross and Skye's gift first, lifting out a brand new Carhartt jacket and gloves. He unwrapped Cecil's next: a pair of good work boots, some long johns with a button seat, and a set of hand tools. Billy turned the items over and over in his hands, as though they might break. He shook his head. There was a small silence, which no one filled with the right words. Billy flicked the zipper of the jacket back, forth, clicking. A jazzy version of "The First Noel" oozed out of the speakers.

"Thank you," Billy said. "You all . . . you spent way too much on me. This is more'n I could ever do."

"You been working hard," Cecil said.

Billy reached into his sweatshirt and dropped a pile of three packages onto the table. They were wrapped in white tissue, tied neatly with red ribbon, labeled with each of their names.

"You first," Billy said, passing one to Skye.

"There's an 'e' in my name," she said.

"I know. Done it on purpose."

He passed one to Cecil, and Ross.

Skye unwrapped the paper and held the small carving up to the light. It was a small statue of a woman hand-feeding a fawn.

"Why, it's beautiful!" She hugged him. "Billy, thank you."

Cecil's carving was an eagle, wings spread wide, a snake writhing in its beak. Billy gave Ross a calling fox, with a litter of three small kits next to her.

"This must have taken you days and days to do," Ross marveled.

"Somebody give me a good knife, once," Billy said, flipping it into the air and catching it. Ross looked at Skye and raised his eyebrows.

"They're all so beautiful," Skye repeated. She cleared the mantle of the manger scene and set her gift atop it in the center.

"Let's eat," Cecil said.

Billy ducked his head. "I really ought to be getting back. They got things they want me to do."

"I can fix you a plate to take with you," she said. "Plenty for your mother, too . . ."

"That's all right," he replied. "There's food there."

"Thanks for the boots, Cecil." Billy said. "I'm sorry I can't stay."

"You can't very well take all that on the bike," Skye said.

"I was going to keep these things here . . . where I'll use 'em."

"That's silly," Skye said. "I'll drive you home."

Ross and Cecil exchanged a look. Billy fixed his gaze on the floor.

"I'd rather you didn't leave." Ross said, taking Skye's hand.

Her apron was already on a hook by the door. She nodded to Ross. "You two can put the food out and I'll be right back."

Ross started the car up while Skye got her coat.

Billy gathered up the wrapping paper and put his jacket carefully back into the box. "Didn't mean to make such a mess," he said. "I do wish I could stay."

"No problem at all, Billy," Cecil said. "Family is family."

Billy wished them a merry Christmas, and Skye reminded Ross to stir the gravy. Ross and Cecil watched them drive into the night. Whorls of snow spiraled up into the air from the drifts. Usually they would have bickered about the temperature trudged out to the barn thermometer to settle the contest. Tonight, they stood at the window weighing shared disappointment, until Ross turned to Cecil and said, "Flip a coin over who sets the table." Cecil handed him a quarter and called tails.

Billy directed Skye as she drove through Country Court, instructing her to follow the gravel lane then turn right, left, and another left. Skye had never been inside the park, and she felt keenly how majestic the house she shared with Ross must seem by comparison.

"This is it." Billy said. Skye glanced out the window. The place was tidy, and there were lights on in the trailer. There were several cars and pickups parked outside. Straw bales stacked around the perimeter to keep out the winter draft and snow. A pup in the yard, asleep in its dog box, the roof painted the same rusty brown as the carport. Billy already had his seatbelt loose and his door ajar when Skye rolled the station wagon to a stop.

Brandie Vance came to the door in new jeans and a pressed shirt. Her hair was tied back in a ponytail, a bit of gray working its way up from the roots. Her eyes were dark and deep-set. Skye had hoped to talk to Billy, but he simply leaned his head in the door, thanked her, and took his boxes from the backseat. He crunched across the frozen ground up to the porch. Brandie stepped aside to let him enter. Skye waved at her; Brandie only nodded and slipped into the trailer behind her son.

It was around 9:00 p.m. on Christmas night when Ross's phone blinked and let out a piercing tone. Skye was on her third glass of wine, and Ross was looking forward to turning out the lights and taking her to bed early. He jumped out of bed and hurried to check the camera. He was in his boots and out the door before Skye could pull on her pajamas.

"Watch the camera," Ross said. Then, he jumped into Cecil's truck and was gone. She stared at the laptop screen, pulling her robe closed and shivering a little. There were three men in hooded jackets, but she could see their faces plain as day. One looked familiar, but she could not place him. He walked directly to the camera and raised a pistol. There was a white flash, then the dull throb of blue screen. When Ross and Cecil arrived at the deer dump, the poachers were already gone.

The game warden arrived the next day to investigate. He took the footage and some photos and asked a few questions. Cecil and Ross were slow to clean up the mess: it was bitter cold, and Billy was off work until after New Year's. It was nearly a week before the weather broke and they could get to the mess. They set into a rhythm, picking up pieces of the deer and tossing them into the fire. The acrid stench of burning meat tinted the air a gritty brown, and they took turns adding brush to the fire to raise smoke. Between the roaring of the fire and stomping through the brush, the men never heard Billy. He stood at the edge of the ditch, in the boots Cecil bought for him and that same old, red hooded sweatshirt.

"Where's your coat?" Ross called, grinning.

"You had the sheriff put papers out on Uncle Reed," Billy said to Cecil.

"Huh?" Ross said, "What's the matter?"

"He's gonna go to jail."

"Won't be nothing new for him, will it?" Cecil said, leaning against his shovel.

"What are you talking about?" Ross asked Cecil. Cecil kept his eyes on Billy.

The boy clenched his hands into fists. "They wasn't hurting nobody."

"They were polluting a stream, illegally dumping carcasses, and poaching," Cecil snapped. He pointed his shovel towards a headless carcass, a ripe line of flesh missing where the back straps had been cut out. "There's fifty, sixty pounds of meat wasted."

"Who died and made you game warden?" the boy said. "We eat the meat that we can."

"You should have told me," Ross hissed at Cecil.

"He'll have to do time," Billy said. "He can't afford no fine. He lives on disability."

"He gets around good enough to hunt and sell dope," Cecil said. "I'm sure he'll cough up the money somehow."

"Billy," Ross said. "I did not know a thing about it—"

"He did though," Billy said to Cecil, pointing. "You knew who he was as soon as you saw his face. You could have talked to him like you done me, and given him a chance to make it right. Now they got him on all sorts of charges."

The boy had worked his way down the slope and stood chest to chest with Cecil. "Admit it," he said, "You knew."

Cecil nodded. "I suspected."

"You should have done it man to man," Billy snapped. "Instead of hiding behind the law like a damn coward."

Ross held his hand up. "Slow down, now. We're all friends here."

"Friends? Fuck no," Billy said. "You think you're going to feed me and tame me same as that deer. Well, I ain't your pet."

"That isn't it—" Ross said.

"And you?" Billy hissed at Cecil, "You think I don't know better than to pick up the change you leave in the truck to test me? Don't test me. I done passed all your tests."

Billy strode over to his dirt bike, threw his leg over the seat. Ross could see the hurt in his eyes as the boy fired up the motor and cast his heel against the kickstand. He peeled out, scattering gravel, and veered up the road. Then he was gone.

Cecil picked up a deer leg, and tossed it onto the pile.

"Better get back to work," he said.

Days went by, then a few weeks. Every now and then Ross and Skye would see footprints, Buck's tracks alongside them. Cecil said to give the boy time to cool off. Ross caught himself taking the road past Country Court, hoping to glimpse Billy. Skye left meals in the barn for Billy in a cooler, hoping he'd pick them up. She slipped notes into the care packages, a few dollars here and there, but it all remained untouched.

By the end of February, Billy's uncles were indicted, charged, and convicted. The sheriff's search of the property yielded all sorts of contraband, and Reed Vance made the front page of the paper when the incident sent him up to Orient prison for three years. Billy's other uncles got time served, a year's probation, and a fine.

At the township meeting that night, the trustees recognized Ross and Cecil for their work in catching the poachers. A photo was taken for the local paper, the game warden and Sheriff Hallinan flanking them. Neither Cecil nor Ross managed much of a smile in it. Cecil went to the AmVets for a beer and Ross and Skye headed home, headlights bouncing along the snow. An inch or two had fallen since suppertime, and Ross wasn't surprised to see footprints from the woods, leading to the barn. Skye saw them, too. She started for the barn, but Ross called her back to the house.

"I think we best leave him alone tonight," Ross said. "He'll come to us when he wants to."

Billy waited in the stall. He petted Buck and bribed him with sweet grain until Ross and Skye went inside. He waited while they settled in. An hour passed. Another half hour, and the house was dark.

Billy coaxed the deer into the cargo bed of the Gator, urging Buck to sit low and close to the floor, legs folded beneath him. He slipped the vehicle into neutral and pushed it out of the barn. He ought to be able to get enough momentum on it to coast the slight incline to attain the road, then they were home free. Billy heard a soft thud and click when Buck hopped out. He stopped, led Buck back into the cargo hold and gave the Gator another shove. Buck hopped out again. Billy gave up and let the deer trot alongside as he coasted into the open, snow croaking under the slow-rolling tires. The weight of the vehicle cracked the icy drive, sending up a sound stark and concise as the report of a rifle. The Gator lurched and rolled backward slightly.

The noise startled Skye out of bed, and she hurried to the window. "It's Billy."

"Call Cecil," Ross replied, clambering down the stairs.

"Billy!"

Billy turned and saw Skye. He fired up the Gator and whistled for Buck. This time, Buck jumped into the cargo hold and stayed. Billy took off as fast as he could up Church Road with Buck bouncing along beside him, head bobbing, their two shadows dark against the snow.

Cecil was there within minutes, the vinyl seats of the truck crackling cold when Ross slipped into the passenger side.

"Hurry!" Skye said.

"He won't get far," Ross said. "Gator's just about out of gas."

"I filled it up tonight," Cecil sighed. "Figuring we'd need to clear snow tomorrow."

"I think I know where he'll go," Skye said. "That old house, with the basement. He kept Buck there before we took them in."

Cecil turned off Church, to the tractor lane leading back to the old estate. His headlights caught fresh tracks: the wheelbase of the Gator was narrow, easy to follow.

Cecil pointed ahead and said "I think I see something."

As they crested the hill, Skye gasped. "Holy shit. He's got Buck."

"What the hell is he thinking," Ross said.

Buck's eyes glowed red and large in the glare of their headlights. The deer knelt on the floor of the cargo hold. Billy glanced back every now and then, driving with one arm on Buck's back. The deer raised his nose up to the air, catching scent as they drove.

Cecil pulled up close and honked, flashing his lights. He motioned for Billy to pull over. He saw Buck teeter.

"Shit," he muttered.

"Billy! Stop!" Skye shouted.

"Drop back," Ross said. His voice was reedy with nerves.

Cecil downshifted as snow, mud, and gravel flicked up on the windshield. Billy's head jerked and the Gator lurched low when it hit the pothole, bouncing the vehicle upward.

Buck's body spun free of the vehicle, rolling through the air as if in an undertow, Ross's arms braced against the dash. Cecil cursed and prayed for the truck to stop as they absorbed the impact of the deer rolling up the hood, into the windshield. When the truck stopped, Buck rolled off the hood and to the ground.

Skye rushed to the deer, put her hands on Buck's neck and abdomen. She sounded like she was choking or heaving, repeating, "What have you done, what have you done?" when Cecil and Ross got there.

"He's breathing," Cecil said.

And he was. Buck's chest heaved. His stomach had black splotches from internal bleeding, his small body slowly filling with and drowning in its own blood. Billy's boots pounded up to them. He knelt next to Skye, and lay his head on the deer's neck, sobbing that he didn't mean to, that he was sorry, that it was all his fault. Cecil could smell the musky scent of Buck's hide and the deer's ragged breaths were hot on his hand.

"I just wanted to get my deer," Billy said.

Ross put his hand on the boy's shoulder, but Billy shrugged it off. Ross clamped down again, this time harder, and snatched the boy to his feet.

"You know what to do," Ross said. "You better do it and get it over with."

"No, no—" Billy cried.

Ross took a handful of the boy's coat and grabbed Billy's knife, jerking it loose of its clip.

"What are you doing?" Skye said. "Let him go."

"He's going to put him down," Ross said.

"No, Ross," Cecil said. His vocal cords felt clogged.

"Do it," Ross said, shaking Billy. "You've got a good knife."

"I can't," he whispered.

"You dumbass," Ross said. "Do it."

"No, Ross," Cecil said, trying to steady his voice. "Don't."

"Quick and clean," Ross said.

"No!" Skye said. "All of you shut up!"

She stroked Buck's head, cradling him. His eyes were dimming, his tongue hung out of his mouth and a bit of wine-colored blood trickled from one corner of his mouth onto Skye's jacket.

"Do it." Ross ordered Billy. He pressed the knife into the boy's hand. "It's the least you can do."

Billy's hand folded around the knife. He drew a deep breath, pulled back his arm, and threw it into the field. It circled end over end over end through the sharp air, then disappeared with a small thud into the field where the graying yarrow and dried brown stalks of ironweed peeked up through the snow. Ross told Billy that he was one dumb son of a bitch.

"I know," Billy replied.

Billy crouched down by Buck, and sat on his haunches, rocking. Skye didn't even look up. "I'm sorry," Billy kept saying. "Skye, I'm so sorry."

"All of you shut up," Skye whispered. She tried to soothe the deer, running her hand along his neck. "Just shut up."

The four of them sat with Buck. Skye held the deer's head in her lap, while Billy petted Buck's side. It took a while. Finally, the deer shuddered, his legs seizing stiff. Buck sighed, and his hooves rested on the ground. A great retch of blood and bile reddened the snow, and it was over.

Skye was silent, riding in the cargo and holding Buck on the ride to the far side of nature preserve. The ground was too icy and would not give for burying, so they drove to a pile of large field stone along the property line. Cecil and Billy lifted Buck to the ground. His body was starting to stiffen. Ross, Cecil, and Billy gathered one stone after another, piling them on top of the deer. Skye helped, staggering back and forth from the rock pile to the cairn.

"At least we kept the coyotes off him," Billy said, when the job was done.

Afterward, Ross drove the Gator home, while Cecil and Billy dropped Skye off.

"I'm sorry, Skye," Billy said. "Tell Ross I'm sorry."

She nodded, thanked Cecil for the ride home, and went inside.

It was well past two in the morning when Cecil finally got Billy back to Country Court, hoping and praying no one would see the two of them smeared in blood, dried tears streaking their dirty faces. When Billy got out of the vehicle, Cecil grabbed the boy's arm and said, "You call me anytime you want to. All right?"

Billy nodded and whispered "Thank you. I'm sorry. I didn't mean to."

Cecil wanted to offer the boy some comfort, say the right words, but he did not. It would not change a thing.

Deprivation of Body, Generosity of Spirit

Akāliko: timeless, unconditioned by time or season.

When it all came apart with Brian, Tess called Brooke—rather than any number of other friends—because she knew that Brooke would not allow her to devolve into self-pity. They'd been friends their whole lives, playing varsity basketball in high school, rooming together at Baron. The two of them ran the college co-op bookstore, selling dusty, outdated volumes of *Norton Anthology of English Literature* and *Principles of Biochemistry*. The books gave the girls' hair a not-so-faint scent of decaying paper, a scent they fought with pyres of incense and bowl after bowl of weed. They had study parties, spaghetti dinners, muumuu movie nights, beginner ballet classes in the backyard, a failed composting experiment, and two illegal tabby cats. After graduation, Brooke left for the Peace Corps, but Tess stayed in the county to run her father's grain operation. For many years, Brooke had Zach, and for much longer, Tess thought she had Brian. Their lives fell into a rhythm of couplehood as they rehabbed her family's old farmhouse. They hooked her grandparents' 1961 Aeroflyte camper to Brian's truck and spent lazy summers along the river, taking weeklong jaunts to Savannah, Santa Fe, Austin, and other points south when the weather turned foul each February.

Now, Tess felt like a nerve ending rubbed raw and left twitching. She could not think about Brian without tearing up; the skin around her eyes was dry as paper, creased lines radiating out from each corner. The scent of juniper and cold air snapped at her lips as she took one deep breath after another. She didn't want to remember the scene at the farm: Brian packing his things into the truck and driving away from her, from them, driving towards Randy's house.

There were signs I missed, Tess thought, steering the jeep along the narrow road. The inordinate amount of time Brian spent on call at the firehouse. The way he insisted on "guy night" each week. Golf in the summer, bowling in the winter, deer camp in the fall, a week on the Florida coast each spring. Tess's tongue turned to felt and shame brought heat to her cheekbones when she thought about that night on the farm computer. She was logging in to look for a message from a colleague in Wichita about a grain hybrid that Monsanto was pushing hard to Ohio growers. Shuffling papers on her desk, she didn't realize she clicked on Brian's credentials. She glanced up to see a chat window, a window he shared with Randy.

I can't go on like this, it said.

I don't know how to tell Tess, Brian replied.

I love you, Randy wrote. *You love me . . . What's holding us back?*

I think I stayed with her so long because she kept me away from you, he said.

Tess read on and on. Three years of Brian's correspondence with Randy. Months of love letters to another man before that, someone Tess did not know, a police officer from the city. And others—mostly hookups. Many others. She printed the emails out and sat waiting for Brian at the kitchen table. It was just after the solstice, and dark by 4:30 in the afternoon, when Brian walked in the door, stomping the snow from his boots. The silver nameplate on his uniform refracted a glare across the kitchen when it caught the light.

"Sit down," Tess said.

"What's up?" he asked. His pace slowed as he approached the kitchen table, wary as a hound. He lowered himself into a chair.

She pushed the stack of emails toward him. Brian read them with a hand curved over his mouth. Tess felt almost sorry for him. She waited for him to tell her it was a lie, a joke, a misunderstanding. He leafed through each one, turning the pages faster and faster, his face darkening. There was tightness to his jaw when he finally spoke.

"What the fuck," he asked, "are you doing snooping in my business?"

"All you had to do was tell me." Tess said. "I would have been content to leave."

He circled around the table, his face so near hers she felt her throat thicken.

"You better keep your mouth shut about this."

"You worry about you." Tess said. "I'll worry about me."

Brian spun her toward him, gripped her shoulders and backed her against the wall. Later, Tess told her friend everything except that. She never told anyone about the sudden reach of Brian's hand for her jaw, the shove, the slap, his breath in her eyes, the bruises on her shoulder blades, the marks on her wrists and arms. She would only tell Brooke that it got ugly and that she had changed the locks at the farm.

Brooke asked if that was all that happened, and Tess lied, "Yeah." After the briefest too-long pause, Brooke ordered Tess to *Akāliko*, stat. "It's a healing place," she said. "Come see me and rest. The last thing you need is to be alone right now."

Tess eased the Jeep into the drive at *Akāliko* and tried to steel herself for the public display of calm that this visit would require of her. She cut the engine and listened to the river thrashing against the dingy gray snow in the valley. Brooke flung open the door and ran towards her with her arms open. Pulling her into a hug, Brooke rocked her side-to-side.

"I'm so glad you're here! So so so glad!"

Tess rallied enough to thank Brooke for having her. She'd tried so hard, after all, to get Tess excited about the annual New Year's party. There would be a DJ, a whisky tasting, potluck meals, cross-country skiing, yoga classes, and workshops on spiritual harmony. Tess was disinterested in each of these, but determined to bear it all for the sake of company. She shrugged her backpack to her shoulder, while Brooke hefted the crate of food Tess brought for the potluck from the cargo hold.

"Bare feet and off-grid in the ashram!" Brooke reminded her, leading Tess into the foyer. She'd been skeptical a few years back, when Brooke first announced her intention to move in with Andrew and run the ashram. He'd come into the property at *Akāliko* after his parents gifted it to him. Then they headed west for states where marijuana had recently been legalized, to build multi-purpose communities in dispensaries and expand their empire of spiritual wellness workshops and low-level weed trafficking. Tess had to admit she'd been wrong; Brooke thrived here. She all but glowed as she gently plucked the phone from Tess's hand and tossed it into a handwoven basket.

"How are you doing, honey?" Brooke asked.

Tess sat down on the floor to unlace her boots. "I want to die."

"Great!" Brooke said. "I can see you're going to be a real charmer this weekend."

"It's true," Tess said. "What do you want me to say?"

Brooke's boyfriend Andrew wandered in. A shamanic healer by trade, his tone always made Tess feel as if she were being lectured. Not just lectured but lectured in an NPR voice by someone who spouted Zen-wisdom desktop calendar aphorisms. Andrew had carved these sorts of sayings—sayings that Tess found just a tad too smug—into the woodwork above each door in the ashram. *Timeless,* proclaimed one doorway. *Unconditioned by time or spirit,* smirked another.

Bullshit, Tess thought. Time changes everything. Except maybe these two.

Brooke and Andrew remained in a hazy, honeymoon phase years after Tess and Brian casually introduced them at the farm's annual harvest party. At the time, Brooke had recently returned from her Peace Corps stint in Guatemala, heartbroken and mooning over an acrimonious breakup with Zach. Tess thought Andrew would be a fleeting distraction, a fun rebound romance. They were on-again, off-again for two years, while Brooke ran hot-cold, leaving him again and again for other men, other countries, other gurus, returning intermittently to rekindle things at her convenience. It wasn't until Andrew cut ties with Brooke and became engaged to a svelte, blonde ski instructor that Brooke returned to the township for good. She set up her massage table and hung her shingle in the village of Cavalle. Brooke befriended the ski instructor, and then introduced the blonde to a handsome surgeon. Within a few months, Brooke was ensconced at *Akāliko* with Andrew, and the ex-fiancée was living in a subdivision in New Albany, wearing mall khakis and making hors d'oeuvres.

"Tess?" Andrew asked. "You still in there?"

"Tess is preoccupied with healing.," Brooke said, patting Tess's arm.

"It's ok," Andrew nodded, placing a hand on his chest. "We understand."

"I mean, I'm grateful you guys let me come here—" Tess said.

"Let you?" Brooke said. "We *want* you here."

Brooke stared at Andrew. He blinked, ran his hand through his beard. "We sure do," he said, *mala* beads clicking in his hand. "We hardly ever get to see you."

"Well, I hope you're ready to have some fun," Brooke said, brushing a chunk of auburn hair back from her face. "Let's get this stuff into the kitchen."

Tess followed Brooke and put the crate on the counter, letting her and Andrew rifle through it. They ooh'ed and ahh'ed at the home-canned jars of vegetable soup, blackberry jam, peaches for a cobbler.

"Is this your starter?" Andrew asked, spinning around the jar of beige, spongy-looking sourdough.

"Sure is."

Andrew lifted a bag of flour out of the crate, frowning, and then set it aside. "I didn't know Pillsbury made whole wheat flour."

"We grow grain for that company," Tess said, patting her bag of flour. "Good grain."

"But organic makes such a difference . . ."

Tess bit back a sharp reply, reminding herself that Andrew had been all but brainwashed into rejecting all normal food by hippie parents. Tess's lunchbox had been full of Hostess Twinkies; his had probably been full of handcrafted kale bars.

"It's true," Brooke said. "Andrew went to a seminar with a man who is a professional techno-emotional cuisinist—"

"Are you freakin' kidding me?" Tess asked.

"No seriously, just listen—"

Tess tried to follow the logic as Brooke drew out a complicated theory weaving intuition, the *Bhagavad Gita*, "mindful cookery," and "culinary-emotional intent."

"You're overcomplicating it, dear," Andrew said, wrapping his arms around Brooke's waist and beaming at her. Tess waited for him to pat Brooke on the head as if she were a hapless puppy. "This chef can tell by the way the bread tastes if the person kneading it was angry, or discouraged, or upset, or in love . . . it's amazing."

"Indeed," Tess said.

"I was skeptical too," Brooke giggled. "But I can tell by the way Andrew makes my tea that he loves me."

Andrew kissed her, and their lips lingered. Tess tried not to hate their guts.

"Why don't you let us catch up?" Brooke said, gently pushing him back a bit, glancing at Tess.

Andrew squeezed Brooke's hand and said, "I'll be in the meditation center."

"Enjoy yourself," Tess said, cringing as soon as the words flew out of her mouth.

"You should join me sometime." Andrew's calm smile was soothing, but Tess shook her head.

"Self-reflection? Ha! Tess never touches the stuff. We prefer brown liquor," Brooke said.

"Thanks," Tess said, after Andrew left. "I never mean anything the way it sounds, lately."

"I know, kid," Brooke said. "I've been there, myself."

Brooke showed her upstairs to the tiny loft where Tess would sleep. The room was made of polished timber so beautiful that Tess felt as if she were suspended in amber.

"You guys have done a ton of work here," Tess marveled.

"Andrew and I planed all these beams," Brooke said watching Tess take in the room. "We're thinking of adding on more sleeping quarters, but for now . . . welcome home."

"Nice bean bag." Tess said, gesturing towards a circular, tufted tapestry cushion on the floor. It was thick, with intricate embroidered rabbits and fawns.

"It's a zabuton," Brooke said.

"Where we come from," Tess reminded her, "it's a bean bag."

Brooke laughed. "Everything here is special."

Tess flopped down onto the zabuton. "Especially you."

Brooke lay down next to her.

"Doesn't it get a bit overwrought?" Tess asked. "All of it?"

"You know," Brooke said, "I was drifting around so much when Andrew and I first got together that I find I really treasure this . . . purposefulness. I'm so busy minding the small things that the big things fall into place. And, I mean, we space out sometimes too, it's not like this is a Netflix-free zone."

"You probably know every line from *Gandhi*," Tess said.

Brooke hit her with a throw pillow. "Thanks to you."

Tess laughed. They lay silent for a while. Tess heard a lone, winter fly buzzing and listened, following the sound to the skylight. She pointed at it, and Brooke nodded. It buzzed again. Brooke glanced around theatrically. "Andrew's busy. We can kill the little sonofabitch!"

She swatted and missed. They laughed and fell quiet again.

The fly landed on Tess's knee. She smashed it. Brooke grinned.

"Done," Tess said.

"How are you, honestly?" Brooke asked.

"I'm really, really devastated," Tess said. "Totally betrayed and heartbroken."

"Well . . . that's understandable. Here you don't have to think about him at all. Just make yourself have fun this weekend . . . who knows, maybe you'll meet someone?"

"I don't want to meet someone. I want him to come back."

"Why?" Brooke snapped. "Why on earth would you want Brian back?"

"I still love him," Tess said.

"What are you, like a total doormat?" Brooke said. "He was terrible to you."

He was. Tess knew it was true. Everything she was hanging on to about what they had been was a lie, but she wanted more time to tell that lie to herself before coaxing herself into letting go of it. She still woke each morning expecting the weight of Brian's arm across her waist. Now he woke up that way with Randy. Tess could not stand it.

"Brooke," Tess said, biting back tears, "Would it hurt your feelings if I went to Cavalle tonight and slept in a hotel?"

"Why? No, no, and no!" Brooke said.

"I just . . . I really want to be alone, okay? I feel like crying all night. I don't want to do that in a sleeping loft while you guys are having sex, like, ten feet from my bed."

"We aren't going to have sex," Brooke said. "It's full moon, and we're observing Five-Precepts."

Tess reluctantly asked what the fuck Five-Precepts meant, launching Brooke onto a tangent about deprivation building sensual response, restraint shoring up spirit of intimacy. Tess focused on a shelf of animal figurines. A zebra. A jackal. A water buffalo. Anything but the mating rituals of Brooke and Andrew. Or Brian and everybody.

"By the way," Brooke said, "Zach is in town and he's coming to the party. Did I tell you he called me?"

"No," Tess said. "How's Andrew with that?"

"Andrew is always chill. Zach called to see if it was all right, and I said I didn't mind. I bet he thinks I still have a thing for him."

"Don't you?"

"Um, no. I'm completely, utterly content. I mean . . . we're amicable."

"When is the last time you saw him?"

"When I tossed his backpack off a moving bus in Peru," Brooke said. Tess high-fived her, and Brooke rolled onto her stomach.

"He had it coming," Tess said. "But I'm glad you two are all right now."

"Check this out," Brooke said. Her eyes lit up, gossip at the ready. "Zach's . . . companion is some girl he met at Burning Man. She's bringing a portable disco lighting system and a trunk full of costumes. He said she's a contortionist."

"At least I'm not the only one getting dumped for some tchotchke," Tess said.

"He's not dumping me for her . . ."

"You sound pretty interested."

Brooke's tone dropped low. "Can you at least pretend to be interested in something other than feeling sorry for yourself?"

"I'm trying," Tess said. "How would you feel?"

"I would feel, like, maybe grateful that your future doesn't include that asshole, that the universe has better things in mind for you than getting treated like dirt by Brian Crowe."

"You said that last time," Tess said.

"Last time he messed up, you said it was the last time too."

"This was different. Last time, all he did was wreck my truck."

"Yes. I guess that's true, babe." Brooke squeezed Tess's hand.

"Where's the bathroom?" Tess asked.

"Over there," Brooke said. She hefted herself up on one arm and leaned over the edge of the loft to point out to a wood-paneled cubby that Tess initially mistook for a closet. "It's a dry toilet. When you pee, sprinkle a little sawdust on it. When you shit, sprinkle a lot of sawdust on it," Brooke said.

Tess immediately determined not to shit for the next two days.

"Where do you shower?" Tess asked, clambering down the short ladder to the main level where Brooke and Andrew slept like ascetics on what appeared to be a giant zabuton.

"Oh, outside in the summer. In the winter, we bathe in the washtub on the deck."

Tess eyed the closed bathroom door. "People pay you money to stay here under these conditions?"

Brooke's short laugh came just a hair too late, and Tess realized she had hurt Brooke's feelings. She cracked open the toilet door. "Hey. I'm just kidding."

"Hundreds of years of innovation in plumbing and electric. Wasted on us," Brooke said cheerfully. She paused, listened, and laughed. "Are you holding your pee?"

"I can't pee when you're listening," Tess said, pulling the door closed.

"Still? After all these years?"

"Run some water."

"Andrew will never forgive the waste of this," Brooke chided, but she went to the small sink in the bathroom and turned the lever. As the water ran, Brooke said, "When you want to take a bath, just fill the tub halfway with snow, then pour in boiling water. It's the perfect temperature. You'll like it. Trust me."

"Wow," Tess said, closing the door to the toilet. "I feel so conscientious, not flushing anything."

"Well, hopefully," Brooke said, "some of our mindfulness will rub off on you."

"Oh, wow," Tess said, "Will I be special then, too?"

Tess awoke early the next morning to find Andrew and Brooke engaged in a sun salutation in the meditation room. Andrew brought his finger to his lips when Tess opened the heavy, engraved door. The room was magnificent: mirrored walls on two sides and a wood-burning stove that heated water and circulated warmth up through the gleaming teak floor. Alabaster walls caught the light, and floor-to-ceiling windows afforded a view of the mountains. Neutral-tone beige yoga mats, sitting blocks, and meditation pillows sat stacked in neat towers. Red prayer shawls and elaborately embroidered tapestries hung from the vaulted ceiling.

She asked where they kept the coffee, and Andrew stopped his yoga to make it for her. He fussed over hand-grinding the beans, fetching clarified water from a designated bucket, measuring out the proportions just so. Tess gulped it down, and asked for a second cup.

"I really don't know if I could drink another," he said.

"That's all right," Tess replied. "More for me."

Tess enjoyed watching him parsimoniously spoon two small heaps of grounds into the old-fashioned percolator. They sipped the brew in silence that was, Tess thought, less than meditative, while Brooke made small talk on a list of things they needed for the party and sent Andrew to town to fetch them. After he left, Brooke glanced out the sliding glass door and topped off her own cup, firing up the stove to make a third pot.

"I love him to pieces," she said, "But the coffee rationing is ridiculous."

"If a man kept me from a second cup of coffee, I would never let his dick within a mile of me again," Tess said.

Brooke looked amused. "Oh, darling. You haven't changed a bit."

"Hey," Tess said, swirling the sludge in the bottom of her cup, "read my grounds?"

"I don't know . . ." Brooke said. "I haven't done that in a long time."

"You predicted Brian," Tess said. "You owe me."

"Well," Brooke said. "Maybe I can foresee his imminent demise."

"Make it slow and painful."

Tess put her saucer on top of the empty cup, closed her eyes, and made a wish. She slid the cup across the counter, and Brooke filled it.

"You drank from one side only?" Brooke asked. Tess nodded. Brooke touched her hand to the side of the cup every few moments to see if it had cooled. After a moment, she lifted the saucer and looked at the cup. Her eyebrows shot up.

"What?"

"No. It's nothing . . ."

"Bullshit. Tell me now," Tess said.

Brooke's laugh was hollow as a clapperless bell. "I looked at it wrong."

Tess almost believed her. She opened her mouth to speak, but Brooke frowned and shook her head no. "Shhh . . . I'm reading."

Tess waited, wishing she had made more coffee to pass the time. Brooke looked in Tess's eyes and said, "What I see is a journey, and you are standing on top of a mountain. You're holding a man's head, and he's kind of like a lion, and his hair is in your fist. You're holding it over the mountain like this . . ." Brooke extended her arm.

"A severed lion-man head?"

Brooke nodded. "I've never seen anything like this in the grounds before."

"Ok," Tess tapped the counter with both hands, drumming the marble. This didn't make any sense. Brian kept his hair short. She wasn't interested in this griffin, or sphinx, or any monsters. It was Brian's fate, her fate, that she needed foretold. "Then what?"

"I don't know," Brooke admitted.

"What do you mean you don't know?"

"It's not science."

"So I maybe chopped off someone's head? And that's all you got for me?"

"Yes, and well . . . you seemed very proud of yourself. Triumphant."

"Give me that."

"You can't read your own grounds," Brooke said, pulling the cup away from Tess. "It's such bad luck."

"You'd better not be messing with me."

"I'm not." Brooke rinsed the grounds down the sink.

"What did you see?"

"Nothing, really. What I told you."

Tess persisted and pestered, but Brooke hurried off to collect some friends from the airport. Her car wasn't even at the mailbox before Tess went to the sink and peered into the cup.

It was no use. Clean as a whistle.

Tess went for a hike. She walked off the trail, following a deer path where the pines grew straight and tall as telephone poles, and deep crevasses plummeted down to the river past cliffs of flinty gray shale and pink limestone. After a while, Tess sat on a large rock that overlooked the river, trying not to think about Brian. She focused on the scent of the forest, the cawing crows. It was cold, and Tess shivered. Brian once told her that people with late-stage hypothermia hallucinate warmth. Maybe that's what she had done with him, with their life. She jogged back up to the house, letting the bitter air burn her lungs.

She tried not to think of Brian as she stepped into the bath, soaping and rinsing herself, scraping her knee raw against the metal washtub. She stood up in the tub and caught a glimpse of her reflection in the sliding glass door. She'd lost so much weight that her stomach was concave. She stood in the chill until her nipples hurt, whitening from the cold. Her thighs were covered in goose pimples and tendrils of wet hair stuck to her shoulders. Shuddering, she wrapped herself in a towel and stepped inside.

"Hello?" a voice said.

A woman stood at the bedroom door. Long red hair hung down her back in a froth of curls. She wore striped leggings, a smock-like print dress, and a furry hat. A man stood behind her, his brown dreads stuffed under a scruffy green toboggan. He waved.

"Tess?" he said, taking off his sunglasses. "Hey . . . it's Zach."

"Zach Rosenberg?" she asked. He smiled. "My gosh, I didn't recognize you with the . . . hair and all."

"Yeah, yeah, I know . . . Sorry we scared you," he laughed. "This is Evah."

"Nice to meet you," Tess said. Evah wriggled like a puppy. Tess didn't know whether to pat her on the head or shake her hand, so she held onto her towel.

"Where is everybody?" Zach asked.

"Andrew and Brooke went into town," Tess said. She slipped Brooke's bathrobe on over the towel, tied it at the waist, and faced Zach. He pulled her into a hug. They hadn't seen each other in years. His matted dreadlocks made Tess want to reach for the scissors. She suspected that he fancied himself a good freestyler, a man of the people, fluent in elementary Spanish.

"So how was Venezuela?" she asked.

"Revolution ain't all it's cracked up to be," Zach said. "I was mostly leading hiking parties for eco-tourists through the jungle, but we got robbed so many times by traficantes that I thought I'd come back to the states for a while and let things cool off. You?"

"I manage the farm for dad," Tess said. "Spend a lot of time on the river."

"Where's Brian?"

She said it. "We broke up."

"Awww, man . . . That sucks," Zach said. "You guys were together for—"

"Five years," Tess said. She struggled to smile, "It's for the best, I think. We were so young when we met—"

"What, like 25?"

"Yeah. And you change, you know."

"You haven't changed at all," Zach said.

"I've changed forever," she said. "I don't know yet if it's good or bad."

"All Zach's friends are, like, freaking out over turning thirty," Evah said. "But I think it's when your life begins."

Tess resisted the urge to ask Evah if she was old enough to buy booze and whether she could indeed count to thirty. Tess said, "Why don't you guys settle in? I'll be right down."

Before leaving, Evah turned and touched Tess's arm.

"Are you ok?"

"Yeah, sure . . ." Tess said.

"Then why were you crying?"

"What are you talking about?" Tess said.

"I heard you . . . when we were coming up the stairs."

"I wasn't crying."

"Yes you were."

"Um, no . . . I was not. You're mistaken." Tess squared her shoulders.

Evah exchanged a look with Zach, then shrugged. "Hope you're okay."

Tess closed the door behind them. She was not going to cry in front of someone she barely knew, and Zach. Damn. She needed time alone and space to grieve, for God's sake; *Akāliko* would afford her neither. She packed her backpack to leave, but faltered when she thought about how much it would hurt Brooke. She had to stay long enough to make it look like she tried, or Brooke would rightfully accuse her of failing to try. She ran her fingers through her damp hair to iron out the tangles, dressed, and forced herself downstairs.

She found Evah standing on the dining room table in the great room, setting up a portable disco ball and several small speakers to "bang out" what she assured them was a twelve-hour-long playlist of trance and electronica. Zach was making some kind of horrible-smelling cabbage bread in the kitchen and had dirtied every dish in the house doing it. Tess rummaged in the hall basket and snuck a look at her phone. Nothing but a long voice mail from Brooke asking her to check the pantry and make sure they had plenty of organic flour.

By afternoon, *Akāliko* was humming with the influx of revelers from Brooke and Andrew's crowd. Tess recognized a few people from around town. She made small talk with Sara and Michelle, the couple who owned the ski shop. There was a whole passel of lefties from the Baron underground: a couple who repurposed wool army blankets to create small-batch hybrid denim fashions that they sold for a small fortune to hipsters on both the left and right coasts. A couple of gentlemen farmers enthralled a group of locavores with a florid description of the sheep-castration process. Todd, who ran a forage-centric CSA, bantered with an environmental lawyer about the dangers of arugula. His beautiful raw-food wife was a self-styled internet personality who somehow made a living by recording ukulele parodies of pop songs on YouTube. Tess wandered over to where Brooke and Andrew were sitting on tapestry floor cushions, in a circle playing a board game.

"I'm in over my head," she told Brooke. "You're collecting eccentric friends again."

"I keep the good ones," Brooke grinned. She whispered, "I hear you met Evah?"

Tess nodded. "She's one of those if-you're-not-open-she'll-pry-you-open kind of people," Tess said.

"Arm hair so thick you could braid it, bless her heart. Poor Zach."

"Your eyes still green over him?" Tess glanced at Brooke.

"Please. That water done run under the bridge," Brooke said. Tess smiled at her friend's rare relapse into country parlance.

"You're awful critical of this new girl of his."

"Well she's far too young for him."

"True. A grown woman would have been long gone around the time he did that to his hair." Tess shook her head. "So cliché."

"We're being mean," Brooke admitted, taking a circular breath. "I don't want to throw off my energy."

"You're no fun anymore."

"Me?" Brooke arched an eyebrow, but her gaze drifted towards the sound of Zach's voice coming from the next room. "Poor girl doesn't know what she's in for."

Tess excused herself to the kitchen to start the bread. Zach stood sipping maté out of a straw while Evah iced a vegan, sponge-like cake that she explained to Tess was crafted out of carrots and spelt flour.

"What's the occasion?" Tess asked.

"My birthday," Zach said.

"Your birthday is in May," Tess said. "We were like, the last two people to get our drivers' licenses junior year."

"Good memory," Zach said. He tipped his chin towards Evah. "She just got hers."

Tess hoped that she did not wrinkle her nose.

"The icing is made out of unpasteurized soy cheese," Evah gushed. "C'mon, it's good!"

Angry raisins puffed out their chests at Tess, as if daring her to try a bite. "I wish I could," she begged off, "But I . . . I don't eat sweets anymore."

"Cooool . . . I'm paleo," Evah sang, using the wooden spoon as a microphone. "But not on birthdays!"

"Will I be in your way if I start the soup and bread?" Tess asked.

"Of course not," Evah said. Zach drifted off after a few minutes, leaving Tess to struggle at making small talk with Evah. Tess soon learned that she needn't struggle much at all. Evah was happy to ruminate on how she didn't work because she felt weighed down by furniture and belongings, so she stuck to seasonal jobs in the service industry that let her travel and experience the world.

"How do you . . . get by?" Tess asked.

"People are always there for me when I need them," Evah said. "It's like the universe just puts them in place for me."

Tess turned her attention to loosening the ring at the top of the mason jar of soup. The lid slipped off—it hadn't sealed. Tess sniffed at the jar, and a thick, sour smell emanated from it. She slid the jar away, making note to put it in the compost heap, when Brooke stuck her head in the door.

"We're having a cleansing meditation session in the rinzai room," Brooke said.

Tess dumped the bag of flour into the bowl, sending up a hazy cloud that she hoped to disappear behind. She made a well in her palm, filled it with salt, and stirred it in with her hand.

"Come join me?"

"Maybe next time," Tess said.

"Andrew's really good at this sort of thing," Brooke said. "Seriously. Trust him a bit."

"It's not him I don't trust," Tess said, pouring in the sourdough. "And I just started this bread."

"Go on if you want," Evah said. "I can finish it."

"That's ok," Tess said. She drizzled olive oil over the lumpy mess in the bowl, and felt the grainy dough molding together in her fingers when she squeezed them into fists.

"It might help you handle your feelings," Brooke said.

Tess sank her hands into the mix and said, "To hell with rinzai, I'll heal when I want to; there's a feeling."

There was a small silence, underscored by laughter from the next room.

"Get it together your way then," Brooke said. "I was just trying to help."

"Please," Tess said. She felt her eyes well up, hot with tears. "I can't think about it right now."

"Okay," Brooke said, "Okay."

After she left, Tess began kneading, smacking the bread down onto the baking stone. Tess concentrated on window-paning the dough. She jumped when Evah put a comforting hand on her shoulder.

"I understand, girl. It's why I avoid committed relationships. Life is a lot easier if you don't have to worry about pleasing anyone but yourself."

"What would this world be like if all of us did that?" Tess asked, despising Evah even more.

"You know that old saying?" Evah said. "… 'Love is the delusion that one man differs from another?'"

"All right," Tess said. "Enough."

Tess extricated a doughy hand from the bowl and stepped back. Evah's arm fell to her side. The girl frowned.

"Everybody has a story," Evah said. "Including me."

"Huh," Tess said. "Spoken like someone who lets other people solve their problems."

Evah turned on the water and filled up the mixing bowl with castile soap. The scent of lavender wafted over to Tess, tickling her nose.

"I grew up in eastern PA," Evah said. She jerked her head in the direction of the window. "Old-order Amish. I left when they tried to make me get married. I haven't been back. I had to learn to let go of everything that hurt."

Evah was now whirling the spatula with her hand, leaving a pattern of perfect, interlocking swirls. She covered the cake with a sheet of wax paper, and put it aside, then popped the spatula in her mouth. "So, I like my freedom now that I have it."

"How old are you, really?" Tess asked.

"Twenty," Evah said. Tess studied her for a moment, then cut the dough in half and handed it to her. The girl flattened it with her palm, pushing it with the heel of her hand, turned it over and began again. Tess smiled at her.

"Drives me crazy when people show off making stuff I used to dream about buying at the store," Evah said.

"Please," Tess said, "Reach over and set the oven timer for fifty minutes?"

The rest of the afternoon passed quickly. There was lunch to eat, kitchen to clean, and soup to stir. Zach, Tess, the lawyer, and the lesbians went cross-country skiing. Brooke led a yoga session in the meditation room. The raw-food wife sat strumming obscure indie-rock songs. Later, Evah opened a huge suitcase full of costumes and handed them out. There was a tutu. A headdress made of peacock feathers. A jackalope costume. A Richard Nixon mask.

What an ungodly nightmare this will be once everyone is drunk, Tess thought.

By 7:00 more partygoers were pouring in and dinner was ready. Brooke sat Tess next to a bearded fellow who attempted to capture her interest with statements like, "I only make pies with indigenous wild apples." Tess got up three times during dinner to visit the whisky bar. After her third double, she asked him what kind of music he listened to. The fellow leaned in, earnest and willing to enlighten her, musing at length on his affection for French political hip-hop.

Andrew stood on a chair and rang a spoon against his wine glass.

"Friends, fools, lovers," he said. "I am so glad you are all here with us. This is a special New Year's at *Akāliko*." Andrew stepped down from the chair and offered Brooke his hand. "Stand up please , honey?"

Brooke wiped her mouth with her napkin. She looked almost shy. Andrew led her over to the fireplace, where he sank onto one knee, and took a small velvet box out of his pocket. Brooke's hand flew to her mouth. She looked at Tess, who smiled and concentrated on arranging her face into a façade of happiness. Fierce happiness.

Tess smiled and clapped at the right moments, but her mind drifted backward. She remembered Brian kneeling in front of her last Christmas. Brian getting choked up, fumbling. Brian asking her the same thing Andrew was asking Brooke. *Yeah* . . . Tess had said. *Yes.* Now Brooke was saying yes, and the room was breaking out in ecstatic cheers, singing, "For He's A Jolly Good Fellow." Then Brooke and Andrew were surrounded by people embracing, shaking hands, and congratulating them.

Brooke took Andrew's hand and tried to make her way to Tess, tears streaming down her face. Zach stopped Andrew and shook his hand. Brooke hugged Zach, who lifted her hand in the air and kissed her ring. Tess worked her way towards them and saw Evah kick on the sound system, sending disco lights spinning around the room.

"Let's get this party started!" Evah bellowed into the microphone. "Give it up for Andrew and Brooke!" The walls of *Akāliko* shook from drum and bass, people surged to the dance floor, and she was grateful to Evah for rendering conversation impossible.

Tess hugged Andrew and Brooke, screaming congratulations over the music. She made a show of dancing with the two of them, then stood on the perimeter of things for a couple of songs, clapping and cheering while they danced, making sure to catch Brooke's eye every now and then. She wanted to be happy for them, she did. But after a very short while, all the air went out of the room, and the scent of the dancers' sweat drove Tess into the kitchen where she helped dry the dinner dishes and swept the kitchen floor clean. She kept herself moving until she had a chance to slip a bottle of good small-batch whisky into her pocket and ease out a side door. Hurrying in her stocking feet across the frigid brick sidewalk, Tess snuck around to the meditation room. Mercifully, the door was unlocked. She sat herself down on a yoga mat and drank until she passed out.

Tess awoke to the din of the still-pounding beat of trance music. She rolled over onto her stomach. Moonlight filtered in through the windows. She glanced at the clock. It was already a New Year . . . My God . . . it was two in the morning. She stood up, capped the bottle she'd been drinking, and stashed it behind the sitting blocks.

She wandered back into the great room. It was dark except for the strobe light and spinning colors from the disco ball. Evah had changed into a sequined leotard and rainbow shimmering tights. She danced atop the table, writhing and undulating with a hula-hoop. In the corner, someone was passed out in someone else's lap. There were a few feet sticking out from under the pool table, and Tess immediately decided she didn't care who they belonged to. God, her head hurt. She fumbled to the kitchen for a glass of water. As her eyes adjusted to the darkness, she saw Zach, costumed in a pair of leather chaps and a magenta vest made out of fake fur.

"Hey," he said. "I thought you left."

"What the hell are you wearing?" she asked. "A Muppet?"

He laughed. "My work uniform. Did you know I was a stripper when I lived in Cali?"

"This surprises me not at all," Tess said.

He began a gyrating dance, moving towards her.

"Something is wrong with all of us," Tess said, covering her eyes. "Especially you."

Zach laughed. Tess's glass clinked when she drew filtered water from the refrigerator, one of Brooke and Andrew's few concessions to modernity. The dispenser groaned, an animal sigh that she wished she could echo. Zach put his hand on her shoulder.

"Nothing's wrong with you, Tess."

"I need to go lie down again," Tess said. Her voice cracked.

"Brooke told me what happened with Brian," Zach said. "I'm sorry."

"Me too."

"I'm shocked," Zach said. "I thought you two were really good for each other."

"Stop," Tess said, starting to cry. "Please stop."

Zach put his hand on her arm and she looked up at him. He dipped his fingers into the glass, stepped toward her, and rubbed the cool water across her eyelids. She put her hands on the counter behind her to balance herself. He leaned toward her, pressing his chest into hers, his hips moving her toward the counter. He smelled like sweat that was not necessarily his own, gin, and salt. His eyes were all irises, inky and shimmering.

"Are you on shrooms?" she asked.

"Yeah," he said, nodding. "Good ones."

"Got any more?"

No one paid attention when they slipped through the great room. They passed Evah, who was grinding against the fellow with the beard as a rapper cadenced in lilting, staccato French. The couple underneath the table had disappeared. The door to the meditation room whispered against the wood floor when Zach closed it behind them.

Tess chewed the shrooms straight, the dense acrid taste and leathery texture drying out her mouth. They unrolled yoga mats and sat passing the whisky back and forth. Tess talked. She had never told anyone the whole story: the humiliation of discovery, her swift turns from beloved to betrayed to battered. They fell silent. Zach put his hand on hers. Tess took a swig of whisky. When she passed him the bottle, he leaned in to kiss her, smiling as liquor spilled from her lips to his. She pulled him in closer, the bottle clinking dully on the wood floor when it slipped out of her hand.

Tess shivered when his hands moved from her waist to her breasts. It had been years since anyone touched her except Brian. They undressed quickly, working their way across the floor to the pile of yoga mats, leaving a trail of clothing in their wake. Zach paused, naked, to throw a couple of pieces of wood onto the fire. Backlit by the glow of the stove, his hair fanned out in all directions like the spikes on a dinosaur. When he closed the grate, the room went dark, and she let herself fall into it all: the deprivation of spirit, the generosity of one body comforting another.

Tess froze when she heard the door open. She saw Andrew, silhouetted in the doorway.

"It's hot as Hades in here," Andrew said. "I thought for sure the stove would be out by now."

The lights snapped on, blinding Tess, illuminating the clothes on the floor. Brooke stepped into the room behind him, giggling as she stumbled over the threshold. She caught her breath.

"What's this?" Brooke said.

"Oh, hey, Brooke," Zach said, covering his bare ass with a tapestry. "Excuse us . . ."

Tess sat up, crossing her arms over her chest. Zach leaned over, hiding her nakedness.

"Tess?" Brooke said. "Really?"

"It's cool," Zach said. "Give us a minute—"

"Cool?" Brooke said, hands on her hips. "I don't think this is cool at all."

Andrew turned his back to give them privacy while Tess and Zach scrambled to cover up, but Brooke's breath was heavy with anger. "This is a sacred space."

"Take it easy," Zach said.

"I can explain—" Tess began. But she could not. The shrooms had kicked in. The lights were cruel and far too white in her eyes, which kept closing and blinking as the rays sent small tracers spider-webbing across the floor. Zach was on his feet, a pillow across his groin.

Brooke kicked their clothes at the two of them. "Get dressed."

"Brooke, wait a minute—" Tess stuttered, reaching for the right words, reaching for her sweater, pulling her pants on.

Brooke turned to her, "What were you thinking?"

"I'm thinking it's no big deal, because—" Zach tugged his shirt over his head. "We're all adults . . ."

"Stop," Brooke said. She raised up both palms, as if pushing against an invisible wall.

Zach and Tess were both dressed by then. Andrew clasped Brooke's hand, his expression a mix of bewilderment, confusion, and concern.

Brooke pointed at Tess. "You did this on purpose. You're hurt, so you hurt me? You're miserable. So you can't stand me being happy?"

"What? Are you crazy?" Tess said.

"It's no big deal, Brooke—" Zach began.

"How could you?" Brooke said to Tess.

"It was nothing . . ." Tess said. The room whirled. "Shit."

"Hey. It's been a long time," Zach said, kindly. "We're way beyond that."

"Like that ever mattered to you," Brooke said. "You . . . you—"

"Brooke?" Andrew asked. The four of them stood, tense as coiled springs, in the paneled room. The fire crackled, snapped, threw sparks. Tess could hear the sound of her own breath. The room loomed around them, dwarfing their reflections in the mirrored wall, their voices echoing off the wood floor.

"Babe . . ." Andrew said. "Are you alright?"

"I want them both to take their shit and go."

"Hold on . . ." Zach said, "You're overreacting."

Brooke poked a finger towards Tess. "She was my friend. You're my ex. This is my meditation room, my house . . ."

"It's actually my house," Andrew said to Brooke. She stopped short, then turned to face the windows overlooking the mountains. Tess could see her friend's reflection. Brooke was so angry her face had taken on a pallor of stone; she seemed as rigid as the Buddha statue that gazed on them benevolently from the altar.

She kept her head lowered, but reached for Andrew's hand. "It's our house. I want them both to leave."

"I don't think anyone should drive," Zach said. "We both took some stuff."

"Took some *stuff*?" Brooke clenched her teeth so hard Tess thought she could hear them grind. "Is that your excuse?"

"No one meant to hurt you," Tess said.

"I was with him for years," Brooke said. Tess felt her heart compress, pause. She looked at the floor.

"I didn't mean to," Tess said. "It was an accident!"

Zach laughed, then clapped a hand over his mouth. Brooke leaned against Andrew's side, burying her face in his shoulder.

"We've all had a lot to drink," Andrew said. "We'll sort it out in the morning. Let's go upstairs. Now."

Brooke glanced from Zach to Tess to Andrew. Her shoulders sank. She turned to leave, pausing at the door. Without turning around, Brooke said, "Sleep wherever you want tonight, but in the morning, I want you both gone."

Tess called after her but was answered only by the stomping of Brooke's feet against the beveled floor. Andrew followed, closing the door behind him. Tess straightened up the mats. She blushed at the wet spots that she didn't know whether to conceal with a pillow or leave open to dry. Zach smiled at her.

"That was fun," he said. "For an accident."

When Tess went into the great room, Evah was still dancing. She beckoned Tess over to her, but Tess ducked her head and hurried up the stairs to Brooke's door. She knocked. She thought she heard Andrew and Brooke talking, but the urgent undercurrent of voices ceased when she knocked. No one answered. Tess called Brooke's name a few times.

"My keys are in my bag," Tess said. No answer.

She went back downstairs to the kitchen. The soup was bubbling in the crockpot. Tess gathered up her mason jars, stacking them back in the crate. The spoiled jar still sat on the counter. There was a thudding, heavy sound from the stairwell, and she hurried over to find her backpack at the bottom of the stairs, her things scattered. Tess picked up her toothbrush, a fleece jacket, a pair of socks. She crammed them back in the bag and closed it with an angry tug at the zipper.

She'd had enough. She was tired of Brooke's sanctimonious wholeness. Tired of Brooke's petty jealousies and unresolved feelings. Tired of Brooke pretending to be all Zen and enlightened. Tired of Brooke's pretentious friends: these assholes so certain they rose above the toxicity of human pathos by virtue, cleansing herbs, weird music, and self-congratulation. She never wanted to come to this party anyway, and Brooke had insisted, pushing, pushing, pushing for Tess to heal when it was impossible to do so because the whole ashram's heart was as raw as a steak. To hell with all of them. She reached for the spoiled jar. She tipped the jar into the crockpot and stirred the contents into the soup.

In the foyer, Tess laced her boots, grabbed her things, and went to the Jeep. It was almost four in the morning. She could probably get a room in Cavalle. It was closer and an easier drive than going all the way home. She started the engine and let it run for a few minutes, staring ahead at the light snow falling in the bluish glow of the moonlight. The clear black of the sky made the stars seem brighter, closer, and colder. She wondered what Brian was doing. If he felt badly for how he treated her. If he felt anything at all, other than the desire to hide his hurt, desire, and burning shame. She wondered if that shame was all they had left in common. Tess felt her eyes burning and was searching for a tissue when there was a tap on the window. Zach.

"You can't drive," he said. "You're drunk and shrooming. It's New Year's."

"I'm going to the motel in Cavalle," she said.

"You'll end up in jail."

He opened the passenger door and got in, rubbing his hands together.

"Brooke's going to kill me," Tess said.

"Pretty salty," he said. "It never occurred to me she would give a shit."

"I should have known," Tess said. Zach looked at her, but she did not elaborate.

"What about Evah?" she asked.

"We're not like that."

"Yeah, no kidding."

Tess burst into laughter and he laughed, too, until it wore thin. They sat for a moment in silence, the dull whir of the fan still blowing frigid air across their knuckles, eyelashes, knees.

"You can't drive. We'll set the alarm early and have you on the road before Brooke even wakes up."

"No," she said. "I'll take back roads and go slow."

Zach reached across her and grabbed the keys from the ignition. He was out the door before she could even unbuckle her seatbelt. Tess chased after him, trying to keep her footing. He was nimble as a goat, bouncing from drift to drift and ducking in and out of the pines. Zach climbed to the top of a rock and held the keys aloft. Tess jumped up beside him. He steadied her, his arm on her back. The whole expanse of the valley lay before them. It was a sloping drop with a few outcroppings, limestone flecks catching the moonlight. Below it, the river curved silver and the ground sparkled with snow.

Zach twirled the keys on the end of his finger.

"Stop it," Tess said, breathless. "I don't have a spare."

Zach pretended to fling them over the edge, fumbling at the last minute. Tess lunged and slipped. She felt branches, stones, ice, and snow. She struggled to stop herself, unsure whether to curl up or open her arms to break the tumble. She could hear rocks falling after her. She felt a strange, searing throb in her side. When she landed, she could taste the thin metal trickle of blood in her mouth. She lifted one limb at a time. When she tried to move her left leg, she cried out.

"You all right?" Zach called. She could not tell if his voice was above or below her.

"I did something to my leg," she said. "I don't know."

"I'll get help," he said. She listened to him struggle up the hill, and then to the few moments of silence while he was inside. Soon he returned with Evah, and they helped her to her feet, hopping along a winding side path, back to *Akāliko.*

Tess awoke under the glare of fluorescent lights, the hum of some kind of monitor. She knew she was in the hospital. Someone kept saying, "Brian . . . Brian . . ."

Shut up, she thought. God I wish that idiot would shut up.

Tess ran her hand across her face. Her face was still there, although it was a little sore on one side. Her chest cavity ached. Her teeth felt like they were wearing little sweaters, and her feet were cold. Why were hospital blankets always so terrible? She looked down at her body, saw her leg in a cast, and swore.

"Hello," a voice said.

Tess turned her head toward its origin. Evah sat beside her making prayer ties, the bright red fabric cinched around a circular orb, fragrant with sage. She leaned over and pressed a cold cloth to Tess's forehead. She said, "I just fed you an ice chip, and I think it made you drool."

Tess said. "How long have I been here?"

"Oh, just since last night. They knocked you out to calm you down . . . you were calling for Brian, plus the pain."

Plus the pain? Tess thought. That is the pain. All the pain. "What time is it?"

"About seven," Evah said. "You missed New Year's Day."

Brooke snoozed in a chair on the opposite side of Tess's bed. She stirred at the sound of their voices, blinking sleep out of her eyes and pushing her hair back when she saw that Tess was awake.

"Thank God," Brooke said.

"You don't believe in God," Tess replied. "So why are you here?"

"Liability," Brooke said.

Tess snorted. "Thought that stuff was for the bourgeois."

"You need to cut this shit out," Brooke said. Tess looked away. Brooke was right. She did need to cut that shit out, and a lot of other shit along with it. The blip and beep of the vital signs monitor did little to bridge the silence.

"Brooke," Tess said, "I'm sorry."

"It's not just your fault," Brooke said. "It's mine."

"It's Zach's fault," Tess said. She tried to crack a smile, but her face throbbed. "Ouch."

"He's downstairs buying a sandwich," Evah said, "But he'll be up in a few."

Evah passed Tess her medical chart. Tess read it out loud. "Oh wow. Two cracked ribs and a hairline fracture in her fibula, various abrasions, and a loose tooth?"

"You didn't have to be so extra . . ." Evah joked. Tess didn't laugh. It hurt too much.

"They're going to let you out tomorrow morning, as long as you don't throw up. Which by the way, everyone at the ashram, including Andrew, has some terrible diarrhea," Brooke said.

"Oh, God . . ." Tess sighed. "That's my fault."

"What did you do?" Brooke asked, eyes narrowing.

"Nothing," Tess said. She closed her eyes and whispered, "I'm still a little woozy."

She knew her friend did not believe her. Tess pointed at Evah. "She escaped the Amish."

"Yeah, she told me."

"You were right. Remember the coffee grounds?" Tess asked Brooke.

Brooke frowned, and shook her head. "No . . . Come in for a landing, please . . ."

Tess tried to sit up but could not. "It was Zach. The dude in the cup was Zach. I saw him, he was a lion, his hair was just like a lion when he put more wood in the stove . . ."

"Just try to rest," Evah cooed.

"I didn't behead him," Tess told Brooke.

Brooke shrugged. "You missed your chance."

Tess turned to Evah. "I fucked your boyfriend."

"Big deal," Evah said. She tied another prayer knot, winding the white cotton cord around the clump of sage, her hands a blur as they circled the red fabric. "For that matter, so did I."

"Me, too," Brooke said, quickly adding, "Not lately . . ."

The three of them laughed, Tess's sounding raspy and causing her to clutch her ribcage to fight off the knife of pain that shot around her torso with the rapid intake of breath.

"Why are you here?" Tess asked Evah.

"Same reason you are."

"Oh, hell," Tess said.

Evah reached for the plastic mug, took the lid off of it, and selected an ice chip. She held Tess's gaze before bringing the spoon to Tess's lips. Tess closed her eyes and felt the ice sting her teeth until she trapped it between her tongue and the roof of her mouth.

Evah straightened back and smiled. "That's better," she said. "Let me know when you want more."

A Line of Four Silver Maples

Word was out in the township that Roby was back living in a trailer in Country Court. The double-wide belonged to the Vances, people who weren't relation to him but who Roby kept calling family. Paul knew the malleability of that term because Roby was his blood cousin. They were raised up next door to each other with only a line of four silver maples and a broad, open, expanse of lawn separating their houses. "Shoutin' distance" is what Paul's father called it. Only most of the shouting came from Roby's father, Ennis, and most of the shouting was directed at Roby. So, Roby was often at Paul's house, nose pressed to the glass of the storm door asking if anyone could come outside and play.

Paul had eight years on Roby, and the boy had drifted off his radar when Paul left for college, moved to Columbus and took a job teaching school. Paul's heartbreak over losing his longtime lover gave him good reason to return to home to Laurelton, albeit under the premise of caring for his ailing father. By then, Roby had long since disappeared into construction work around Columbus. Roby was always changing jobs, getting fired, arguing with the boss, or flitting in and out of doomed ventures in self-employment. He had such bad luck: perennially left holding the bag by some unsavory partner; winding up in small claims, jail, bankruptcy, or lien. Last Paul heard, Roby was in the middle of his third divorce, ducking his soon-to-be ex because the girl wanted her truck back.

That early spring, Paul could smell the heavy perfume of apple and cherry blossoms on the breeze despite cold, overcast skies. Stacking bags of mulch to spread in his mother's flower beds, he was so lost in the shadows of his own mind that the first he heard of the vehicle was its radio blasting Charlie Daniels' twangy, undulating "Long-Haired Country Boy."

Paul looked up to see a vehicle overshoot the driveway: a red Ford work truck with a deer dent on one side. The motor groaned when the driver put her in reverse. Paul noticed the broken slider, one side tinted glass, the other with half a Harley-Davidson sticker peeling off. The truck had no tailgate and its bumper was held up with 8-gauge wire. One well-muscled arm hung out the window, thick with ink: dragons, a mermaid, a melting skull, the Confederate flag next to the Eagle-Globe-and-Anchor. Roby.

Paul last remembered Roby as a skinny twelve-year-old: all knees and elbows and the hungry look of a horny kid hoping for something, anything to let him stick his peter in it. Now, even slouched in the bench seat, Roby's bulk made the truck appear toy-like.

"Hey, cuz," Roby drawled, teeth gleaming. "Long time no see."

Paul smiled and said, "Come on in, cousin. Good to have you back home."

Paul's mother was fast asleep in her chair with the cat on her lap, Bogsy's enormous paunch warming her legs as they snored in unison. Paul adjusted the blinds to take some of the glare off Helen. Roby strode into the room, and sent Bogsy bicycling four feckless paws across Helen's stomach.

Roby laughed and caught Bogsy, hefting the poor thing into the air. The old feline arched indignantly. Helen's eyes flitted open.

"Put my cat down," Helen said. "Or you'll pick your own willow switch."

Roby chuckled and bent to gently drop the cat to the chair. "Aww, I wouldn't do nothing to a cat," he said.

Bogsy ran for his life.

"How are you?" Roby asked, kissing her on the cheek.

"Glad to see you, Roby," Helen lied.

Helen offered him a seat but did not stand on account of her sore legs. Paul's eyes met his mother's. They chatted obliquely while Roby coughed gently and intermittently into his hand. Paul sensed that Roby had read his unwelcome straightaway. If nothing was offered you—a slice of cornbread in buttermilk, some homemade chocolate cake, a glass of iced tea—you could bet you weren't received. Paul noticed the tightness around his mother's eyes whenever she smiled at Roby. Helen's thinly veiled irritation gave Paul a quiver of guilt.

He remembered how it hurt his father when his mother inked the kids' names on foam cups before each family picnic, her pretty mouth flattened into a straight line. It was as if she thought the misfortune and grit in which Uncle Ennis and Aunt Linda and cousin Roby lived would somehow backwash into the mouths of her own children. Ennis noticed, and worst of all, Roby noticed. Paul knew that Helen's not-so-faint sense of superiority made Roby seek her approval with even more fervor. Helen withheld it then and now.

"You mind if I get myself a glass of ice water?" Roby asked.

"Why sure, help yourself," Helen said. "My legs are awful weak."

"Cups in the same place?"

"Just where you left them."

Neither Paul nor Helen took thought of the small cash Helen kept hidden in a coffee can in the cabinet just up right of the kitchen sink. They heard Roby open the refrigerator and rustle around.

"Mind if I make a sandwich out of this ham?" Roby asked.

"Course not, go ahead," Helen said.

They heard Roby open the cupboard door, sneeze, then run some water. It would be months before Helen noticed the money was missing from the coffee can. Paul would remember the racket Roby made in his kitchen and blush with shame for suspecting him, and more shame for being right.

Helen leaned in to speak to Paul, pursing her lips and gesturing towards the kitchen with her chin.

"What's he doing back here?"

"Go look if you want to know."

"We don't know his condition—"

"He seems all right."

Helen need not remind Paul that Roby had been arrested. Once for a fight with an ex that turned ugly, another time for petty theft of materials from a job site, and then a year of state hospitality in Kentucky for selling cocaine.

"That was years ago, Mom," Paul said.

"Take care not to cast your pearls before swine," Helen said, and adjusted the pillows in her easy chair. Roby returned a moment later, stuffing a red bandana into his back pocket.

"You're looking good, Auntie," Roby said, sitting down and taking a big sip of water.

"Well, sugar," Helen murmured, "Aren't you sweet as ever . . ."

Bogsy growled a low, rumbling sound from his hiding place beneath the coffee table next to Roby's chair. Roby reached down and scooped the cat up again, cradling Bogsy to his chest as the cat writhed. Roby scratched Bogsy's ears, chuckling. "It sure is good to be home."

Paul showered, changed into a clean shirt, and drove to Shelly's, wondering if his baby sister knew about Roby. Shelly and Roby were close enough in age to be in school at the same time, and so Shelly treated him like a little brother and let him hang around her and her friends. Paul was living in German Village by the time Roby came back from Kentucky and took an apartment in Buckton. Roby was working steady and claimed to be sober. She didn't know that Roby didn't need to drink when he was chewing down pills. Pills that made him smarter, stronger, faster—but just a tad less meticulous with everything from measuring the framing to mixing the mud on site to arriving on time, or even arriving at work at all. When Roby lost his job, she took him in. The arrangement didn't last two week. Later, Shelly told Paul that after how Roby acted in her house, she wouldn't piss on him if he was on fire. With secrets of his own to keep, Paul dropped the subject. She didn't want to keep company with Roby, and that was that.

But he ought to tell her Roby was back. He'd hoped to talk to his sister alone, but Wayne's truck was parked cattywampus in the driveway. It was plastered with stickers: *VOTE REPUBLICAN: HOTTER WOMEN, LOWER TAXES, DON'T TREAD ON ME, COME AND TAKE*

IT. A decade ago, Shelly wouldn't have been caught dead in a truck like that. Now, it was marital property.

Paul trudged up the muddy path, dodging piles of dog shit and keeping an eye out for Boomer, Wayne's overly affectionate dog. Thankfully, the coast was clear. On his last visit, Boomer had snuck up on Paul and attempted to mount him so suddenly that he had found himself face-forward in the dirt, while Wayne howled with laughter and took his time pulling the hundred-pound, stinking mutt off him. Shuddering at the memory, he pounded on the door of the pole barn that Wayne called "the shop."

"It's open!" Wayne bellowed.

Shelly had the baby hanging from one breast, his tiny face grotesquely concentrated into a puckering scowl, one hand cradling him to her chest and the other holding up a wad of wires while Wayne anchored them to the wall with a drill gun. Her long blonde hair was usually a frothy web of waves, but now she kept it pinned up so that the baby wouldn't pull at it.

"Go for power," Wayne said. The TV snapped to life, revealing a screen split into quadrants.

"Look at that!" she said to Paul, "We got *eight* deer-cams now."

Shelly had changed so much once she started running around with Wayne Padilla—changes that Paul didn't welcome. She'd gone from a prissy prom queen to hillbilly huntress since meeting her husband. How seriously could you take a man who anglicized his name as pa-dill-uh and open-carried in Walmart, swaggering around in camo fatigues and posting "constitutional conservative" talking points on Facebook. To a degree, Paul blamed himself for Shelly's desperate attempt to cling to and fulfill their parents' expectations, which he'd dashed in ways they discussed openly—Paul "abandoning" the family farm to become a science teacher—and in ways they didn't dare acknowledge.

They'd sent Shelly to Barron College with stern warnings for her not to get above her raising. Shelly had held to it: earning her degree, then dutifully returning to the west end of the township and tending bar at the AmVets. When Wayne came along as an Otis Elevator repairman with a country drawl and a penchant for outdoor pursuits, she'd been swept off her feet. But there was an avid stridency to her hunting and fishing that made Paul wince for its showiness. Now here she stood underneath a 12-point buck that she had taken herself, first year out.

Wayne pointed to Shelly's bow. It was a high-end model with sleek camouflage print and walnut detailing on the recurve. "I wanted to start her out with a crossbow, you know, cause they're easier to learn with," Wayne said, "But she wouldn't have it. Said that the guys at the AmVets told her they was for pussies and I laughed so hard I didn't know whether to kiss her or wash her mouth out with soap."

Shelly pressed close to Wayne and Paul felt a shiver of irritation run through him. He reminded himself that this was his sister's husband. . . but he still wanted to punch Wayne in the throat. Instead, Paul smiled back and placidly accepted a beer. After all, Wayne and Shelly were just about all the company he had.

Paul was no social magnet. Plain of face, tall and mild-mannered, he was too bland to arouse even nominal speculation. His mildness matched the understated, neutral tone of his classroom, and each year he seemed to fade along with its beige walls and eggshell-colored laminate cabinets and dull steel sinks. He wanted to stand out, but he did not know how. Or for what. Escaping notice might be a boon for others like him, but for Paul it offered neither solace nor refuge. So, he suffered the small talk, hearing the deer story for the hundredth time until Shelly went in to put the baby down for a nap. He crunched his beer can with his heel, then said, "Roby's back in town."

"Well hot damn in the morning," Wayne said. "Don't tell Shell. She'll put a cap in him."

"She still pissed?"

"You know your sister."

"What did they squall over, anyway?" Paul asked.

Wayne spit a stream of tobacco into a Styrofoam cup, thought for a moment, then said, "Shelly tried to help that boy. He showed up on the back steps with his clothes in garbage bags and grocery sacks. It was pitiful. All he had to do, and I mean all—was stay off the drink. Within three days he was at the nip and mean as a snake. Roby come unwound when she called him on it, and told him to find another place to stay. Roby raised all kinds of Cain, cussing her and throwing things around the yard, beating on the door. Then, he drove by with his friends and shot a gun off." Wayne ran his hand across his lips. "She had to call the law."

Paul tried not to look surprised. "They pick him up?"

Wayne shook his head, stuffing a napkin into the cup before tossing it into a trash can. "When I got there the sheriff came and said he was gonna put them both in stir."

"Wait . . ." Paul said, "They were gonna take *her* in?"

"She kicked Roby in the nuts and the deputy saw it." Wayne shook his head. "These days they arrest 'em both. Damn law's so poor it does you just as much good not to call it."

Paul frowned. "He hit her?"

"She says no," Wayne said, "But I don't know that she'd tell me if he did."

Paul nodded. That was true. Shelly was a tack, and a brass one at that. She'd never admit a weakness. "Then you'd both be in jail huh?"

"You know it," Wayne said. Paul's heart softened a little. He remembered asking Shelly before the wedding what she saw in Wayne, a big old rawboned farm boy who seemed to be made entirely out of calluses, vulgar parlance, and mechanical knowhow.

"That man loves me to the point of sheer stupidity," she had said. Her face turned childlike as she added softly, "He does the dumbest stuff you ever saw in your life to show off, but he'd kill for me."

Paul had looked at her, shaking his head. "You want that little sister?"

"*Want* that?" Shelly said. She turned suddenly serious. "Someday he may have to."

Wayne was walking around the shop tidying things up. The dull thud of an empty oil carton hitting the metal trash can jolted Paul back to the present.

"She didn't know Roby was all twisted up on that oxy... When he first come back, and they started running around again, she told me how glad she was he was home. How she was hoping he'd do better in the country, here with the family again . . ." Wayne tossed Paul a glance. "Then look what it got us."

"I'm just going for a beer with him," Paul said. "I'll see what I can find out."

"That's your sister," Wayne said. His tone was coppery, and Paul winced.

"Daddy told me to look after the family," Paul said. "He wouldn't like it one bit for us to just turn our back on Roby."

"That family may mean something to you. But I don't know what it means to him."

"Blood is blood," Paul said. "You know that."

Roby had a crowd gathered around him at the bar when Paul walked in the door at the Breeze On Inn. Roby sat at the bar with his new girl, a woman Paul had gone to school with but whose name he couldn't remember. Roby had his arm around the woman's puffy shoulders, and was running his thickly callused finger down the glittering beads of an earring so long it grazed the straps of the woman's sheer tank top. Her hair was brown at the roots, red in the middle, and blonde at the tips. Paul could hear his cousin all the way across the room.

"We were going at it on these like, 80-grit sheets in the camper," Roby said. "Her knees was all scraped up."

The woman ducked her head, letting her hair hang over her face then tossing it over her shoulder as she giggled. "80-grit!"

The men standing around them laughed. Roby leaned into the woman's collarbone, then nibbled on her ear. She swatted him away. When Roby dodged her, he saw Paul.

"Hey, cuz!" Roby yelled, "Come meet my best girl."

Roby introduced him to his friends, and bought a round. Then Paul bought one, then someone else, then Roby and Paul again and soon nobody was keeping count. The best girl of Roby's went out for a smoke and didn't return. Paul handed the barkeep his keys. Roby tried, again and again, to call his "best girl," but the "best girl" was no longer answering her phone.

Neither Paul nor Roby could drive by last call, and now seemed as bad a time as any when the barmaid told them to start the long walk home. The moon was full and hung low over the cornfields that grew wider and longer as they staggered their way past the AmVets, the post office, the library. Roby whistled at the low-slung line of ranch-style condos in the new subdivision.

"Used to hunt deer where that water tower is now," Roby said.

"Dad hated it, too," Paul said. "An eyesore."

"Your dad," Roby said, as if reading Paul's mind. "He taught me how to be a man." That was true. Paul remembered his father taking Roby fishing, shooting hoops with him in the driveway. Roby grinned, "Remember that time he picked my daddy up by the throat for telling Shelly she had nice legs?"

"Must have been quite a lesson," Paul said, and they laughed a bit. "I been back with mom at the farm since he passed away."

"I sure miss him."

"Pretty hard not to," Paul replied.

"I didn't make the funeral," Roby said. "I didn't have a suit or gas money and I was too ashamed, when I was still torn up on hard stuff."

"You past all that now?"

"I let it go after I hurt Shelly," Roby said. "That about broke me. She's like my sister, you know?"

Their boots scuffed along the gravel, kicking up tiny pieces of rock that punctuated the silence.

"It meant a lot to me, you coming out tonight. Being seen with me in public. It seems like everybody done give up on me."

"Don't give 'em no more reason to. They'll come around."

"I hope so." He sighed. "I'm gonna need help."

Roby's eyes were clear and pooled with tears in the moonlight. Paul remembered the last time he saw that look on Roby's face. Paul was babysitting him, and Roby misbehaved. Paul had swatted him across the bottom and sent him to his room where Roby screamed and ranted and raved, repeatedly throwing a baseball against the wall in a flawless imitation of Ennis. When Paul finally had enough and flung open the door, Roby shrank against the wall, raising his hands up, pleading surrender. Paul remembered feeling terribly ashamed of Roby's fear.

"I'm sorry, Paul," Roby had said, covering his face. "I'll be good. I'll be good I promise."

He was saying the same thing now.

"What can I do?" Paul asked.

"Just what you done tonight," Roby said, "Treat me like a human being."

Roby stopped by the farm to see Paul nearly every day. Paul didn't mind him coming around. Paul was grateful for the company, the disruption of his near-monastic routine. Monday to Friday, September to May, Paul taught all grades of chemistry at the high school. Saturdays he helped Helen with her errands and mowed the yard. Sundays they had church and then Paul would visit Shelly and Wayne and the baby. It had the feel of lather, rinse, repeat, as did all of Paul's days. A necessity in a place where one long look, one smile too wide, even too long a conversation with another man or a pastel dress shirt would put Paul under suspicion. His solitude and silence were his shield, and Paul hadn't realized how suffocated he felt by life in Laurelton until Roby appeared.

Roby was always doing something. Frying a big batch of shrimp up, making gumbo and calling up a passel of friends in to feast and play guitar in the yard until all hours. Taking a canoe down the river, fishing all day amongst the live oaks in the dank watering holes where Paul's father used to take them as boys. Rigging up a potato gun with PVC pipe, just to see if they could still do it, and nearly blowing a hole in the side of the storage shed. Even just an afternoon of cornhole or picking off groundhogs with a .22 was fun with Roby.

Paul took to returning the visits. Hanging out with Roby's crowd, Paul was startled to find that people liked him and that he could make them laugh. They went to a party and Paul got so rowdy that he threatened to punch someone who called him gay. Roby had his back and threw in a few good fists himself, and they ran to the car peeling out of the driveway and laughing like a couple of teenagers.

"Man, you shoulda seen the look on that guy's face when you went animal on him."

"Animal?"

"Yep. Animal."

Paul let go of the steering wheel and pounded his fists on the roof of the truck, howling. Roby joined in and they goofed the whole way home with Roby intermittently shouting, "Son of a bitch!" and Paul letting out another baling yowl.

That night they built a fire in the ring next to Roby's trailer and listened to the local bluegrass station croon songs they remembered from childhood. Old hymns wafted promises of peace across the fog rising from the swamps. Songs about green pastures, homegoing, eternal peace.

Paul woke up in the morning, the apricot glare of daylight in his eyes. He hurried home and got Helen to service on time, speeding a little along Church Road past the nature preserve. Helen tried to make small talk, smoothing her church dress and failing to mask her disapproval of his late hours. Paul dodged explaining where he had been or what he had been out doing.

"Now Mom," he said, "You don't need to worry about me. I'm making new friends."

"Will wonders never cease," she said. He looked at her, and there was a little gleam of both humor and hurt in her eye. Paul knew she appreciated all he did for her. He had been trying hard for a long time to convince himself, and her, that it wasn't too much to ask of him.

Helen patted his knee. "It's about time."

It had all started simply enough: Paul had been weeding the garden, sweat running down his back so hard he'd already taken to dousing himself with the hose to cool off. When it finally rained, the angry sky did so simply to heap humidity atop the heat's misery. By 11:00 in the morning, Paul retreated into his office, the air conditioner blasting. Helen napped in her chair with the cat on her lap. Bogsy opened and then closed one green eye as Paul slipped past.

His cell phone was lit up with a handful of messages—a bank deposit, the weather update for the day, a couple texts from Roby:

What are you doing?

You busy?

Want to goof off and do a little fishing?

Paul didn't mind, though he never had been much of an outdoorsman. Roby was the one who thrived in the woods.

He went out and returned dragging sticks bowed with squirrel and rabbit, good meat deer on a lorry, ice-capped buckets of catfish.

Paul paused, then typed:

yes, as long as there's booze and shade.

"You're not gonna believe this place," Roby said, steering the truck onto a narrow driveway. He passed Paul the blackberry wine cooler they'd been swilling out of a gallon jug. "The guy's got 300 acres along some kind of hippie commune, and that wood runs all the way to the county line."

He noticed Roby's hands shook a little as he steered down the lane. Roby spoke rapidly. "I was doing finish plaster work on the house and he come by for an inspection. I started joking around with him, and in a few minutes I had the guy—he was real odd, wore this white karate type outfit—trying on stilts and using the hod to plaster. His parents, they grow medical marijuana, and I was like, "Y'all are my kind of people . . ."

They turned the corner and the double row of trees opened onto a wide lawn, revealing a two-story modern compound, with huge glass windows and solar panels on the roof. Paul laughed, trying to sound nonchalant. "Doesn't look like anybody's home."

"They're in India. Two-month honeymoon with the new missus." Roby sat up taller in his seat. "Asked me to keep an eye on the place. They call it a 'ashram,' whatever that is."

Paul took in the meticulous landscaping, sculpture garden, and stained-glass windows. He whistled low.

Roby waved at a security camera and grinned, then waved his middle finger. "That thing don't even work. He thinks this is effin' *Mayberry*."

"More like *Twin Peaks.*" Paul took a draw from the joint that they passed between them, eyeing the driveway as it narrowed into a lane. Roby steered them towards the woods. "Do you think we should just get out and walk?"

"Hell no!" Roby said. "I got us in 4-wheel."

Paul felt good, a humming in his chest cavity from the cool drink and a pleasant mellow feeling from the wine and the weed. They finally parked the truck in a small clearing, then hiked in another quarter mile, slapping at mosquitoes and winding their way along the deer trail that snaked through thin underbrush. The trail ended at an abandoned stock pond, serene and deep. Water lilies the size of dinner plates bloomed on its surface. Lush woods of silvery beech, mottled live oak, and black walnut surrounded them.

"It's like another world," Roby sighed. They passed the hours in relative silence, only occasionally noting the changing light as the sun shifted downward through the trees. Paul felt a little woozy. Instead of wearing off, his buzz was getting stronger, fuzzier. The gallon jug was empty now, a deep plum ring staining the bottom. After a while, Roby ran his hand through his hair, and said, "You ever hear anything about my dad?"

Paul shook his head. "Last I heard Ennis was down to Orient for two years."

"Oh, he got out of there after a while and got another church to take him on."

"That man could fall headfirst in a outhouse and come out smelling like a rose."

"He's got no more God than a liverwurst sandwich." Roby paused. "Guess I don't either. You know what though?"

Paul didn't know much at all, other than the wine was giving him a dizzy head and significant heartburn. "Huh."

"Only thing he told me that helped me, might help you, too. It's better to be hated for who you are than loved for who you ain't."

Paul felt all the blood drain from his face. What did Roby know? He jumped when he heard a strange chirp. Roby froze.

"Sounded almost like a Nextel phone," Paul said.

Roby shook his head and frowned. "Nah. Just a cricket or something."

There was a small pause, a question in the air, as they stood, cupping their ears. After a few moments of listening to the woods hum, Paul relaxed against the tree. Roby sat next to him, shoulders hunched up, tense. Paul turned and looked his cousin in the eye.

"You ain't like him, Roby." Paul slurred.

"You're drunk as shit," Roby grinned. "We better get you out of here."

Paul kept his eyes on the frayed laces of his boots to keep his balance. He noticed that the ground was black, silky, and cut soft by deer hooves. Roby trailed behind a few yards. When Paul stepped out into the clearing, he froze. The South County Sheriff cruiser blocked Roby's truck. The sheriff himself leaned against the truck with his arms crossed, and a deputy coolly trained a gun on Paul.

Paul raised his hands, dropping his fishing rod. He glanced over his shoulder.

Roby had melted into the woods.

TC's face folded into confusion. "Paul?"

Paul had taught Chem II to the sheriff's niece that past semester. She'd won a state commendation for her work on a science project. Paul smiled weakly and asked "How's Amanda?"

"All right, doing good." TC waved for the deputy to lower his gun.

"What's going on here?" Paul asked.

"Well, sir," TC said. "We was hoping you could tell us the very same thing."

When they read his charges, Paul felt so weak he was afraid urine would run down his leg. He was unaware that he had possession of a stolen truck, its seat filled with methamphetamine and a bunch of pills marked OC-80. Paul did not know he was also committing criminal trespass. Not to mention, he was fishing without a license.

"I'm . . . I'm a teacher," Paul said.

"Well . . ." TC said, "That isn't the problem."

TC prevailed upon him to confess, but Paul didn't say a word. He was not about to sing on family. Blood was blood. "I told you all I know."

"You expect me to believe," TC said, "You were just out fooling around, and you didn't have no idea that you were driving a hot vehicle? That you don't know what oxy is and are just as solid ignorant about that crank in the truck? That you did all this on your own?"

When Paul wouldn't talk, they arrested him. For everything.

"Mr. Burress," TC begged. "Please."

Paul just shook his head, declining a lawyer for the time being and asking to be tested for the drugs they found in the car, thinking that would clear him, even as the handcuffs bit into the soft flesh of his wrist. He tried explaining all this to his sister when he called her from jail, but there was a long pause, her nervous breathing rattling the line between them.

"My god" Shelly seethed. "You are dumber than a box of hair."

Roby was breathing heavily, and sweat stung as it trickled down his neck and into his skin. He was cut all to ribbons from running through the cornfield where he ditched the first car he'd stolen that day. He looked in the window and saw Aunt Helen stir a little in her sleep.

When Roby snuck in, Helen shifted her thick legs and uncrossed her ankles on the footrest. She never awakened, though, even when her car keys clinked gently against Roby's callused palm. Bogsy hissed at him. Roby gave the cat a good shove with his foot. As Roby crept out the screen door Bogsy fled into the yard, arching his back against the tires, tail leaving a smudge in the dust along its fenders.

Roby glanced through the window and saw Helen, still snoozing in the chair.

He went to the car, and eased it into neutral, giving it a good shove to roll it down the driveway. The movement startled Bogsy, and the cat sprinted underneath the porch.

Roby hesitated. It was one thing to take the car, it was another to leave that cat. Cussing softly under his breath, Roby threw the parking brake on, got down and scooted on his belly into the crawlspace. His shirt grew damp from the thick, untended earth, and grit made its way into the waistband of his jeans. He reached and finally clasped the cat firmly by the collar and the back legs. When Roby tossed Bogsy indoors, he caught the screen with his forearm and left a smear of blood on it. By the time Helen woke up, the blood would have turned brown. She'd hobble over to the door, notice it, and spit on her apron, rubbing out the stain, never realizing what it was. That was the problem.

Helen, Shelly, Wayne—they never saw who Roby was, wanted him to be someone else. Someone who never got fired, high, or dope-sick. Someone who knew the right thing to do and always did it, and never let anyone forget about it. Roby remembered his daddy, Ennis, pointing at Helen and saying, "You can put on all the show you want. Better to be hated for who you are than loved for who you ain't."

That was the problem, Roby thought. Nobody ever saw the good he did, who he was inside. Everybody remembered every mistake that he got caught for and some he didn't, but nobody caught him doing good, like putting back that old lady's cat. Roby dwelt on that the whole way down the road, until he turned into the empty driveway at Shelly's house.

Shelly waited an hour to see Paul, an hour that gave her plenty of time to cuss his infernal stupidity. She had hurried out so fast she had on mismatched flip-flops, her purse bulging with cash from the house safe. Paul finally emerged, looking calmer than she thought he would. Shelly listened while TC read off the charges and slid the bail sheet across the counter.

"Is there anything you didn't get arrested for?" Shelly asked, counting out the bills.

"I wouldn't know how to do all that if I tried," Paul said.

TC looked up from processing Paul's paperwork, and exhaled through his nose.

"I thank you Sheriff" Paul said. "You treated me decent."

TC and Shelly exchanged a look.

"Let's go," Shelly snapped. "They charge me a dollar a minute when I'm late to daycare."

In the car on the way home, Shelly listened while Paul laid out his case. "What on earth are you going to tell mama?"

"Same thing I told you," Paul said, bracing himself as she took a hard turn into her driveway.

"Here's your chance," Shelly said. "There's her car."

Paul looked up to see Roby stepping out of Shelly and Wayne's new garage, carrying Shelly's bow with one hand. Roby had two shotguns tucked under his arm, and a .38 in his belt. Shelly rolled down the window, and began yelling at Roby.

"Put that back," Shelly growled, pointing to the bow. "Or so help me, I'll kill you."

"No, you won't," Roby said, putting the shotguns in Helen's car. His voice had a strange evenness to it.

"You're holding the damn thing upside down," Shelly said.

"Pawn shop won't care, little girl," Roby said. He grinned and waved. "Hi, Paul."

"Hey," Paul said.

Shelly made to open the car door, but Paul took her arm. "Please don't."

"Let me go!" Shelly snapped. "He's robbing my house—"

"Shelly!" Paul said sharply. "He is. Now calm down."

Roby walked around to Shelly's window, put a hand on her shoulder and squeezed.

"Don't touch me," Shelly said.

"Look," Roby said. "I'm only doing this because you were such a cunt to me when I was dope-sick."

"Fuck. You."

"Easy, Shell." Paul was afraid. He could see an edginess in Roby, a palsied nervousness in his cousin's eyes that Paul had not seen before.

Roby said, "I need your keys and your phones."

"No."

Roby chambered a round. Every sound seemed amplified: the car window's complaining squeak, Roby's boots popping gravel as he circled round to collect Paul's things. Shelly sat perfectly still.

"Please," Paul said.

Shelly stuck her lower jaw out, dug in her purse, and handed the phone and keys to Paul. "This will all go into my police report."

Paul said, "Don't leave like this cuz. You might want to come back someday."

Shelly laughed.

Roby took a pocket knife out of his back pocket and plunged it into the front passenger tire. The air hissed out, whining as the tire flattened.

"Hear that?" he chuckled. "I feel like that all the time, girl."

Roby circled to the rear of the vehicle and flattened all four tires. Shelly pounded her fists on the steering wheel. Roby walked to Helen's car, stopping to wave at Paul.

"They won't give you no time," Roby said. "You're respectable."

"Hope so . . . I didn't tell them a thing. Can you do me a favor in return?"

"A favor? What kind of favor cuz?"

Paul pointed to the bow. "You don't need that."

"I'll pawn the sonofabitch—" Roby grinned. "Oughta bring at least a hundred."

"I took the fall for you." Paul reached into his back pocket, and slowly tossed his wallet to Roby. "Here. Hundred bucks in there. Couple of credit cards. More than you'll get for that bow at pawn."

"Give me hers instead," Roby said. "I don't want your money."

Shelly sat breathing heavily, one hand over her mouth, eyes closed. She nodded. Paul fished around in Shelly's purse, and passed her wallet to Roby. Roby placed Shelly's bow on the ground.

"You'll always be blood to me, Roby," Paul said. "Thank you."

"You done good, Paul," Roby said, as he got in Helen's car. He threw it into gear and backed out, swerving a bit. They heard the dull thud of the bass from the radio before Roby even cleared the end of the driveway. Roby waved, grinned, and was gone.

Shelly got out of the car, and picked up her bow. They stood watching the dust rise behind Roby. She began to run, jogging lightly at first, her gait unsteady in the flip-flops, one blue, one yellow. Paul tried to keep up, but she was fast. By the time Paul caught up, she was standing on the neighbors' porch, her feet cut and dirty, shirt soaked with sweat, still clutching the bow as she cradled the house phone in her ear and told the whole story to the dispatcher.

The state police found Helen's car a few weeks later down in Kentucky. One of the handguns turned up at a pawn shop in Virginia Beach, and another was used later to murder a man in Champaign. None of the family ever saw Roby again. For a while, they heard rumors: he was in Florida, maybe Georgia. Eventually, they heard nothing at all.

Paul was mostly exonerated by the grainy video of Roby waving at the security camera they passed at the ashram, a gesture Paul thought indicated welcome, not intent to trespass. His lawyer got all the charges dropped except for contempt of court. He walked with a couple years' probation and a reprimand from State Fish and Game. Paul resigned from his teaching job and went to work at a grocery, managing inventory and scheduling unreliable employees, designing endcaps of soda and snack cakes under the hum of fluorescent lights. He had a union card, profit-sharing, a 401k, and much lower expectations in this new vocation.

Late of an evening, usually on a Sunday when the store was closed, Paul would turn on the bluegrass program and let the strident fiddles, and high lonesome sound lull him into a bit of the past. The glorious summer when he learned that he had a streak of danger in him and could live a little or even raise some hell if he felt up to it—be just like anyone else. His thoughts would turn to Roby, and wonder where he was and if he ever would come back. When the radio wept one sad, high, lonesome sounding song after another, Paul would think of them as they had been ten or fifteen years ago, young and with some hope. He still had some, foolish as it was.

Home, Grown

Hannington was driving, grinning each time the car careened around one of the hairpin curves that led from the interstate to Cavalle. The mountains were encased in fog that evening, and the famous blue-gray shadows were just tinting the hilltops as the sun set. Kalli usually drove herself down from New York, but Hannington had insisted. She found herself marveling anew at a familiar landscape: the outcroppings of rust-and-peach-striped sandstone strafed with glittering pink granite, the sheer drop of limestone that gave way to the river valley below.

Hannington cleared his throat and said, "I read that the ridge is blue because of the gases emitted by vegetation that only grows here. Nowhere else."

Kalli nodded. This was something every schoolchild from Marietta to Erie could tell you, but it was sweet of him to study up in preparation for this visit. She was bringing him home to meet her family, and loved that he'd put so much thought into this visit. She had put a lot of thought into it too. Mostly thoughts of trepidation and nerves that jangled like a banjo. There would be probing interrogations awaiting them, interrogations involving livelihood, matrimony, state of grace, and intentions. She still blanched at the memory from years ago of her Uncle Rex offering a piece of land to a man she had only been seeing for a few months. Kalli was the only girl, and after all that Uncle Rex and Aunt Evalyn had sacrificed to raise her as one of their own, she wasn't sure how the family would take it to see her wearing this man's ring before even asking their blessing. She caught herself turning the ring on her finger and made herself stop. She still wasn't quite used to how the platinum chilled and warmed along with the ambient air, like a cold-blooded thing. Hannington put his right hand over hers, and said "Nervous?"

"No baby," Kalli lied. "Not at all."

On the next uphill grade, she pointed out the Roadkill Café and the burnt-out juke joint caved in next to it. When she was a girl, Uncle Rex took her and Boyd and Curtis to watch a snake handler there. Kalli had been all of six years old, but she remembered the way the man from the Pentecostal church stripped his shirt off and stepped into the pit, neck undulating from side to side. The snakes' coppery leather skins writhed and clung and slithered around him in the disappointingly small pit, hissing and clicking at her and Boyd and Curtis through the chicken wire. Rex swore them to secrecy, but Kalli peed the bed for a week afterwards, and when Aunt Evalyn found out why, she pitched a fit. Now there was nothing in that lot but the boarded-up cafe, the shell of the bar, and a few abandoned rigs, all of it feathered with waist-high foxtail and chicory laced over with kudzu.

By the time Kalli finished telling the story and explaining all the nuances to Hannington, they were in Cavalle proper. In town, they passed by the general store. Paint peeled from its red roof and the dingy stucco exterior and gasoline price marquee were dim and empty of numbers. A few doors down, the new Valero station gleamed. There were a few booths inside, and its parking lot stood full of idling pickups whose windows were branded with decals: a coal miner in profile, the words *The lower I go the more she likes it.* The bug shield of one spectacularly rusty Dodge proclaimed *I'm not a-strokin, I'm a CUMMINS.*

"Welcome to my ancestral home," Kalli said.

Hannington laughed low, and glanced at the GPS. "Says thirty minutes to go the next twelve miles?"

"There's another curve or two coming up."

Kalli felt queasy as the car rolled to a stop, watching Hannington take in the first sight of her family home. Rex had built the place himself, from a prefab kit that had to be hauled up the mountain's narrow sand road in bits and pieces, tacking on new rooms here and there, adding a screened-in sun porch. Kalli had forgotten that the siding on the newer sections didn't quite match, and that there were a few gray shingles pixelating the roof where it had been repaired.

"Here we are," Kalli said, forcing a smile. She spotted Boyd standing in the shadows of the camper he and Curtis slept in and waved to him. He dipped his head to spit in a chaw cup, raised it in greeting, and melted back into the darkness.

"Who was that?" Hannington asked.

"Just Boyd," Kalli said. "He don't talk much. You'll meet him later."

Hannington raised his eyebrow at her abandonment of verb-noun agreement, and she wrinkled her nose at him. He knew her whole story; that Aunt Evalyn took Kalli in when she was just a baby after her parents—both of them high as kites—raced a railroad train to its crossing outside Buckton. Aunt Evalyn and Uncle Rex had raised Kalli up right alongside their own boys, Boyd and Curtis, bread-and-buttering her all the way through college; Rex sold quarts of corn whiskey to help pay her tuition. Seeing it anew, it was hard for Kalli to believe that the five of them ever managed to cram themselves into the little narrow-ribbed house. Floorboards sang everything but "The Star-Spangled Banner" when you walked down the hall. There wasn't a square or level angle in the whole doily-draped place. Kalli thought of the sleek loft she kept in Brooklyn and Hannington's immaculate and chic townhouse in Queens, and wondered what on Earth he'd think of Aunt Evalyn's faux wood paneling, painted-over wallpaper, and knick-knack shelves teeming with collectible ceramic plates, thimbles, and angels.

"Wow," Hannington breathed. Kalli felt every fiber in her body go taut. "You never told me this place was so quaint and cute . . . Like something out of a picture-book."

"Aunt Evalyn and Uncle Rex keep it looking sharp," Kalli said, and exhaled hard.

In the driveway, Hannington admired the purple cast of the pines against the craggy mountains inking a blue-black line across the sky. The stars seemed to press against their faces. Kalli inhaled the scent of mountain laurel, sassafras, and green peaches, wishing for something stronger to shore up her nerves. She tugged on Hannington's hand and led him inside.

Her aunts were holding court in the living room, their banter drifting out into the night air. She and Hannington kicked off their shoes in the green-carpeted sun porch. Kalli heard her Aunt Beulah's voice rise above the others drawling, "If I can't have me a young man, I don't want me one at all!" The treble roar of female laughter drowned out the sound of their entrance.

She and Hannington stepped into the golden light of the living room where the women sat with their feet up on overstuffed teal and white jacquard cushions. A stranger could tell at a glance that these were sisters; all four of them had the same high cheekbones and bottle-blonde coiffed hair, the same penchant for low-cut tops and pearl-pink manicured nails. Aunt Mae delicately ashed her cigarette into one of those smoke-suppressing ashtrays from the Home Shopping Network. Tears ran down Aunt Helen's face, her thick curls quivering as she laughed. Aunt Evalyn fanned herself with her apron, gasping for air. Aunt Beulah sat regal as a princess, chin high, eyes flashing.

"Why Kalli!" Aunt Evalyn cried, springing to her feet. "Come in, come in . . ."

"Hey there," Kalli said. "I want y'all to meet Hannington."

There was a brief pause as the women assessed him. Then they feasted. Mae lingered rather too long with her hug, then squeezed Hannington's bicep and encouraged the other sisters to follow suit. Beulah remarked twice how handsome he was and just as tall and strong shouldered as anybody. Hannington beamed, cheeks glowing from their attention.

She had tried to prepare him. He had been highly amused by Kalli's warnings: that Aunt Helen would not be wearing her teeth during dinner, especially if there was corn. Lots and lots of people were going to ask him if he knew Jesus as his personal savior. She told him that Curtis and Boyd bore harmless resemblance to photos of Confederate POWs—in body and in spirit—and advised him not to drink anything they gave him without watching them drink it first. There'd be a lot of rebel pride displayed on shirts, forearms, flagpoles. He should brace himself for mortifying questions, ranging from "Now what kind of Chinese person are you?" and "Are all your people tall?" to "Tell me the truth. Do you'uns *really* eat cats?" Hannington had laughed. He reminded her that he had been Chinese his entire life and even more so after taking a job in corporate finance. He was used to holding his own.

Watching them, Kalli felt as if a stone fell from her chest. Hannington produced a velvet-trimmed box of exquisite chocolates, a Valero gift card for Aunt Evalyn, and a wooden crate of Asian pears that peeked out of green tissue-paper nests.

"Got them in Chinatown, special for you," Kalli said.

"She means the pears," Hannington quipped. "I live in Queens."

Kalli winced, but the women collapsed in laughter.

"You must be something special too, though," Aunt Evalyn said to Hannington. "Kalli don't never bring anybody home to see us."

Kalli felt her tongue salt with guilt. "Who can blame me?" she said, putting her arm around Aunt Evalyn's soft shoulder. "I'm afraid you'll steal him away."

Now Aunt Evalyn held up Kalli's left hand appraisingly, admiring the setting of rubies clustered around the small diamond. She turned to Hannington. "You sure do mean to get the papers on her, don't you?"

"You bet I do," Hannington winked. "Same as I would a good huntin' dog."

"And I was worried about you getting along all right down here," Kalli said, shaking her head. "Looks like you do just fine."

Her aunts were entirely charmed. Curtis pumped Hannington's arm a little rough while Boyd merely nodded from a lawn chair, spitting genteelly into his chaw cup. They were friendly enough though, and even more so after learning that Hannington had served in the army to pay for law school, although Kalli kicked Curtis's knee when he said, "The U.S. Army, right?"

Her Uncles Rex, Harlan, and Derle stood to shake hands when she took Hannington up to the campfire to say goodnight—then grew so taken with him, they invited Hannington to sleep out in the poutin' trailer, only elbowing each other on the sly when Hannington asked what a poutin' trailer was. "You marry Kalli, you'll find out," Uncle Rex winked, squeezing her side. "Good to have you home, girlie."

Walking back down to the house, Kalli let herself wonder if maybe things were changing a little bit here . . . maybe. The one thing that most certainly had not changed were the sleeping arrangements of unmarried couples. Hannington was directed to the fold-out couch in the living room, and Kalli relegated to the porch since the aunts were bunked two-to-a bedroom. Hannington guffawed over the teased hairstyle she sported in her high school graduation picture and examined Aunt Evalyn's collection of ceramic angels while Kalli unfolded the quilts Aunt Evalyn left stacked on the arm of the couch.

"Really?" he asked, running his hands through her hair. "Separate beds?"

"No turtledoving here . . ." Moving out of his reach, she bumped into a stand of cut-crystal angels that Aunt Evalyn called the "Heavenly Host." "Oh shit. We break one of these we just leave quiet and head straight for the interstate."

"There are so many of them," Hannington marveled. The angel statuettes were frozen in postures of childlike adulation, their oval eyes trained upward towards heaven where all of them were doubtless as firmly ensconced as Billy Graham. He held one up. "What if I turn their faces to the wall so they won't see our hanky panky?"

"The good Lord and Aunt Evalyn see and hear everything," Kalli said.

He slid his hands around her bottom and she play-swatted him away. "I guess they'll watch over me while I sleep."

"You'll need watching, if Boyd and Curtis get to wilding," Kalli said, as she tucked a corner of the quilt into the sofa. "They sewed my last boyfriend up in his blankets like a human burrito."

"I bet at your Aunt Mae's we could fool around."

Kalli laughed, snapped a pillowcase at him. "You'd have to sleep with one eye open."

"Where are you going to be?"

"In the hammock on the screen porch."

"Outside?"

"I have an electric blanket, and a .22 automatic for the bears."

Hannington shook his head. "I'll sleep out there, you stay inside."

"No baby," she said, smiling at him. "I'd have to teach you how to shoot."

"I was in the Army, woman." They kissed again. "I'm not useless like your other boyfriends."

"Who told you that?" Kalli asked, pulling back a bit.

"Aunt Mae," Hannington said, eyes twinkling. "And Curtis, and Aunt Beulah, and that one uncle whose shirt was unbuttoned all the way."

"That's Derle." Kalli rolled her eyes. "He ain't nothing but a fart in a skillet."

"Oh wow, that's a good one." His face turned suddenly serious. "Am I doing ok? You know . . . with your family?"

"You sure are," Kalli said. "You fit right in."

"Good. I really like them."

"Good," she said. "Me too."

Kalli went to the porch and made her bed on the hammock. She found it hard to fall asleep to the sounds of the forest, and missed the roar of the BQE. It was the first time in ages they'd slept apart, and she missed the feel of Hannington's solid, strong body next to her, the weight of his arm around her waist. She even missed the way his full lips quivered when he snored. It had gone better than she hoped, and for that she was grateful. Tomorrow, they'd have a big family dinner and then Sunday they'd be back on the road to New York, a true hillbilly haul. She could stand it that long. Kalli let the cool night air fill her lungs, and drifted off.

The next morning, the aunts were awake at dawn, cooking and milling around the kitchen brewing pot after pot of coffee. Kalli didn't wake until eight o'clock, when she heard Aunt Beulah wondering rather too loudly if "the girl" ever would roll out of bed. By then, Hannington had already eaten, showered, and helped her uncles set up for the noon meal. After fortifying herself with caffeine, Kalli tried to redeem her sloth by making the gravy. But she put too much flour in the roux and had to be rescued by a beleaguered Aunt Helen. Then, she torqued the hand mixer too high and splattered cornbread batter all over the kitchen. After that, the aunts assigned her idiotic tasks like counting Styrofoam cups and taking a spoiled sandwich to the dog. Finally, Aunt Evalyn suggested rather too crisply that Kalli ought to quit wasting her vacation indoors and show Hannington around the land.

Kalli walked up the hill towards the sound of laughter and found the men gathered around an ancient Chevy with its hood popped open. She stared at their backs: broad shouldered, dark-headed, tan. Finally, her eyes rested on Hannington standing in the middle of them with his hands on his hips, nodding along with her cousins and uncles. He wore a short-sleeve, pearl-snap button up plaid shirt that appeared to be one of Boyd's or Curtis's and an Ohio State ball cap. She extricated him from the men, and they hiked a trail that wove around the wooded mountainside to the bottom of the ridge.

Kalli smiled at Hannington's deep intake of breath when they stepped out of the forest into a pasture that teemed with wildflowers. She taught him how to draw the sugar out of honeysuckle, laughing as he marveled at the pale citrus and cream-colored blossoms that were buttery to the touch. Kalli led him to an old deer blind, but it threatened to cave in around them, so they made love standing up against a beech tree, her legs wrapped around his waist, leaving both of them breathless and spent. They made a little blanket out of their clothes and dozed on the ground afterwards, eating some dried persimmons Aunt Helen had sent along as a snack. Kalli rose and began to dress, snapping her clothes against the trunk of the tree to shake off the red, sandy dirt. Hannington asked if she wanted to go further into the woods and explore a few of the deer trails that spurred off the main trail.

"Let's go on back to the house," she urged. "I'm worried we'll happen onto a bear, or somebody's still or something."

"These things happen on a regular basis?"

"That's why I moved to Brooklyn."

"I don't know why you'd want to," he said, chewing on a sassafras twig. "I could live out here forever."

"You don't know it the way I do," Kalli said. "Not entirely, just yet."

When they returned, Aunt Evalyn made Kalli sort plastic cutlery while Hannington played horseshoes with the men. She suspected he had a nip or three with Boyd and Curtis because his face was reddening a little. She was glad that he was settling in, but she noticed that his speech—which had just a whiff of Mandarin cadence and a touch of New England vowels—was taking on the flat A's and abbreviated gerunds of her family's drawl. If it wasn't from the liquor, she hoped he would stop.

After the grace was raised, they stood in front of the buffet, set out on long rectangular folding tables that sagged under the glut of ham, game turkey, mashed potatoes, two pots of gravy, biscuits, cornbread, innumerable cream and fruit pies, banana pudding, glazed sweet potatoes, and greens simmering in the slow cooker. Aunt Evalyn was filling a plate. She looked at Kalli and raised an eyebrow. "Rex," Aunt Evalyn called, "You want white or brown gravy?"

"Brown," he said.

Kalli got up from her seat with a start, and patted Hannington's arm. "I'll get your plate, honey."

"You don't have to. I'm a grown man." She glanced around, unsure how to explain to him that there was an order to meals: the men ate first, then the children, and the women didn't take one bite until everyone else had been fed. It would not do for the aunts to see Hannington filling his own plate like he hadn't anyone to look after him.

"Would you go sit down?" Kalli hissed, nudging him with her elbow.

"I can do it myself," he said, playfully nudging her back.

"No, you most certainly cannot." She smiled. A little louder, she cooed, "You stay set down, sugar. I'll get it for you."

"I could get used to being waited on," he said, winking at Aunt Mae, who nodded at him approvingly. When Kalli returned from the buffet with her own plate, Hannington was sitting at a picnic table with her aunts, praising the food and enthralling them with tales of his early childhood in Shanghai.

"Did you know that they were so poor they didn't even have a box fan?" Aunt Mae said. "We always at least had a fan."

"Yes, I know." Kalli took a bite of deviled egg, and it was so delicious, she made a note to go back for seconds.

"Didn't have it as bad here as you think," Aunt Evalyn winked. Aunt Beulah inquired about his family in the Orient. The Orient. Dear God. Kalli opened her mouth to speak, thought better of it, and filled it with the rest of the deviled egg, instead.

"I don't have family in China anymore," he said. "My parents moved us to Queens when I was ten, and now they live right next door to me."

"Hannington bought his parents a house," Kalli said. The women fell into a pleasing hum of "oh, how lovely" and "isn't that nice . . ." that made Hannington blush a little.

"I wanted us to be close together," Hannington said.

"Why, we do the very same thing here!" Beulah said. "Stick close by."

"That's near as good as putting them in a trailer in your own yard," Helen agreed.

"I get to see my mother every day."

"Well, young man," Evalyn said. "Aren't you sweet?"

"My mother adores Kalli," he added. He was laying it on a little thick, so she raised her eyebrows at him. Mrs. Yan did like her, but "adore" felt a bit performative.

"We sure wish Kalli would get herself home to us a little more," Aunt Evalyn said. "I think she got to be about half ashamed of us after that law school."

"I didn't either," Kalli said. "I run down here to see you every chance I get."

"She talks about you all the time," Hannington said quickly. "It's wonderful how you were able to raise her in the family. In China, if you are orphaned you are pretty much on your own."

"Oh, heavens, no. In this family nobody is allowed to be alone." Kalli spotted Boyd at the buffet, and he smiled at her with his eyes before grabbing a couple deviled eggs and beating a hasty retreat to the sun porch, where the men were eating.

"Why on earth would you *want* to?" Aunt Beulah asked. "Idn't natural."

"What's unnatural is a good Ohio girl, running off to New York City."

"I don't know that I'll live anywhere else," Kalli said. "I love my job and they sure keep me busy."

"Too busy if you ask me," Hannington said. "I'd like her to get out of the prosecutor's office and into entertainment, finance, any kind of law that pays more money and actually lets you start a family, take a vacation—"

"We're on vacation now," Kalli said. She felt the pressure in her chest again, like a rubber band being pulled taut. She was afraid it would break. He had never talked like this before.

"A family would be a fine thing for a girl like Kalli." Aunt Evalyn rested her elbows on the table, and laced her fingers together, and arched her eyebrows in Hannington's direction. "I keep after her to hurry up . . ."

"Hannington, do you want to have a baby someday?" Beulah's eyes were keen.

"I'm flattered you ask me, ma'am," he demurred, "But we only just met."

God bless him, Kalli thought. Beulah slapped his arm and giggled, but Evalyn honed in. "Kalli has land sitting here waiting on her whenever you want it."

"I didn't know you had land," Hannington said. She imagined his mind tinkering with numbers, calculating. He slathered butter on an ear of corn, and grinned. "We could probably build a beautiful home down here for half what we give in rent."

"Certainly a double-wide," Aunt Evalyn said.

"If I wanted a double-wide I coulda had me one a long time back," Kalli said. A small silence fell. The mashed potatoes had turned to clay in her mouth. She gulped her iced tea.

"Nothing wrong with a double-wide," Aunt Evalyn said.

"Good homes for people just starting out," Aunt Beulah added. "Humble people."

"Now, now," Aunt Mae said. "Our girl's done real good up there and ought to do what pleases her."

"Wait too long and you can't do what you please," Aunt Evalyn said. "You'll just be old and alone."

"Enough about us . . . How are Boyd and Curtis getting along?" Kalli smiled, kept her expression wide open. She knew full well how Boyd and Curtis were getting along, and so did all her aunts. The boys—if 35- and 37-year-old men could indeed be considered "boys"—lived off income from the gas wells, filling their days hunting ginseng and chasing other men's wives and complaining about Obama down at the AmVets. Curtis walked in to fill his plate and smiled at the Aunts. "Did I hear my name?"

"They're getting along real good," Aunt Evalyn gushed, putting a hand on her son's arm. "Curtis here has an interview next week."

"No, I don't," Curtis said, brushing crumbs off his *Don't Tread On Me* t-shirt. "They canceled it on me since the mines are still down."

"Well, maybe you'll find another job," Hannington said, helpfully. Kalli wished she could have stopped him. "What do you do?"

There was a brief pause at the table. Hannington searched Kalli's eyes, but there was no way now to explain that "what do you do" was such a rude question here, where people's jobs weren't rewarding career choices or paths to prosperity. Curtis studied Kalli's face. He popped a deviled egg in his mouth, swallowed it hard, and said, "Only job I want is down in the mines. But Hillary Clinton come and closed them up."

"Give me a break," Kalli said, daring Curtis to spar. "All by herself, she did that?"

"Damn straight."

"Appalachian Power said the coal's all been dug, and the work ain't coming back." Kalli said. "You know that well as I do."

Curtis glanced at Hannington as he loaded his plate up with the last two deviled eggs. "Kalli don't like coal. But she likes her lattes hot. You're a smart man . . . riddle me that?"

"No more politics, you two!" Aunt Evalyn said. Curtis smiled mercilessly, and sauntered off with a "yes, ma'am."

Evalyn frowned at Kalli. "Why do you two carry on like that?"

"He started it, I finished it." She heard Hannington ask Mae what was going on with the mines, and saw Mae blow her cheeks out and roll her eyes. Kalli pressed on, knowing it would only make things worse. "What, he can speak his mind, but I can't?"

"How much is a . . . double-wide?" Hannington asked Aunt Evalyn, squeezing Kalli's hand under the table.

"Depends," Aunt Mae said. "On your options."

"You have to figure on a deck," Aunt Beulah said. "These days, anyway."

"You can get one for thirty, maybe 28-5 if you barter good," Aunt Evalyn said.

"Did you know that it's fourteen miles and back to fetch a quart of milk?" Kalli asked. Her blood was still pounding from the exchange with Curtis.

"Must be why it's so peaceful," Hannington replied, smiling.

"The electric goes out all the time."

"Used to happen all the time in Shanghai," he shrugged.

"Hell, half the time the power goes out and we don't even notice," Mae said. She wiggled her eyebrows at Hannington. "You find other things to entertain you."

Kalli stabbed at the ice in her tea with a spoon. "How on earth would you make a living?"

"I hear they have banks down here."

"Good, good banks," Aunt Evalyn sighed. "Don't need no bailout."

"And we would be nearer your family."

Her aunts smiled, blonde heads bobbing and murmuring "mmhmm" in unison.

"I'm near them right now," Kalli said, "And I sure love it."

There was a small silence, a flutter of hurt. The aunts looked at their plates, but Kalli sat straight, staring defiantly. These family pileups never failed to leave her raw, as if she'd just been sanded by a mine belt. Hannington stared at the tablecloth, and she knew she had shamed him. He would never ever speak to his family the way she had just spoken to hers.

"Oh, honey," Aunt Evalyn said, "We're just teasing you because we love you."

"I'll get you some more ice tea." Kalli snatched up Hannington's glass. He followed Kalli into the kitchen, carrying his plate. She took it from him without a word and put it in the wash bin. He slipped up behind her and gave her a hug. "Kalli, come on. That was rude."

She didn't answer, just shook her head. Hannington didn't understand the barbs behind the words, didn't hurt the way she did over the jokes that papered over real resentment. "They do this every time I come home. Curtis picks a fight with me. The sisters hassle me to move back, marry a Republican, have a baby or three."

"Shhh shhh . . . I was just humoring them," he said. "If we did build something, it'd be a getaway—a vacation place. We aren't leaving New York."

"You've given them false hope . . ."

"Oh, come on . . . What's the harm in talking about it?" he asked, "I'm not serious yet—"

Kalli did not know how to make him see that playing along wasn't really playing, not with the aunts. This was a blood sport, and bull hooking Kalli was the prize. She felt a lump rise in her throat. "Don't you see how they pick and pick at me on purpose until I get mad, then they complain that I don't get along with nobody," She choked back a sob. "It's like to drive me crazy."

"Well . . . could just be a little more tolerant?" Hannington shrugged. "What's it matter?"

"What matters is that they don't care at all what I want. They'd rather have me barefoot and pregnant, teaching Sunday School at First Baptist and baking cookies than representing the State of New York in court. Nothing I accomplish counts for shit to them."

"They just miss you," Hannington said. He touched her arm, and she flinched. "I don't know what-all your deal is—"

"What-all?" she mimicked.

"Ok, ok . . . I didn't mean to appropriate the norms of your culture."

Aunt Mae cleared her throat in the doorway. "Can't you two quarrel like normal folks?"

Hannington gave Kalli a squeeze and stepped back a bit. "Oh, darn it, Miss Mae. I was just stealing a kiss."

"Take her in the woods for a good long walk," Mae said, bumping her hip into Kalli's as she reached for her leopard-print cigarette purse. "Take her mind off things."

"We tried that," Kalli said.

"Try harder," Mae threw over her shoulder as she sashayed towards the door. "It's good for your complexion. At your age, sugar, that counts."

After the meal, her uncles began to snap open cases, pull guitars and mandolins and fiddles from plush resting places, and draw lawn chairs into a circle. The aunts disappeared into the kitchen, the sounds of plucking and tuning cut only by their muffled laughter and the clink, scrape and rumble of dishes being run under the sink faucet. As she washed and scrubbed alongside them, Kalli said little. She peeked out the kitchen window and saw Hannington smiling and clapping as he listened to her uncles sing "Nine Pound Hammer" and then "Heaven's Bright Shore" . . .

Good Lord have mercy. They had Hannington singing.

Now Hannington was laughing too loudly at some idiot remark made by Curtis, and Boyd had to grab Hannington's arm to keep him from tumbling off his perch on the tree stump. She saw Hannington take a deep draught of clear liquor from a quart jar, and let Boyd coax a pinch of chaw into his palm.

Well, don't that beat all, Kalli thought. He's gone native.

Hannington was impersonating, imposter-ing, whatever you wanted to call it—he was embarrassing the living hell out of her. She dried her hands on a dishtowel and went out to the garage where the women's purses were piled up atop the deep freezer. Aunt Evalyn and Aunt Helen were clearing off the table for a round of euchre and conveniently failing to notice just how far into that bottle the men were getting. Kalli fished through her handbag for the car keys.

She didn't mean to be gone as long as she was, just a ride down to Laurelton and back. She found herself wandering the aisles of the Wal-Mart Supercenter, staring at stacks of tires, the vast selection of deodorants in pastel plastic casings, seemingly mile-long stretches of skinny jeans, tube tops, flip-flops. When the store's PA system announced its 10:00 p.m. closing, Kalli jolted herself from her reverie. She'd been gone over two hours. A rush of anger and shame coursed through her body. It wasn't right, leaving him to fend for himself with her family, even if he were doing better at it than she was.

When Kalli pulled into the drive, Hannington was leaning against the tailgate of Rex's pickup truck. Curtis waved, and Boyd spit into his chaw cup, avoiding Kalli's hello.

"Aunt Evalyn is about to skin you alive," Curtis said.

"Why?" Kalli said. "Ain't you got it coming first?"

Boyd spit again, and looked away.

"Hello, Kalli," Hannington said, extending his arm for a handshake. "I believe we've met before . . ."

"Is that right?" Kalli said. "You seem familiar, but I can't place you."

"Why'd you run off?" Hannington asked.

Kalli couldn't answer. She tried to think of a comeback, but the fact was, she didn't have one. "You been into that liquor?"

"I been having fun with your family and missing you." Hannington took an unsteady step, recovering his balance on Boyd's arm.

"Baby," Kalli said, reaching for him, "Let's get you to bed."

"Aww, leave him alone," Curtis said. "He's a grown man."

"I'm not going to bed with you," Hannington said. "Not now."

"You're drunk."

"Yes," he said, "But I'm not stupid."

Kalli heard Boyd spit, and she felt heat rising up her neck, embarrassed that her cousins were audience to it. "Is that right?"

"We've been treating him good while you was gone," Curtis said. "Not that you care."

"Mind your own business," Kalli said. She turned to Hannington. "I do care."

"Coulda fooled me," Curtis said. "You run off and left him, treated him like nothing but a n—"

Kalli froze as if slapped. "I don't like that talk." She looked at Hannington, but he studied the woods, unwilling to meet her eyes. "Hannington. Is that word ok with you?"

"I'll say what I please," Curtis paused to take a drink, "Same way you do."

"I don't come all the way home to watch you act ignorant in front of company."

"Let it go, Kalli. Doesn't matter," Hannington shrugged.

But it did matter. It mattered a great deal to her.

Curtis drained the last of his beer, crushed the can, and said, "Why don't you come on up to the trailer with us? They're going to pick and sing a little more."

"Yeah, sure," Hannington said. He steadied himself, tried to stand. Boyd steadied him again, holding his spit cup out to keep from sloshing it.

"Hannington—" Kalli cried out.

"What?" His face was tense in the glow of the fluorescent light. The air smelled sweet and sick with citronella candles and wood smoke. "You can go off when you want, but I can't?"

"You are making a fool out of yourself and me both."

"Already been done," Boyd said. "From what I can tell, you're all three being assholes."

"Boyd can talk!" Hannington said, joy springing from his voice. He threw his arms out.

"Of course he can. He just don't care to," Kalli said. Boyd shrugged and started walking uphill towards the campfire, Curtis on his heels. They paused when Hannington called for them to wait up.

"Come talk to me," she whispered, lightly touching Hannington's arm. "Please, don't."

"All right." Hannington held her gaze for a moment, then he turned to her cousins. "I'll be up in a minute."

The boys disappeared into the darkness. Hannington held out his hand to Kalli, pulled her onto his knee. The truck springs groaned beneath their weight.

"I know he upset you," Hannington said. "But do you realize . . . do you realize how bad you made the boys feel? How bad you make them feel all the time?"

Kalli's mouth went slack from shock. "What?"

"You didn't have to embarrass him," he said.

"You're going to put up with that shit?" Kalli snapped.

"No, but I don't take it personally. Except when it's personal."

"It is personal. He does it because he knows it makes me mad."

Hannington sighed. "Then don't get mad. You're playing right into his hands."

Kalli's head spun. He was blaming her now, too? Just like the rest of them?

"You're a big-shot New York lawyer," Hannington said. "It's hard for those two men, living up to what you do."

"What am I supposed to do—just stand there and take it?"

"You don't have to be so outspoken about everything. Everything's not a fight, honey."

She closed her eyes and said, "You sure have bought the hog, haven't you?"

"Everyone has flaws, Kalli. Even you. It's not up to you to point them out and make sure they know it." He looked her in the eyes. "You're being a brat."

"I'm being myself!"

They stood for a long moment, her arms crossed over her chest, his hands on his hips. She caught herself turning the ring on her left finger with her thumb, and stopped.

"You do what you want," he said. "I'm going to enjoy your family."

Kalli closed her eyes and listened to him walk away. She went indoors and turned off the porch light, realizing that's just what Aunt Evalyn did when she was mad at Uncle Rex. Kalli sat on the couch, tears running down her face, trying to keep her crying quiet so she could suffer it in solitude. She wanted to feel something familiar, something other than the rickety need that hung between her, her pride, her feelings, Hannington being half-right, and all of it being wrong.

She stood up, and with sudden energy made Hannington's bed on the couch. She patted the pillows just so, then turned down the sheets. They were the color of wild rose petals, satiny cotton that warmed at the touch. She crept to the bathroom to brush her teeth and wash her face, avoiding the aunts. She didn't need another reminder of ways that she was found failing, or worse yet, the sympathetic glances from women who pitied Hannington and believed that he was putting up with far too much from her. She couldn't stand up under their scrutiny, and no one could stand up under hers. Even herself.

Kalli awoke when dawn was just creeping in, a flaming orange line burning through the treetops along the ridge, framed up in the picture window of Aunt Evalyn's living room. Hannington hadn't come to bed. Mist rose from the hollers, muffling the chatter of squirrels and the early calls of songbirds. She shivered into a fleece and brewed a cup of coffee, pouring an extra one for Hannington. Kalli went up to the boys' trailer and tapped lightly on the door.

"Hannington!" she stage-whispered. Someone groaned and shifted inside.

"Go away," Curtis mumbled.

Kalli opened the door. The scent of men sweating whiskey and stale beer pushed her back. Boyd lay spread-eagled on the floor, fully dressed. He had a wadded-up sheet for a pillow.

Curtis was passed out in an easy chair rocker. The remains of a poker game lay scattered across the camper table. He groaned, rubbing a hand across his eyes. "Kalli. You still got your drawers knotted up?"

"Using racial slurs makes you seem like an even lesser man than you are."

"Ok," Curtis nodded. "I'll keep that in mind."

That was it. She crept over to him, then pulled the rocker low to the floor, watching him wriggle and struggle for his balance. "You know better than to piss with me, boy," she hissed, then tugged his beard so hard it made him howl. She dodged Curtis's swatting hand, ignored his cussing and went to the back room where Hannington lay crashed out in an upper bunk.

She touched his arm. His eyes flickered open, caught hers, and his smile faded. He closed his eyes and sighed. Kalli's heart felt like someone pinched it.

"Hi" he said finally.

She took his chin in her hands and drew his eyes towards hers.

"Go back to sleep. You smell like booze . . . weed . . ." She sniffed in his direction, "Deer jerky and . . . death."

"Love you, too."

"I'm sorry," she said. "I don't know what's wrong with me."

"That's all right," he said. "I gave it plenty of thought."

"What'd ya come up with?"

"Everything," he said. "And nothing."

She lowered her head to his shoulder, letting him feel the coolness of her tears. He hesitated. Then he ran his hand across her hair. She pushed the blankets aside, hefted herself up and got into bed beside him, putting her arm around him. He slid his leg over hers.

"I'm sorry," she said again.

"You should be. But I understand a little more than you think, after last night."

"You gonna stick up for me now?"

"Always. Except when you're wrong."

"Hold me tighter," she said. "Please."

"Take those damn shoes off," he muttered, pulling her closer. She kicked her flip-flops off and settled into him, curving towards the warmth of his body. Hannington rolled over, easing his hipbones atop hers.

"Uncle Rex catches us, you're dead," she whispered.

"What a way to go . . ." He leaned in to kiss her.

"You have got to brush your teeth," she said, gagging. "What did they give you?"

"We drank some liquor that Rex hid in the yard," he admitted. "The boys thought it was hickory. But Uncle Rex came over and told us he buried it because it was scorched."

Kalli started laughing and couldn't stop, barely managing to tell him he got exactly what he deserved for tipping cups with poor company. Hannington play-threatened to breathe on her again, tickling her underarm until she shrieked "Stop it, hickory breath!"

A boot thudded into the door and they both jumped.

"Knock it off!" Curtis yelled.

"See what I mean?" Kalli said, shaking her head. "Never alone."

"Is that such a bad thing?" Hannington said. They lay back down, crowded against each other in the bunk. Kalli pulled Hannington's arm around her, tighter.

"Maybe not," Kalli said. "Not always."

He turned to her, smiled, and shook his head. "I don't guess so."

"Stop," she pleaded, "Stop puttin' on the pone."

They lay like that for a while, wafting in and out of sleep until one of the boys got up and started stirring. The screen door slammed shut. Kalli heard footsteps near the window and rolled over to peer through the shades. Curtis was peeing on a tree just a few yards away from their window.

"Use the flush toilet, you philistine!"

He waved over his shoulder. "Morning, Kalli!"

"May you find your way to the nearest electric fence."

Curtis laughed, zipped his pants, and headed down to breakfast.

"What's going on?" Hannington asked, rolling over.

"I made peace with Curtis," Kalli said. She stroked his hair. "You want some breakfast?"

"Sure do." He started to sit up, then fell back, blanching and pale. "Oh, wow."

"Brush your teeth," she said. "I'll be outside."

Kalli waited for him by the campfire. It barely smoldered at the center, a ring of gray-white ash pooling up around its edges. She held her hand above the white, feathery substance, testing its heat. There was none, so she put her hand into the dust itself, shocked at how light it was, like a cobweb. She dusted off her hand and put wood on the fire, stoking it to flame. Finally, it caught, and she warmed her hands over it, more for the comfort than for the heat.

The men sat with Uncle Rex on the porch, sipping coffee. The lights were on in the kitchen, and Kalli could see her aunts bustling around in their loose cotton house dresses. Kalli was still standing there when Hannington emerged from the trailer, drying his face off with a paper towel. Everything felt all right, somehow, if a little gauzy: Hannington smiling at her, his face still flushed from the hangover. Her hands gray with ash, ash that smeared across his crumpled, stinking shirt when she leaned into him. As they walked up to the porch, she took his hand in hers, cradling her fingers in its warmth.

Search, Rescue, Recovery

That whole week brought havoc to Stowe Valley Camp and Canoe. A domestic dispute among tent campers drew the sheriff out twice on Monday. On Wednesday, a thunderstorm felled several trees and knocked out electric to a whole block of RV glampers. It was humid as hell and insufferable along the hiking trail due to the swollen, rotting carcass of a llama that wandered over from the neighboring farm and dropped dead in the woods. Thursday, my kids were goofing around with a nail gun and we wound up taking a family trip to Urgent Care for tetanus booster shots and stitches.

By Friday afternoon we were so far behind on prep for Father's Day weekend that I left my son, Jacob, to run the camp store. Diana was helping me replace Edison outlets on the RV hookup stations, which is to say that she was handing me tools, listening to me cuss, and preparing to knock me off the ladder with a 2x4 if I got electrocuted. The hot sun beat down on us. I was hacking at molten plastic, ripping out miles of fried wire and muttering that I should have had the foresight to pursue a career in accounting or insurance sales. Anything but following in my father's footsteps as the sole proprietor of a four-star outdoor recreational facility. Diana touched my arm, jolting me from my complaint.

"Kenneth," she said. "Look."

She pointed to a small crowd gathering around some kayakers at the put in. When we got to the river, the man—Steve was his name—was bellowing that they could not find their boy. Steve had one of those dumb navy tattoos: a mermaid whose breasts jiggled when he clenched and unclenched his fist. Marla, the mother, had a sweetness to her face that seemed to say "Please," and I was certain that she spent her days at a cash register, meaning it when she told people to have a good day. The girl with them was about fourteen. She kept pulling at a bunch of those Silly Bandz bracelets on her wrist, nervous as a hare.

Was their boy here? Had we seen him? Steve's eyes sunk deeper in his head when Diana shook her head no, twisting a strand of blonde hair that had fallen loose from her ponytail.

"Goddamn it . . . I can't take much more of his shit," Steve said. I looked at him.

"Devin . . . sometimes he runs off." Steve said that the boy had learning issues. That Devin wasn't quite right, and was young for his age. While Steve rambled, Marla stared at her shoes. She wore a pair of soaking wet sneakers that made squeaking sounds when she shifted her weight, and I remember being distracted by the flatulating squelch.

"Devin's always rambling off a-looking for something," Marla said, voice trembling. "He always comes back . . ."

"We'll find him," I said. "Don't worry." Diana called the sheriff while I radioed the volunteer fire department. My buddy Ross and his girlfriend organized a search of the grounds. Some tent campers brought bottles of water and snacks to the family while I hustled to hitch up the boat trailer.

"Dad," Jacob said. I looked up. "I know that kid from school."

"Who is he, again?" I asked.

"He played t-ball with me that one year," Jacob said. "Remember? Flaps his arms all the time and had to leave the team?" Jacob held up his phone and showed Devin's picture. The boy's face was cherubic, naïve. I remembered seeing him in the hallways after school, ducking his head low and letting his bangs fall over his face to avoid my hello.

"They call him 'Lockdown' because he runs away all the time, and then the whole school gets shut in."

"I better not hear you calling him that."

"I don't," Jacob said. "I don't beast like that." Jacob sounded so hurt, and I realized too late that I should have known better than to start yet another argument. We had been at each other's throats all summer. The boy formerly so eager to help with the canoe livery retreated into his PSP, his phone, the computer—anything with pixels. It was infuriating for me to see my son thickening up, turning pale and chubby as a lump of bread dough from hours and hours cruising imaginary cities in stolen cars, blasting away at the cops with a pretend AR-15. At Jacob's age, I was already running rescue with my dad and cutting all the firewood for the campground, chasing real girls instead of picking up digital hookers and dyeing weird colors in my hair.

Diana made me lay off Jacob after he won a prize at some kind of gaming conference and started getting small sponsorships for his YouTube channel. But that victory—and his burgeoning online "fame" with a following of a thousand other nerdy game-wonks—just sucked Jacob deeper into the recesses of the world-wide waste of time and farther away from reality.

"Glitching . . . Dad, you're glitching," he said.

"What?" I dropped the canoe I was loading and its plastic hull barked against the metal carrier.

"So . . . can I go with?"

"Can you be away from Call of Whoredom that long?"

"You're on me no matter what I do—"

I felt a blush of shame creep up my neck. He was right. Jacob shuffled his feet and said, "I rented them the boats this morning. I feel bad for Devin. He's . . . he's kind of lost all the time."

"All right, all right." I nodded. "Sure, you can go. I understand."

"Yes!" he said, pumping his fist and running up the hill. "Yeah!"

"Hug your mother," I said, "She's real worried."

He nodded, his blue-tinted hair catching the sun as he sprinted away. Maybe this would be good for him. Lord knows, Jacob could use a dose of reality.

The family was waiting in front of the camp store when I pulled the van around. Jacob helped the women onto the bench seat, gesturing for Steve to sit up front by me.

Steve cleared his throat. "Thanks for helping us."

"How far are we going?" I asked.

He wiped his face with his shirt. "I don't know exactly . . . three or four miles upriver?"

This gave me pause. The family had paddled right past the village of Stowe. Why hadn't they called for help finding Devin, then? I cleared my throat. "Will you know where to put in if we drive along the road?"

"I think so." Steve sounded hoarse, exhausted, and far from certain.

"I remember," Marla said. She leaned forward and kissed Steve's cheek so tenderly that I had to look away. Jacob was talking to Kylie. Both of them were pointing at something on his cell phone, their faces fixed in the thousand-yard stare of the web-addicted.

"Hey, Jacob," I said. "Did you check the straps on the kayaks?"

"Yes, sir. We're game ready."

I saw the girl smile a little, tentatively—and as much as I wanted to jerk Jacob by the arm and tell him that this was no effing game, I could not bring myself to do it. At least he was talking to a human female in real life; that was progress.

The five of us were near-silent as we wound our way along the main road through Stowe's only stoplight. We passed the bar, the post office trailer, and the turnoff for the ashram. We passed a bunch of cars in the watercraft trail parking lot where a large cluster of families were picnicking down on the banks under a huge, brightly colored "Happy Juneteenth" banner. The families had to have been there already when Steve and Marla paddled by looking for Devin. Finally, at Quarry Church Road, Steve tapped the glass and said, "There. We was just down from here."

Jacob radioed the sheriff while I pulled the van into the parking area, sandy soil whispering beneath our tires. Soon, the bank swarmed with EMTs in bright yellow vests, river rats in denim cutoffs and tennis shoes, and the photographer from the local paper. I nodded to Randy and Brian, the divers from the volunteer fire department. Both military-trained, they were the best men we had.

While Jacob and I geared up, Sheriff TC Hallinan asked the family several questions. Was there a life vest in the kayak? Yes, but the boy didn't have it on. How long had Devin been missing? About two hours now, maybe a little more. Does he know how to swim?

"He swam good," Steve said, voice catching. "I taught him."

TC stayed ashore with Marla and Kylie, while I helped Steve into our canoe. The rest of the boats were spread out around us, waiting. Steve nodded. We started to paddle.

I tried to imitate TC's genial demeanor as I asked Steve questions: Was the fishing hole before or after the house with the pink porch? Did he happen to remember if he'd passed the old canal locks?

Steve just shook his head and said, "I'll know it when I see it."

You better, I thought, you damn well better.

I listened with half an ear while Steve talked and talked. He told Jacob where he met Marla, that he loved Devin like his own boy, how much better Devin did outside in nature than in school. Steve smiled shyly when he recalled teaching Devin to fish.

"Loved it just like me," Steve said. "Took to it like a foal to milk."

I half-wanted the silence we'd had in the van, but Steve was obviously a nervous talker. He told me that Devin must have paddled on from where he left him; that Devin should have knowed better; that he had already half wore himself out looking but he'd keep looking if it was the last thing he ever did. "I won't ever give up on Devin," Steve said. "Never have, never will."

By then we were on a particularly lonely stretch of the river bordering the nature preserve. Pockmarked slabs of discarded concrete and sandstone boulders lined the riverbank, and it dropped off to a deep and muddy bottom. People liked to bass fish there, but the previous night's storm uprooted a huge live oak that laid across the river and created a bottleneck.

Steve took a quick breath. "That's it."

Jacob's eyes met mine. He'd paddled the river with me enough to know that water was likely rolling hard below that tree, pulling everything in and down. I've found all sorts of things in whirlpools like that: crushed coolers, dead cows, waterlogged kayaks turning like dowel rods, scrap axles bent into strange and unimaginable shapes. And a few times, I've found people.

"You ok?" I asked Jacob. He nodded, lips pressed thin.

Steve leaned over towards me. His voice sounded like it was being wrung out like a towel. "I didn't want to say nothing in front of his mother . . . but when we was looking, I thought I saw the boat under that log." Steve avoided my eyes and stared down at his hands. "I didn't want Marla to see."

You dumb sonofabitch, I thought. Jacob's head jerked up, and for a moment I feared I had said it out loud. Steve stared at me, his jaw working. I sighed, blew the signal whistle, and radioed the sheriff, pretending not to hear my son whisper to Steve that sometimes I act like a total ass. The water pulled hard towards the logjam, and I had to hold onto the paddle with both hands to keep the current from snatching it away.

It nagged at me, Steve being fool enough to leave Devin alone on the water. Steve abandoned that kid in high-running water . . . And even a half-dry river has no more mercy than wolves give to lambs.

"Dad," Jacob said. "Are you going in?"

"Too dangerous." I shook my head. "We have to wait for the divers."

Steve blanched, and his lip quivered. Then he stood, cupped his hands, and yelled, "Devin . . . Devin!" The echo came back to us on the water.

My son—my sweet son—knelt on the floor of the canoe and patted Steve on the back.

"Don't worry," Jacob said. "We'll find him. He probably just wandered off—"

"Easy. Let's not get our hopes up," I said.

"He was just trying to help," Steve said. He reached over and touched Jacob's shoulder. "It's all right, son."

TC, Kylie, and Marla stood on the riverbank. Fire and rescue trucks idled roadside, and a couple medics were high-stepping through the waist-high weeds with an empty gurney, defib kit, and oxygen tank. The lights of the emergency squad strobed red, white, and blue across the water's surface. I could smell the river, the mix of fish, decaying leaves, and sand. The sound of its current filled our silence while the divers worked: Randy manning the jon boat while Brian dove. I heard the radio crackle when the search party from downriver reported there was no sign of Devin. The volunteers at Stowe gave the all-clear a few minutes later.

I studied Steve. His face had the creased wear of someone who used hard drink, and I wondered how much patience a man like that would have with a boy like Devin. He clearly thought the boy was a burden—cussing that he was tired of his shit. What kind of a father does that? I know you can't judge a man until you've walked in his shoes. And I know that panic, shock, and fear will do strange things to a person's mind, but if that was any child of mine there in the river, I would not stop diving until I found him, or drowned myself trying. And I just kept thinking: why didn't Steve stop for help?

Brian surfaced, hanging onto the boat with one arm and lifting his dive mask with the other. He spoke quietly to Randy.

Steve stood, nearly tipping our canoe. "What's going on?"

"Gonna run the line," Randy said. "Found a boat."

"What's it look like?"

Brian rubbed his eyes, avoiding ours. "Blue kayak."

It was surely one of our rental craft. Steve sat heavily and brought his knees to his chest. Jacob bit his lip and folded his hands. Brian put the regulator in his mouth and tipped backward into the water.

We could hear everything; the birds chirping like it was just any other day. The winch grinding as it drew the kayak up out of the river, water pouring from its hull. Steve leaned over the edge of our boat and vomited into the water.

"I want Marla," Steve said, gagging. Jacob looked at me, unsure.

"Drop me off with the divers," I said to my son, jerking my head towards the dive boat. "He should be with his family right now."

The boat was stuck good. I took over running the winch so that Randy could help Brian. Recovery took them a long time because the water was muddy, the press of the current was exhausting, and the tangle of submerged tree roots and debris made it hard for the divers to see more than an arm's length in front of them. When Brian asked for a body harness, I radioed Sheriff TC. The word "coroner" echoed off the water like the chopping of an axe.

Marla buried her face in Steve's shoulder. Jacob waited on the bank with the family instead of paddling back out to me, and I could not blame him. This was more than I bargained for when I brought him along. I saw him scoop out a place to sit in the sand with Kylie. The two of them looked so small, sitting with their thin, tan arms wrapped around their knees, waiting.

Marla wailed so loudly when Devin's body came free that I thought the river might stop moving. Kylie jumped up, hand on her forehead, Jacob's arms steadying her as she swayed, crying. Steve turned his face away.

Randy and Brian and I struggled to get Devin on board. One of his legs thudded against the hull, and his jean shorts ripped, exposing his nakedness. Rivulets of muddy water flowed down his body. He had a bunch of those plastic bracelets on his wrists, just like Kylie's: a dinosaur, a bird, a fish. There were deep, red scratches on his throat where his shirt tangled and cinched his neck. There was an expression of amazement on his face.

I helped the divers in and we paddled furiously to shore. Brian and Randy pulled Devin's too-still body from the boat and immediately began CPR.

In a drowning, we're trained to always attempt to revive—even if there's no hope. It makes it easier on the families to accept the loss. I held a thermometer strip to Devin's forehead, his body shaking limply with each set of twenty pumps, three resuscitation breaths. We all startled at the sound of a hiccup, but only a thin stream of brackish colored water trickled out of the boy's mouth. Brian wiped it away, turned Devin's head to the side, and continued to resuscitate. I heard a rib crack, then another, like the sound of corn popping in a kettle, brittle and wet at the same time.

The first impulse when drowning is to hold your breath. Then the CO_2 builds up in your body, and eventually you'll have an involuntary reflex to inhale. Water goes into your lungs, and your organs slow their function. Often, drowning victims go into mammalian diving response, which slows breathing and heart rate, so that the body uses less oxygen. But mammalian response forces your body temperature down, which is why medics work on a drowning victim until the victim warms up—once a drowned body is warm, death is certain. Devin's temperature was at 89 degrees coming out of the water. When the thermometer read 94, Brian asked if he should continue.

"Keep trying," I said, glancing at Marla. "Trade out men."

Randy stepped in and took over compressions. I was having a hard time holding onto the thermometer, knowing it was useless, feeling the warmth radiate up from Devin's temples. Randy paused after three rounds and looked at me.

"What's he at?" he asked. The thermometer read 97 degrees.

"You can stop," I said. My throat felt as if it were lined with wool. "It's too late."

Steve spoke up. "What do you mean it's too late?"

"He's gone, Mr. Vance," Sheriff TC said.

Steve pointed at me. "You're just going to let them give up?"

"He's gone," I said. "I'm sorry."

"Get the fucking ventilator," Steve snapped. "What about that oxygen, or the shock thing?"

TC put his hand on Steve's shoulder. "There's nothing more they can do."

"Nothing? Them two didn't do nothing anyway," Steve said. Brian crossed his arms. Randy looked down.

"Take it easy," TC said.

"They didn't do shit."

Brian said, "We're trying to help—"

"Then keep trying," Steve snapped. He knelt next to Devin and shook the boy's shoulder.

"Please don't do that," Brian said. Steve moved Brian's arm out of his way, grabbed Devin's shoulders and shook him, hard.

Marla gasped, "Stop it, Steve—"

"Come on, Devin," Steve said, "Come on, Devin!"

Steve tried to blow air into the boy's mouth.

"Please, stop—" Marla begged.

"Say his name! Bring him back!" Steve turned to look at her, his face fierce as an animal caught in a trap. "Dammit, Marla, rub his feet!"

Marla knelt next to Steve and touched his shoulder. She hugged him to her, pressed her lips into his hair and whispered, "It won't do no good. It won't do no good, you hear me?"

Steve collapsed on top of Devin's chest, moaning, "I'm sorry . . . I'm sorry, boy . . ."

TC led Marla off a ways, and Steve followed them. Kylie sat running her fingers around the Silly Bandz on her wrist, then she removed them, one at a time. Jacob crouched silently beside her as she dropped them into his palm.

"Daddy?" Kylie said. Steve turned to her. She handed him some of the Silly Bandz. They were wet and tangled, the miasma of colors and shapes contorted from being stretched out on the dead boy's wrist. Steve clutched the bracelets, working them in his palm.

While the coroner crouched over the body, the searchers began packing out, stacking boats on trailers. The divers changed out of their wetsuits and the fire department loaded up their medical equipment. Each rescuer filed by the family, offering condolences, while Marla looked blankly up at each of them. Steve stood behind her. Kylie leaned against Jacob.

When nearly all the searchers were gone, I watched as TC took Steve aside, gave him a cigarette, and lit it for him. I tried to guess what they might be talking about—the excuses Steve would make. Every now and then, the sheriff scribbled something in a little notebook. When they finished, they walked over to me.

TC nodded towards the kayak we'd pulled from the river. "That your boat?"

"Yes," I said. "I own it."

"You got the inspection papers at the livery?"

I nodded, and TC said he'd drop by later to get copies. He moved to go.

"Wait," I said. "You been down the river, lately, TC?"

He shook his head.

"I have." I spoke slowly. "That logjam . . . any outdoorsman would know better than to leave a kid in that particular spot."

Steve edged closer. "What was that?"

"I'm asking the questions." TC said. He turned to Steve. His voice was gentle. "Why don't you go see to Marla."

"I think I better stay right here." I could see Steve's pulse pounding in his neck.

"Tell you what, Sheriff," I continued. "I'll take you down the river later tonight if you want. You can see how far this guy paddled past Stowe before he let that woman call for help—"

"I don't know what you're doing," Steve said to me.

"Hell, there's a picnic up at Stowe." I stared at Steve. "Can't imagine why a person didn't stop to ask for help."

TC's jaw moved, slowly, like he was chawing tobacco.

"You better watch it." Steve's voice was the low boil of a bulldog growl.

"Thirty people up there cooking hamburgers. Nobody stopped to ask for a cell phone? For help?"

"You got a lot of nerve," Steve said. "We didn't want to bother them people." I let "them people" hang in the air, and Steve had the decency to look a little ashamed.

"You got some nerve, buddy . . . leaving that boy on the river like that."

"You think I hurt Devin?"

"Nobody's saying anything like that," TC said, sliding his pen into a sleeve of the notebook and closing it with a snap. But by then Marla had noticed what was going on and moved to Steve's side. Kylie and Jacob stood watching.

"Steve?" Marla said. "What's happening?"

"He's full of shit," Steve said, pointing his finger at me. "I would never hurt that boy."

"You seemed to know right where to take us," I said. "I find that odd."

"Kenneth." TC moved between us. "That's enough, now. Get in the van and go home."

"What about the scratches on that kid's neck?"

Marla stammered, "He . . . Devin always touched at his neck."

TC raised his voice a hair. "My department is doing an investigation. Not you."

Steve stared hard at me. His arm clenched, and the tattooed mermaid's breasts jiggled in a blur. Marla's hand was on his other arm.

I held his gaze. "You were the last one with him. Took us right to the spot."

"You knew," Marla said. It was not a question. Steve dropped his eyes to the ground.

I said, "Damn right he knew."

Steve tossed the handful of rubber bracelets in my face and lunged. I pushed TC aside and swung for Steve's jaw just as Marla rushed between us.

My punch sent Marla to her knees, and Steve jumped me as I recoiled. I ate a mouthful of sand and dirt while Steve pummeled me, shouting that I was an asshole, that I had no business hitting a woman. Randy got hold of Steve, and Brian pulled me off to the side, wrenching my arms behind my back. I heard the whirring shutter of a camera as the fighting came to a halt, and saw the local news photographer snapping away with his ancient Kodak as TC pulled me to my feet and snapped handcuffs onto my wrists. When I turned my hand, the cuffs tightened.

TC turned to Homer. "Put the camera away and get the hell out of here."

"I'm sorry—" I said to Marla. She held up her hand.

"You're the one belongs in jail—" Steve said, straining to free himself from Randy's viselike arms. "A grieving mother—"

"I'm sorry," I said. "I'm sorry."

"It's a little late for that," TC said, tugging me into a sitting position. "Wait here."

Marla's jaw was bruised. The coroner—who doctored the living as well as the dead—prepared an ice pack. Jacob had his arm around Kylie's shoulder. My god. He had seen the whole thing. I closed my eyes and kept them closed as Sheriff TC half-led and half-dragged me over to the squad car.

"I don't even know why I put these damn things on you," TC snapped. He shut me inside. "You hit like my grandma."

From the rear window, I saw the EMTs load Devin's body into the ambulance. TC helped Marla climb in behind the gurney. Steve and Kylie got into the SUV with the coroner. The ambulance groaned and bounced its way onto the road.

Jacob sat in the passenger seat with one knee hiked up, elbow resting on it, thumbs twitching against that damn phone. I said, "You ok?"

"That was FUBAR, Dad."

"What does that mean?" I asked.

"Fucked Up Beyond All Recognition."

"I'm sorry," I said. "So sorry about all of it."

Jacob's phone beeped and buzzed. He kept his eyes on its screen, the lights tinting his face from green to gold to blue. I rested my head against the window and watched as TC shook hands with the divers and the fire chief. He lumbered back to the patrol car, looking more tired than I'd ever seen him.

"Took me a lot of talking, but she ain't pressing charges."

"I'm not under arrest?" I asked. TC shook his head. I fell back onto the seat, sandbagged by relief.

"I think you learned what you need to learn," TC said. He started the engine. "But what in the hell were you thinking?"

I was thinking I didn't deserve arms, hitting a woman like that. I thought about my son, and what he had seen me do. About Marla, sitting with her only boy strapped to a gurney, his head lolling and shaking with every bump and incline. I thought about Steve, too—how many times I had done things like that: let the kids drive the car, use the power tools, paddle along the river, play in the woods, pop wheelies on their dirt bikes and—my god, the list was endless. I was thinking that life was so interminably long, and far too short at the same time, and entirely unfair to all of us.

"I don't know," I lied.

TC sighed. "Well, I sure as hell don't know, either."

"FUBAR," Jacob said, looking up at the sheriff. TC squeezed my son's shoulder.

The handcuffs bit into my wrists, a pinching pain that worsened as the cruiser jolted and lurched through the rutted driveway to the main road. I rested my head against the partition, listening to my son breathe, and stared out into the evening, the sun reddening the tree line along the river. Its current moved on and on, indifferent to all our searching.

The Newcomers

Hope and Daniel built the house in Buckton nearly a year ago. They had grown tired of Northpointe: the endless rows of immaculately groomed lawns, cul-de-sacs teeming with shiny Subaru's and midlife divorces. Hope would not become one of those ornamental women of a certain age, active in philanthropy and discreet trips to plastic surgeons, decked head-to-toe in J. Crew and affluent liberal cluelessness. No. She'd spent twenty years raising the girls until they were grown and flown. Sasha was across the sea at St. Andrews happily married to a dashing Scots-Pakistani woman, while Rebecca was in California taking yoga classes, protesting everything, and working at a startup. Hope had stepped down as the chairwoman of the Foundation for Juvenile Diabetes—twenty years of galas, phonebanks, golf outings and art auctions, goodbye!—and was free to do as she pleased and start a life of her own. It was Hope's project and Hope's dream, albeit a dream that Daniel was both pleased and proud to afford her. He owed her that, after all.

When she'd first confronted him, Daniel sank into a chair, pale as a moth. He had been jealous, he said. She was so busy with her projects, with the new house and the business plan. He wanted his wife, he said, but Melanie was interested. He just wanted companionship, that was all. His explanations grew increasingly stupid. He had been foolish and vain. He'd gotten carried away in a silly flirtation, texting, chatter. They hadn't even traded pictures. They'd never so much as gone anywhere together or kissed . . . just . . . talked about it. It was irrelevant. It was virtual.

"Please . . . don't leave me. What can I do to make this right?" Daniel had gripped the wicker back of the dining room chair so hard that she heard it crackle beneath his tensed fingers. His voice came out like the rasp of a wounded animal. "Honey?"

Good. Let him worry for once, about what she might do. Hope told him she was moving to the house in Buckton; he could stay in Northpointe or join her. And another thing: she was getting a dog.

"Come on, you know I'm allergic."

Hope turned to face him. She'd suspected for years that he was gilding the lily on that one, to keep the girls from having pets that he considered a nuisance. She looked into his eyes, her husband, still so handsome. His large, coffee-brown eyes, thick-black hair and olive complexion; the strong shoulders and toned, lanky frame that had once made her purr like a kitten. Then, in a flash she felt a lightning bolt of rage course through her. She smiled, reveling in her cruelty.

"Well then, try Claritin. Maybe it's time I had some loyal companionship."

Hope ripped off the necklace he'd given her for their thirtieth anniversary and walked out of the kitchen, leaving him sitting at the table with his hands covering his stupid, stupid face. She went into their—now, her bedroom—and locked the door. By the time Daniel knocked and asked for his toothbrush, Hope had already googled *animal shelters in Columbus* and filled out an application—only one, a boxer with an underbite. It was love at first sight: nine months old, the runt of the litter, twice-rehomed Queenie was 45 pounds of energy, with a white eyepatch and squishy bulldog nose and three white toes on each paw. This was the pup for her.

Three days after she slipped the door open just enough to hand Daniel his toothbrush and some pajamas, Hope wheeled Queenie indoors in a fetching plastic carrier and opened the door. Queenie galloped out like a bull, careening across the hardwood floor, castanet nails clattering. She went straight to Daniel and began clawing at his dress pants, humping him with focused, tongue-biting adoration.

"Down Queenie . . . down. Come on, Hope, get her. Ok, ok . . . can we talk about this?"

Hope turned her back to hide her smile and scooped ice cream into a small dish. "Awww isn't that sweet. She really likes you."

Daniel put a flattened moving box between himself and Queenie, but the cardboard shield was no match against her advances. "Ha ha ha . . . this is just hilarious," Daniel said. Queenie yipped in response and play-lunged at the toe of his shiny, leather-soled wingtips. "Easy there, easy . . ."

Hope crouched low, tapping a spoon against the dish. "Here you go, baby. Good girl!"

Daniel's mouth fell open, gaping like a cave. "Not from our dishes!"

"They'll get sanitized in the wash." Hope clapped as Queenie all but dove into the treat.

"Hope, stop it, that's gross and besides . . . that's my ice cream."

"Don't be so stingy, Daniel. I thought there was plenty of you to go around."

Queenie's rapt licking and snarfing filled the silence between them.

"I'm not taking care of that dog," Daniel said, finally. "She's your responsibility."

"Nobody asked you to. Anyway, I'm not your child, don't lecture me." Hope turned her attention to Queenie, who was cleaning the bowl so intently that it clanked against the cabinets. Daniel made an exasperated "ack" sound and stormed off. She heard him slam the door to the guest room and she settled into the loveseat, iPad in hand. Queenie wiped her face clean on the upholstery around Hope's feet, snorting with pleasure. She hopped up to the other cushion, nestling in the crook of Hope's arm. While they cuddled, she listened to Daniel in the other room opening and closing the closet door, the whirring groan of the treadmill, the steady pulse of his 8 minute and 30 second mile pace thudding like a heartbeat. He hadn't sneezed once. Not even a good liar, that man of hers. Queenie snored steadily next to Hope, paws twitching as she dreamed.

In the weeks between their big fight and Hope's move, Queenie staged a relentless crusade to win Daniel over. She redoubled her efforts to impress him, prancing across the house to bring him her toys, play-bowing and yipping when he ignored her. It broke Hope's heart the way she trailed after Daniel, throwing herself at him and begging for his scant attention.

"Can't you just pet her a little every now and then?" Hope asked.

But Daniel's attentions toward the little dog contained all the enthusiasm one might have for stroking a salamander. "I'm sorry," he said, "I'm just not a dog person."

So, Hope made it a point to show Queenie extra affection. She would make no such ministrations towards her husband who, in her opinion, ought to be crawling back to her if it meant dragging himself across broken glass. Hope still loved Daniel, but whether or not they would fall back in love with each other and fall in love with this new life . . . well, that remained to be seen. She and Queenie were moving forward with or without him.

With Daniel in Northpointe weekdays, Hope and Queenie set a regimen: mornings, Hope worked inside; unpacking, painting, and decorating. Afternoons, she turned her attention to the garden plants in the greenhouse, planting the flowerbeds, trimming fruit trees in the orchard. She walked Queenie every evening that the weather allowed it, and they both reveled in their laps around the block. In town, that would have taken all of fifteen minutes; in Buckton, the trip around the block was four miles. On weekends, Daniel joined their walks, holding Hope's hand and humoring her as she pointed out all the exciting wildlife: a groundhog, a cottontail rabbit and two kits, a muskrat skittering over the road by a culvert, herds and herds of deer. Once, a coyote. But after a trek past Cecil Hyland's when he was power washing the cattle barns, Daniel gagged and turned back, protesting that, "It reeks of manure out here." She reminded him that now, they lived next door to a cattle farm, not a subdivision.

His ambivalence about the Buckton place ate at her. Hope was hurt when he pointed out that the view from their gazebo featured Shelly's tacky yard: her sagging clothesline heavy with a faded quilt. Three rusty lawnmowers with dry-rotted tires out back of the cinderblock garage, and what appeared to be a charred barrel surrounded by some spray-painted fieldstone. Granted, that was something Hope had not noticed when they picked the build site at the height of summer foliage, but what was the big deal? She was eager for the leaves to return, obscure her view, and restore Daniel's.

He was trying, after all. The night before Mother's Day, Hope let Daniel take her out for dinner. As they neared the bright lights of town, Hope noticed the quickening of his laugh, a bit more pep in his smile. Hope was touched when he re-presented her with the diamond necklace she'd torn off during their fight, expertly repaired and flanked by a pair of earrings, custom-made to match. But the card he'd tucked inside the blue-velvet jewelry box meant more to her than anything: *Hope*, he wrote, *thank you for loving me, for all these years together, for being everything I ever dreamed of and more. Please don't give up on me, you are my forever.* They held hands in the car on the way home, giddy from the wine and exquisite Egyptian cuisine. Hope had just brushed her hair and put a dab of cologne behind her ears when Daniel appeared in the bathroom doorway, nervous and twitchy.

"I—I can't find Queenie," he said, voice shaking. "She won't come when I call her."

"You let her out?" Hope turned to him, eyes wide. "Why?"

"I wanted to help. I'm sorry . . ."

Hope stuffed her legs into jeans, pulled a barn jacket on over her nightgown and went outside with a flashlight. Daniel joined her, searching along the ditch. She shouted for Queenie again and again, her voice thin with worry. It could just as easily have happened to me as him, Hope reminded herself as she trudged along the fencerow, trying not to hate her husband's guts.

A truck rolled to a stop alongside them at the corner of Birch Road. Hope guessed it was Wayne, Shelly's husband, even though she'd only seen him from a distance. Shelly had described him as "outdoorsy" the morning she stopped by with a pie and her friend Margaret, the two of them intent upon welcoming Hope to the neighborhood. Hope blushed thinking how she'd stood awkwardly holding the dessert and making small talk for too long before realizing what the women wanted was a look at her new house. So, she had swung the door wide, and let them in.

The women left their boots sitting on the doormat and wandered all around Hope's downstairs in stocking feet. They admired the blue-floral mosaic tiled kitchen and ran their fingers along the brass fixtures in the bathroom. Shelly paused in front of the family portraits and Hope wondered for a moment if she was put off by the one of Sasha and Fatimah's wedding kiss. But Shelly never skipped a beat, complimenting Hope on the lovely couple and moving on to examine the rest of Hope and Daniel's messy, half-unpacked life: the piles of throw pillows belching out of boxes, her diploma from Cambridge School of Culinary Arts, a stack of colorful baskets Rebecca had sent them from study abroad in Chiapas. Hope began to feel more than a little exposed by their bald inquisitiveness, especially when Margaret raised her eyebrows at the photo of Hope and Daniel standing arm-in-arm with the Obamas. Margaret said, "Gonna find it pretty different here after Northpointe."

Hope had not told them where she moved from. She knelt down to put Queenie in her carrier, hoping the women would take it as a signal to leave, and said, "That's why I picked it. The last thing I want to do is wake up in the middle of a suburb in ten years."

But they did not. Shelly and Margaret took their time, asking probing questions and oversharing about their own lives, children, marriages. Hope learned about Margaret's low opinion of husbands and sheep; that there was more money in breeding donkeys than llamas. Shelly had twice tried to edge Margaret towards the door, where Margaret spotted their Torah scroll and examined it, sighing, "That's beautiful . . . Wow. Jewish farmers, huh? Don't get much of that around here."

"What the hell do you think they did in the Bible, Margaret?" Shelly asked, shaking her head. Margaret looked chagrined, at least, and Shelly herded her friend out the door with an apologetic, "Call if you need anything!"

After that visit, Hope hadn't been overly eager to reach out, but tonight was an emergency. Up close, she could see that Wayne's thick arms were tan and ringed with tattoos; she could smell the beer on his breath. Wayne gave them a pleasing, friendly smile and said, "Hey there . . . You folks need some help?"

"Looking for my wife's dog," Daniel said. "We think she ran away."

"Better hope a coyote didn't get it," Wayne said. Hope's neck snapped towards him Wayne rushed to add, "Now that hardly ever happens, ma'am."

"We have got to find her dog."

"It's a female you say?" Wayne looked off in the distance, then agreed to take a good look around his place to see if Queenie had somehow wiggled past the invisible fence. Hope saw his flashlight beam circling around the yard. The beam stopped, then quivered.

"I found her!" Wayne yelled, his voice echoing through the trees. Hope was off and running, stumbling through the yard, Daniel hurrying behind her. Wayne met them, shaking his head. "Bad news. She's with Boomer."

"What happened?" Hope asked, desperate with worry, sniffing the air when she caught a whiff of acrid smoke.

Wayne turned his flashlight to illuminate Boomer's huge body and Queenie's tiny one impossibly, grotesquely locked in the process of making love by the burn pile. "No! Queenie! Oh, no!"

"It's too late," Wayne said, nodding sagely. "They sure won't stop now."

"Oh great," Daniel muttered. "This is just great."

"Can't blame them," Shelly said, wrapping her coat tighter around her. "Nobody likes a ruined evening." Hope hadn't even heard her approach. Shelly's hair was in a bun on top of her head, her eyes red and swollen. "It's his fault. Wayne here won't cut a working dog."

Wayne shrugged at his wife. "I thought you was gonna stay inside with Brandon."

"He's asleep," Shelly snapped. "Finally."

Daniel looked embarrassed, and even more so when Queenie yelped and Hope strained against his grasp, calling, "My lamb! My poor baby, oh, Queenie . . ."

Queenie ignored her, glaze-eyed and panting. She and Boomer stood clenched back end to back end, skirting in a circle. Hope said, "How long is he going to do this to her?"

Wayne kicked at the dirt with the toe of his work boot. "Awww, could be five minutes, could be an hour. Once they get going, who knows?"

"Hmmm. Interesting." Daniel glanced at his watch. "Honey, do you mind if I—" he stopped short when he saw the look on Hope's face.

"Yes. I mind." She knew that Daniel was desperate to leave and didn't give a damn. Everyone, it seemed, was stuck.

"Come on inside," Shelly said, "It's cold out here."

"We can stay with the dogs," Wayne said.

"Go on in, warm up, honey," Daniel said, clearing his throat. "I'll be in in a minute . . . or an hour."

Shelly opened the sliding glass door, and they stepped inside. A braided rug and sturdy oak table sat in a breakfast nook, heaped with plastic bags from the dollar store, cans of food, a few packs of ammunition and a couple open boxes of nails and screws. Dirty dishes sat piled high in the sink, and wet clothes hung from a folding rack over the furnace vent. The coffee pot slurped and gurgled. She held a finger to her lips. "I just got my toddler down a little bit ago."

"Ahhh, I remember those days," Hope said. Around the corner, she could see a disassembled washing machine, a toolbox, another pile of wet clothes leaking water onto the floor. "Machine's acting up again. Wayne went to town to get the part for it, but they won't have it until Monday. I hate for you to see all this mess."

"It's not a mess at all," Hope lied. "You ought to see my place."

"Oh, Lord, what? You left a magazine sitting out? Don't bullshit me." Shelly's twinkling eyes softened her words. "Wayne thinks it's my job to pick up after him, and last week I went on strike, but he hasn't even noticed." Shelly poured Hope some coffee then slid a jug of milk and a sugar rasher towards her. "Anyway, I'm really sorry. Boomer is a terror."

"It's nobody's fault." Hope sighed and wrapped her fingers around the warm mug. "I was waiting another month or two to get Queenie spayed. She's still practically a puppy."

Through the window, she saw Daniel disappear into the garage with Wayne.

"I bet you ten bucks Wayne has him looking at that egg weld he keeps screwing up."

"Daniel's not real . . . handy. He's an engineer."

"Oh," Shelly said. "That's too bad." From the next room, the voice of an NPR commentator with a Michigan accent complained about the outrageously close proximity of a Burger King to a school crosswalk. Hope smiled as she took a sip of coffee. "Hard to believe those are the problems I used to be most worried about when we lived in Northpointe."

"So, this restaurant of yours—it's going to be like *Chez Panisse*?"

Hope smiled, impressed that the girl knew about Alice Waters. "Something like that."

"That's cool you can grow your own food. Wayne says I don't grow nothing but older and meaner since the baby."

Hope felt a pinch of sympathy for this harried young woman with a grouchy husband. Daniel wasn't perfect, but he never talked to her like that. Never.

Hope said, "You seem quite charming to me."

"Yeah, but last time I made gravy, Wayne threw it in the yard and Boomer buried it."

"Roux is tricky. So . . . where'd you go to school?"

Shelly started as if Hope had pinched her. "How'd you know?"

"I hear liberal arts in your voice . . . plus you have floor-to-ceiling bookshelves in there by the fireplace. Denison?"

Scorn flickered across Shelly's face. "No, are you kidding me? I had a 4.0. I went to Barron."

"Wow. Neither of my girls got in, you must be a real smart cookie."

"They give me a full ride," Shelly sipped her coffee, "But I didn't learn a damn thing that I can use around here."

"What did you want to do with your degree?" Hope asked. Shelly ducked her head, and Hope felt the mistake; people here didn't ask that.

Shelly's voice was firm. "I'm doing it. I tend bar."

"Well, that lets you be at home when the baby needs you."

"With us on separate shifts we don't have to pay a sitter. Besides, the less I'm home the less we fight. I mean . . . the real child in my life is Wayne. Did you see what he did to my cypress tree?"

Hope shook her head no. Shelly pointed out the kitchen window, but it was too dark for Hope to make out much. "While I was at work tonight, he and Boyd and Curtis set it on fire shooting at a bowling ball full of gasoline, about scared the baby half to death. Now he's mad because he can't put Brandon down. We'll be lucky if that child doesn't pee the bed until he's forty." Shelly shook her head and crossed her arms. "Hey, can I ask you a question?"

Hope braced herself. "Sure."

"Why's Daniel such a square peg in a round hole around here?"

Hope hesitated. Should she tell Shelly a lie, a partial lie, or the whole truth? That Daniel was trying to win her back, trying to fit in, trying not to resent his hour-long commute, even though she'd overheard him complaining to a friend on the phone that it was twenty-five miles round trip to the nearest avocado and that they were the only Democrats in the whole township. Hope managed a weak shrug. "He's from Boston?"

"Maybe Wayne could take him out sometime and show him around. Does he hunt?"

Hope snorted coffee, and Shelly handed her a paper towel. "Daniel couldn't shoot a staple gun. Although he could probably design a really terrific prototype. I don't know what it will take . . . an intervention? Like on one of those reality TV shows, maybe, to get him to feel at home here."

"I'd watch that!" Shelly laughed, and then stopped when she realized Hope wasn't laughing with her. "Those sound like pretty good problems to have."

"Not really. That's what this is," Hope said, voice cracking. "We thought this would be good for us." She pushed her feelings, the forlorn sorrow, deep down into the pit of her core and focused on Shelly. What the hell was Hope doing complaining? Shelly lived in grueling poverty with no emotional support and here she was the one crying. "A new start."

Shelly pushed some crumbs from the table into her cupped hand, brushing them into the sink. "I could use me one of those."

Hope could hear in the young woman's story all the things that she wasn't saying. "My turn for a question. What would you do, if you could do anything?"

Shelly thought for a moment. "Law school, maybe? My cousin Kalli did that: lives in New York City with a hot, and I mean hot boyfriend and a fancy loft apartment. She always said I should go, too."

"You could do that," Hope said. "Part time, study while the baby's sleeping."

"Oh, no. Wayne would never allow it," Shelly said. "He thinks all the lawyers should be lined up and shot."

"What?" Hope said. She put her coffee mug down. "That's a little extreme."

"Won't allow Kalli over here because her boyfriend's Chinese."

"Oh, no," Hope said. "That's not right at all. That's your family, plus . . ."

"I know . . ." Shelly said. "You can't tell him nothing, though."

Hope wanted more than anything else, in that moment, to help Shelly. "You can always come by my place anytime you want to talk or hang out."

"Most of the time, I have my hands full," Shelly replied. She grabbed a broom from behind the refrigerator and swept up a few hunks of tracked-in dirt from the floor. "You mind if I tidy up a little?"

Hope didn't. She even helped do the dishes, taking extra care not to clank the pots and pans and wake the baby. They worked in companionable silence until Queenie appeared at the sliding glass door, yipping away. Hope rushed outside and scooped her up. Queenie nuzzled against Hope with an indolent stare of gross carnal satisfaction while Shelly cussed at Boomer and led him to his kennel. They found the men in Wayne's garage workshop, peering intently at some kind of contraption on a huge wooden bench scattered with tools and fast-food wrappers. She paused in the dark outside the open garage door for a moment. If she was not mistaken, the smoky air also smelled a bit like marijuana.

"Try that weld on the balance ring, same as this," Daniel said, coughing a little into his hand. "You'll be all set."

"Hi," Hope said. Daniel glanced up at her, red-eyed. His face brightened when he saw the dog.

"Busted," Wayne said, breathing out a huge plume of gray-green smog, and winking at Hope. Daniel gave Hope a hug, and even scratched Queenie's ears, leaving Hope to wonder just what Wayne had let her husband smoke. Shelly stood at the threshold, kicking the mud off her boots, and laughing at Daniel's failed attempt at feigning sobriety. Queenie exhaled mightily, snorting, leaning against Hope like she'd just run a marathon.

"Ready to go, honey?"

"Nice to finally meet you," Daniel said to Wayne. "Thanks, man."

"Don't be a stranger."

Hope turned to Shelly and held her hand out. Shelly squeezed it.

"Thank you," Hope said. "For everything."

After that fateful night, Shelly and Hope began to wear a path between one another's houses. Sometimes Hope stopped over for coffee, sometimes Shelly knocked to see if Hope wanted to sit on the back porch and watch Brandon play with the dogs. Queenie wobbled along, her belly swollen and rocking back and forth when she hopped and nipped at Boomer. The women would work on the garden or in the greenhouse together until Shelly had to leave for work at AmVets. Hope was grateful both for Shelly's company and her youthful vigor; her knees and back occasionally reminded her of the twenty-year gap between them. Sometimes Margaret joined them, and Hope loved the way their raucous laughter echoed and rang across the fields.

The more they talked, the more impressed Hope was with Shelly and the more she disapproved of Wayne. The man had a brilliant wife stagnating away at home while he whiled away his hours hunting, hanging out with the guys, and making messes Shelly had to clean up. Hope tried to encourage Shelly to expand her horizons, pointing out that if Shelly worked, she could make twice what Wayne brought in from the machine shop. But Shelly changed the subject every time Hope mentioned law school or job applications, demurring politely even when Hope offered to watch Brandon until Shelly could find reliable daycare.

"He's never going to need me more than he needs me right now," Shelly would say of Brandon, though Hope knew it might also be just as true of Wayne. "Maybe someday."

Daniel was amused by Hope's friendship with Shelly, calling them "the odd couple." He overheard Shelly scold Hope that she would help her *hunt* morels, but most certainly would not forage because "foraging is for yuppies." He was not, however, entirely amused by Hope's nettling at him to make friends in the neighborhood. She hoped that Daniel might be a good influence on Wayne and encourage him to be more of a family man. She even managed to talk Daniel into going on a charity golf outing with Wayne and his buddies, but Daniel still limited their friendship to occasional joshing around at the end of the driveway or calling "hello" while working in the yard. She heard the two men talking that afternoon and flushed bright red when Daniel declined Wayne's invitation to go fishing with the guys, citing allergies.

"Allergies to what, this time?" Hope demanded. "Fun? You could at least try to fit in."

"You want me to fit in with those guys?"

"Give it a go. I'm making friends, here." Hope hesitated, wondering if she should tell him just how much she knew about Shelly. "You never find what you have in common with people if you won't even talk to them."

"So, like, the next time we go golfing at Chapel Green, should I join them in making bets about who'll be the first one to sleep with the female caddy? I put up with that shit for six holes, then told them to stop when Wayne offered her twenty bucks if she sat on his face."

"Oh, my god."

Daniel hadn't mentioned that before. Hope saw Queenie dragging a throw pillow towards her doggie bed and wrestled it away from her.

"I have never been more uncomfortable in my life," Daniel said. "The girl was a junior in high school, and every last one of them left Chapel Green so drunk that I fear to ever take to the roads here at night again."

"Okay . . . okay," Hope said, unsure if she felt worse for Shelly or for the caddy. "How is this any different than the way men act with restaurant hostesses or at happy hour at Pointe Tavern?"

"It isn't, and if you'll recall, I didn't tolerate it there, either. My question is, why do you want me to?"

"I don't," Hope snapped. "You don't have to tar everyone with the same brush. So, Wayne is a bad apple. Shelly is a wonderful person, and Margaret may be a little rough around the edges, but she's hilarious and she has a heart of gold."

"Those women seem nice enough, sure. So, why are they married to total assholes?"

"Good question." To Hope's surprise, Daniel laughed. Queenie was pawing at the couch cushion now and Hope gently moved her paw away from the leather upholstery. "No, no, sweetie."

"Look. I'm not asking you to be bosom buddies with them, but could we at least go to the Spaghetti Supper at AmVets? It's a fundraiser for the FFA."

Daniel slid his glasses down his nose and shook his head. "If you want to eat out, let's go into Northpointe. I'll take you somewhere nice and show you off."

"I don't feel like dolling up and going to the city."

"Well, you don't need to worry about that in Buckton. You'll be the only woman there who even owns a dress."

Hope called him a snob, so he doubled down on his refusal, leaving Hope to sulk over her book, curling up with Queenie on the couch in the living room. An hour or so later, Daniel wandered in and got a glass of water. He leaned on the island counter that separated the living room from the kitchen and said, "How can you read with all that racket?"

Hope looked up. "What racket?"

Daniel sighed and pointed out the window to the woods, where she could hear the faint growl of heavy equipment. "They're knocking down trees with a bulldozer. I can't hear myself think."

"Turn on some music to drown it out," Hope said. Queenie sighed, rolling over and snoring lightly. Daniel stood staring out the window, drinking his glass of water.

"I'm going over there to say something."

"Say something to whom?" Hope closed her book.

"What asshole runs a tractor on a Saturday night?"

Hope raised herself up on one arm and peered out the window. "That's Wayne. He probably had a fight with Shelly and is just blowing off steam. And it's not a tractor. It's a Bobcat." Hope felt peevish, so she pushed it further. "There's no neighborhood association here. What do you care what he's doing on his own property?"

"I care," Daniel said. "We have a right to peace and quiet."

"All you're going to do is make him mad and make yourself look like an ass."

"An ass—I'm the ass?"

"Yes," she said. "By going over there acting like we're still in Northpointe."

"What do you want me to do? Wear a flannel shirt? Put one of those used toilets in the yard and start growing flowers in it? Sit at the little crummy bar on the edge of town, drinking with farmers and mechanics?"

"It sounds better than sitting in this house with you, waiting to die."

There was a moment, when they were gazing at each other, that she felt the same keen spark of attraction she felt when they first met. They were undergrads at a frat party, lost in a slow dance until the lights came up, smiling into each other's eyes. Then it was gone, startling them both with their first fully illuminated view of one another. Queenie perched on the arm of the couch, ears pinned back at the tension between them. They listened to the dull buzz of the motor, the rough scrape of its bucket, then the crash of a falling tree.

"That's it," Daniel said, "I'm going out there."

"Take him a beer, and don't act like an idiot."

Hope watched her husband storm across the yard towards the woods. She whistled for Queenie, who lumbered to her feet, groggily. Hope held the door, but Queenie didn't go outside. She simply turned around and went back to her bed, kneading the pillow and turning in a circle.

Daniel walked up to Wayne and stood in the path of the Bobcat. They exchanged a few friendly words at first, but when Daniel crossed his arms, Wayne gave him a curt nod and revved the engine, forcing Daniel to step aside. Then he steered the Bobcat towards another stand of saplings, and knocked the small trees loose with a tearing sound as roots separated from the wet ground.

Daniel began to make his way towards the house, lifting his knees high as if treading water. Hope waved. Daniel did not wave back. She put her hands on her hips and whistled. Daniel's head snapped up. She waved again. He shrugged in annoyance, raising his hands as if asking, *what?* Hope flipped him off with her left middle finger. When he did not react, she raised her right arm and flipped him the bird with that hand, too. She held her pose the whole way across the yard to the garage, arms raised defiantly in the air. Then she got into the car, and drove to AmVets.

Hope parked her car next to Shelly's truck. *Good*, she thought. *I'll have some company.* She paused for a moment before going in, taking in the place. It was a small building, squat, with a green roof. Outside, the sign read DJ DEWEY GRASS: THE KING OF KARAOKE. BISCUITS AND GRAVY $3. SPAGHETTI $3.50. There were no windows, just a small foyer with a thin aluminum screen door that whined when Hope opened it. Inside, she stood face-to-face with a camera screen, and an intercom button. She hesitated, and then pressed it.

"Fancy seeing you here." Shelly's static-y voice filtered through the speaker. The door buzzed open, and Hope was inside. She definitely looked and felt out of place in her yoga pants, black tunic top, and prim silk cardigan, jewelry clanking against her wrists. Hope nodded at the men in work clothes gathered around a table. They nodded back. Hope walked along the buffet piled with pasta and meatballs, a salad of iceberg lettuce and croutons. She slid onto a red-pleather barstool. "How many beers do I get with a spaghetti dinner?"

"Rough day?"

"You know it." Hope laid a manicured hand on the bar. There were several laminate restaurant tables, mostly empty but for the occasional plump couple in t-shirts and hoodies, shoveling spaghetti into their mouths. A Keno machine next to a jar had a handmade sign that said, "TUESDAY

DRAWING WEEKLY—PICK YOUR NUMBER $1 PER BET" in faded ink. A dry-erase board read the name of the previous day's winner: *Ross Berger, $47.85.*

"Wait, why do you win eighty-five cents if all bets are a dollar?" Hope asked.

"House always takes a cut," Shelly said. Hope drummed her knuckles on the bar in time to the music. A man who introduced himself as Derle tapped his beer bottle on the countertop, lifted it to his lips, and winked at her.

"Derle likes to forget he's married," Shelly said, snapping her bar towel.

"Don't we all?" Hope said.

"Point taken," Shelly said. She leaned in to Hope. "I could have killed Wayne earlier. He brought Brandon in here for dinner, then dropped him at his mother's house, and you know that woman drinks. Says he doesn't feel like babysitting."

"That's not babysitting, that's parenting." Hope had arrived angry, and this stoked it.

"Exactly. Then come to find out he's tearing out a bunch of standing timber at the back of the property to put in a shooting range. I don't want a shooting range. They can do that at the Conservation Club if they want to. Grown men out there, playing with their little guns, think they're going to defend Ohio against Obama. Right." She wiped the counter clean, then looked closely at Hope. "You ok?"

"I think we're splitting up. Me and Daniel."

"Awww, you don't mean that," Shelly said. "You guys just think you have problems. Me and Wayne have *problem*-problems."

"You could leave too, Shelly." Hope spoke low, but Shelly still froze and looked around, brought a finger to her lips.

"What? What are you talking about?"

"I'd help you. I'm not saying now, just . . . when you're ready. If you need money for an apartment—"

"My father deeded us that land. I'll die on it." Shelly shrugged. "Or maybe Wayne will."

"I hope that's not true."

"He's bad sometimes, but he ain't that bad."

Hope knew this was not true, and she knew it was a mistake, but the words tumbled out of her anyway, things she'd been meaning to say for weeks now. "It isn't right the way he acts. He works you like a rented mule while he runs around with those brothers two nights a week. He says you can't afford a new washer, but he's always got money for golf, that new quad, tickets to the basketball finals at OSU. I know you're a proud woman and that this isn't easy to hear, but it's not right, and I respect you enough to say it."

Shelly's face had brightened so red that Hope worried she would knock her off her barstool. Shelly whispered, "I cannot do this right now, okay? Just. Stop."

But now that Hope had started, there was no going back. "Daniel told me some things tonight that make me worry for you. Things about other women. Look, I don't want this for you, any more than I want it for me. But I'll be fine . . . it's you I worry about."

"It's me, huh?" Shelly's eyes had hardened to a flinty gray. "Thanks for thinking of me."

"I—Please don't take any of this the wrong way. I know this is upsetting right now, but once you have a chance to get your head clear and think about what I said, I'll do anything I can to help you. Even the spare room is yours if you need it."

"I'll handle it my way," Shelly said. Louder, she added, "That was one spaghetti dinner, right?"

Hope nodded, a peach pit lodged in her throat. Speaking everything aloud made it easier for Hope to put her mind around it, and Hope felt like she could foresee the way it would all play out. Daniel would keep the condo in Northpointe. She would take him to the cleaners for alimony and use the assets to start her restaurant. She would grow tomatoes in a little patch in the backyard, and never ever scold the neighbors for clearing their own land or letting their dogs run. She would keep one of Queenie's puppies, or maybe all of them. She could help Shelly with the baby, and she'd hire her to work at the business, give her a good salary and her own independent income so she could ditch Wayne. It would all work out, Hope told herself, even as she wondered if either of them had the courage or the will to go through with it. With a start, she realized that Shelly was speaking to her, and begged pardon.

"I said, there's karaoke tonight. Dewey Snodgrass is on *fire*." Shelly pointed to a thin man on the stage singing a country song, the gist of which was that he would have a good time tonight because it was Friday, and he had a truck. Blue and red lights flashed over the dance floor, illuminating a group of three women in their fifties, wearing sweatshirts and loose jeans and sneakers. Dewey whirled each of them in a circle, their cropped silver hair flopping in their eyes, heart-shaped filigree earrings bouncing in time to the beat. He scurried back to the microphone in time to finish out the final chorus, taking a bow as the whole bar applauded.

"You should go dance," Shelly said.

Hope knew Shelly was eager to be rid of her. That nothing would change for the younger woman and that she had wounded their friendship quite possibly beyond repair. People didn't come to Buckton to live authentic lives, get back to nature or attempt second chances, she realized. They came here to pretend: to role-play a life that was simpler, but wasn't. For good, clean country living, that wasn't. Who was she trying to fool, anyway? What made Hope think she would be different or that she could make a difference? Shelly had been kind enough not to ask her "who the hell do you think you are?" But it was high time Hope gave that some thought, herself.

"Hey, Dewey! Over here!" Shelly called. "Got a dancer for you."

To hell with it, Hope thought, taking Dewey's thin hand. When the pedal steel started to weep, Dewey hopped up and down like a pogo stick, elbows tucked into his waist and hands splayed out like a Fosse ingenue. Hope joined him, dancing to every song until the back of her neck was sticky with sweat. At one point, she looked over and a very, very sloppy-drunk Wayne had arrived and was half-splayed over the bar, reaching for Shelly's hand. Shelly stood glaring at him with her arms crossed, lips pressed together in a straight line.

Hope leaned into Dewey, dancing hard until someone tapped her on the shoulder.

Daniel. What was he doing here? She spun away from him and tried to keep dancing with Dewey, but Daniel took her arm with more firmness than roughness. Hope jerked her arm away and shouted, "Let me go!"

Hope hadn't realized how loudly she spoke. The whole place fell quiet, although the music still blared and twanged in the background. Dewey paused mid-move, fingers poised in the air, ready to snap. Shelly had one hand on the beer tap, letting it overrun the cup below it, a large cloud of froth piling up at the top.

"Husbands coming out of the woodwork tonight," quipped Derle Wilson, jerking his cap low over his eyes.

"Honey," Daniel said, his face pale and drawn. "You've got to come home now."

Hope felt herself begin to tremble, and glanced at Shelly. Wayne was asleep on the bar, head over one bent elbow, snoring. Shelly closed the tap, turned her back, and took Cecil Hyland a beer, pointedly ignoring Hope.

"Why?" Hope demanded.

"Please, we gotta hurry. It's Queenie."

Every light was on at the house. The moment Hope stepped inside, she heard a strange whimper, a cry of distress. Hope froze at the sound of another whine, this one more protracted.

"She's in the guest room," Daniel said.

Hope brushed past him and all but ran down the hallway. There, in the corner beneath a wingback chair, Queenie lay on her side breathing heavily. Her water had broken and there was a ring on the new carpet, a bit of blood tinged at its perimeter. Hope saw that little Queenie had made a nest, dragging over a bath towel and shredding an expensive throw pillow. The dog lifted her head up at Hope, buggy eyes turned dark black with pain and effort, puffs of pillow stuffing clinging to her ears.

Hope didn't know what to do. Queenie stared at her, as if she did.

"How can I help?" Daniel asked, petting Queenie's side.

Hope wanted to say something snippy or hateful or punishing, but why? This is what Daniel always asked in a true crisis: how can I help? What can I do now? He waited for her, eyes patient, forehead wrinkled in concern.

"Can you bring me a bowl of water?" she said.

Daniel hesitated in the doorway. "Um . . . should I boil it?"

"This isn't *Little House on the Prairie*, Daniel, just get some water," she sputtered, laughing. His face parted in a smile at his own silliness. Hope reminded herself that the vet said not to worry, Queenie would likely be fine, that instinct would take over during the birth. Still, while Daniel was in the kitchen, Hope could not resist googling *how do dogs have babies* and *how to help dog in labor* and *emergency dog c-section.*

Daniel returned with the bowl and knelt next to her. "What do we do?"

Hope shook her head, pressed her lips tight. "The vet and the internet both say Queenie knows best. We just stay with her while she goes through it."

"Ok," Daniel said. He sat cross-legged on the floor next to her, and insisted that Hope give him Dr. Jenny's number so he could put her on speed-dial. Then, he held Hope's hand.

Queenie was panting heavily and pushing. Hope sat next to her, encouraging her, doing the Lamaze breathing she remembered from delivering her girls. She could hear the clock ticking, the dog breathing, the furnace blowing warm air up through the register vent next to her. She tucked the towel a little closer around Queenie and waited. Daniel surprised Hope by purring kind words to the dog, stroking her ears between contractions, helping Queenie sip water.

Hope had not allowed Daniel into the delivery room, heeding a warning from her grandmother, the farm wife who told Hope that, "Once they see what comes *out*, they don't want to go back *in*." Watching Daniel's concern, shoulders hunched and dark hair tumbling over his eyes, his tenderness with Queenie, Hope wondered if she might have given him just a little more credit. Then, or now.

Queenie labored. They waited.

Soon, a grayish-black form appeared, emerging from the dog's birth canal. Queenie pushed out a tiny black shiny sac that writhed like a glob of slimy mucus. The dog bit the birth sac and a watery film gushed out. Queenie licked the puppy clean and pulled him towards her teat with her mouth, cleaning him as he sat blindly, eyes closed, rooting for his mother's nipple. His coat was brindled blue and black, and his tail curled in pleasure when he took his first pull of milk. Queenie ate the birth sac, chomping on the coiled mass of tissue with fervor that made Daniel gag. To distract him, she asked him to look up, *do dogs have afterbirth?*

He did, fell quiet, then said, "Oh god this is gross," and passed the phone to Hope.

"You're a good girl, Queenie," Hope said, fighting the impulse to gag along with him. "So good."

Queenie bore down again, and Hope wanted to weep with relief as she watched Queenie deliver puppy after puppy, until a total of four nursed at her belly, wriggling stomachs and tiny little hind paws combing rhythmically at the air. The pups whimpered and yawned.

Daniel stood up to stretch his legs and left the room. She kept petting Queenie and was astonished when Daniel reappeared with a small bowl of ice cream. He stroked Queenie's head, but he was looking at Hope when he said, "Good girl. I'm proud of you."

Daniel rested the ice cream on Queenie's nest, then put his hands on Hope's shoulders and massaged her back. He cleared his throat and said, "I went back later. After you left. Took Wayne a beer . . . Hope, that guy is a dick."

"I know, honey. He's terrible." Hope said. "We may need to help Shelly."

"I kind of thought so."

Hope was surprised; she hadn't thought he'd noticed. She wanted to tell him everything: that he'd been right and wrong, and that she was sorry. She wanted to tell him about Shelly, and what she feared was waiting ahead of her likely-former friend, and about the rifle-range plans that Wayne had for the backyard. There would be time for all of that later, though. It was late, and she was tired, tipsy, taken down more than a few pegs. Tomorrow was for dreading; tonight, Daniel was with her, and Queenie was all right.

Hope let her head drop back into the hollow of her husband's shoulder. Daniel unfolded his legs and hugged her with his whole body while she leaned back into his firm stomach and he stroked her hair. They sat, cocooned into each other, watching as Queenie sniffed at the ice cream. She sat up slightly and stretched her neck forward, glancing at the pups to make sure they were all feeding. Daniel nudged the bowl a little closer, and Queenie began to eat.

Gimme Shelter

Debra willed the phone to ring. It was Tuesday, the night she usually had dinner with her daughter Celia. They always made their plans by four o'clock, but it was already pushing five and she hadn't heard a word. For any mother this would be worrisome. It was even more worrisome when the child was Celia. Debra jumped up when she heard footfalls and muted voices from the front porch.

Tess stood at the door with a client. Recently hired as the Victim Advocate at St. Francis Shelter for Battered Women, Tess had a no-nonsense demeanor that matched her fleece jacket, jeans, and faded flannel. She was such an exemplary employee that the Board suggested Debra consider priming Tess to replace her as Executive Director when she retired. When Debra relayed this to Tess, she'd used the occasion to suggest that the younger woman begin dressing office-casual, to which Tess replied that nobody trusted Debra because she wore JCPenney loafers like a Nazarene Sunday school teacher. Debra dropped both subjects and hadn't raised them again since.

"Can you let us in? I forgot my door fob," Tess said. Debra sighed and unlocked the door.

"Hey boss," Tess said, "This is Linda Burress."

"Linda Junior," the woman demurred, voice milky.

"Welcome, Linda Junior," Debra said.

Linda Junior's lash-less, unnaturally pale blue eyes blinked. Her face was sweet, doughy-as a pastry. She clutched a leatherbound Bible under her plump right arm, wore a pink-gold cross around her neck, and had a small, worn duffel bag slung over her left shoulder. The bag made a crinkling noise when Linda Junior gave a slight shrug.

"I'll be in my office," Tess said. "5:30?"

"That'll do," Debra said. "Let's get started, shall we?"

Linda Junior settled into a chair while Debra glanced at her paperwork. A glance in Linda Junior's file confirmed that her beloved was *the* Ennis Burress: a sort of ne'er-do-well, half-itinerant "minister" indicted for defrauding every church he founded. Debra had followed the press around his latest fiasco. Expelled from a storefront church the next county over, Ennis and Linda Junior wound up living at Stowe Valley Camp and Canoe. There, Ennis attempted to settle a billing dispute with the campground owner by having Linda set fire to their ancient pop-up camper. Said fire caught a crosswind and spread to nearby RVs. By the time the fire department arrived, there were twenty acres of riverfront forest aflame. The blaze damaged scores of crop fields full of corn and soybeans, and required local medics to treat the llamas at an adjoining farm for smoke inhalation. It made the six o'clock news all over Ohio. The woman did not look like someone who would commit arson for insurance; she looked more like someone who would hand you a *Guideposts* tract and ask you to pray for the unborn. When Debra complimented the garnet setting of her ring, Linda Junior told her that Ennis gave it to her the night that they wed.

"You know what he said to me?"

I can only imagine, Debra thought. She said nothing though, and set her face in a bland, friendly expression as Linda Junior closed her eyes and whispered, "Who can find a virtuous woman? For her price is far above rubies . . ."

"Indeed it is," Debra said. Linda Junior was paying that price right now.

"Isn't that the sweetest proverb you ever heard?" Linda Junior clutched the high neckline of her blouse. "Now, *that* is a good Christian man."

Debra smiled and explained house rules: residents had to stay clean of drugs and liquor. Linda Junior would meet with a counselor to establish a reasonable budget, seek gainful employment, and was required to attend weekly group therapy sessions. Linda Junior's head snapped to attention when Debra explained that residence at St. Francis was conditional: Linda Junior must cut all contact with Ennis or face additional charges.

"What? Why?"

"Because your case is special . . . they sent you here instead of jail."

Linda Junior blinked rapidly, as if Debra was shining a lantern in her eyes.

"Ma'am," she said, "I want to be grateful for all the people helping me, but . . ." Linda Junior's voice quivered when she reminded Debra that wives were supposed to obey their husbands, and how was she supposed to be a helpmate to Ennis if she wasn't even allowed to talk to him?

Debra snuck a quick glance at the blank screen of her phone. No notifications. When she glanced up, Linda Junior still awaited an explanation. Debra said, "I wish I had all the answers. It's a lot to take in. Do you have any other questions for me?"

Linda Junior leaned forward, eyes steady, her voice an inviting, near whisper. "I was just wondering if you know the Lord Jesus as your personal savior."

Debra paused. "I'm a confirmed Catholic, so yes."

"Catholic!" Linda Junior's eyes widened, then shot back and forth as if looking for escape. Debra waited to be asked if she prayed to Mary, if she worshipped the Pope, if she had an alcohol problem—all the prejudicial keynotes.

Instead, Linda Junior said, "Do your people read the Bible?"

"My people?" Debra asked. "I was born and raised in Cavalle."

"Where you're from, you know, your people," Linda Junior said. "Are you Mingo?"

"No," Debra laughed. "Not at all. My mother was a war bride. She met my father when he was stationed in Seoul."

"Ohh . . . was she a nurse?"

"Not exactly." Debra was very uncomfortable with this line of questioning. Most clients knew Debra's history: her abusive, sick husband; her dramatic rescue of Celia; Debra's trial and subsequent acquittal—those were all open secrets in Laurelton. Baffled, Debra said, "Why do you ask?"

"You know all about me," Linda Junior tipped her chin at the thick manilla folder on Debra's desk. "I was just curious if your mother was a nurse. You seem like a nurse to me."

"Oh, I assure you, I did not miss a calling in the medical profession," Debra chuckled, and Linda Junior smiled a little. Debra heard the front door open and close. She lowered her voice a bit. "My mother worked in hospitality, serving drinks at a bar. Sometimes she sang and danced to entertain the soldiers."

"Oh . . ." Linda Junior averted her eyes. "Like Mary Magdalene?"

Debra struggled to keep her face neutral. Linda Junior was pitching her like a tuning fork. "Not quite. She was more like a cocktail waitress or a . . . showgirl. Somehow, she met my father who was a chaplain. He married her and brought her here."

"A minister!" Linda Junior said, eyes widening, "So is my husband!"

"Yes, I know," Debra said, trying not to grind her teeth.

"I can't tell you how grateful I am that the Lord has led me here, to join with a woman of faith."

"I don't know that I'd—" Debra paused, knowing that her "I'm a really bad Catholic" joke would fall flat with Linda Junior, true as it was that Debra was ecumenical to the point of heresy. She said, "I prefer to think of my faith as an attempt to live out St. Francis's suggestion that we 'preach the gospel at all times, and when necessary, use words.'"

Linda closed her eyes and whispered, "My goodness, that's beautiful. What a blessing you are. A powerful witness."

"Yes, well . . . I try," Debra said. From the hallway, Debra heard plastic grocery bags rustle. "Rochelle?" she called out, but the only answer was the sound of the woman's footsteps receding upstairs.

Rochelle, the other shelter resident, had a falling-out with Debra that very morning because Debra refused to petition the judge to drop charges against Rochelle's still-at-large boyfriend. Rochelle had ranted, threatened, and cajoled, insisting that Debra didn't understand. Rochelle said that sometimes violence *was* the answer. That it was just as important as love, and that all Debra's social worker fancy words couldn't fix everything, and that's why there was fighting and fucking. Debra held firm: the charges would not be dropped. Since then, Rochelle wasn't speaking to her; this was hardly a punishment.

The clock on the mantle chimed five. Debra turned back to Linda Junior. "You can meet her shortly. For now, let's show you around, shall we?"

While Linda Junior gathered her Bible and duffel bag, Debra snuck another look at her phone. Nothing.

Debra led Linda Junior through the office spaces on the first floor, explaining that the shelter, once a Victorian mansion, had been donated by the estate of a local steel magnate. Debra pointed out the few remaining vestiges of the mansion's grandeur: pink-marble fireplaces, ornately carved crown molding, a few patches of inlaid parquet flooring that hadn't been carpeted over. Linda Junior ran her hand along the smooth walnut railing of the grand staircase that led to the clients' rooms on the second floor.

"Wow," she breathed. "This place is nicer than anywhere I ever lived."

Debra showed Linda Junior her room. There was a double bed with faded cotton bedspread. Cheery yellow gingham ringed the bed skirt and valances. The floor was linoleum, beige squares swept clinic-clean. Debra cracked the window a bit to let in fresh air. They could hear birds singing. Linda Junior dropped her duffel on the bed, making the springs squeak and cringe. "I hate sleeping alone."

"I understand," Debra said, absently, checking her pockets for her phone. Her heart sank when she realized she'd must have left it downstairs. She was just about to excuse herself to retrieve it when a deep, resounding belch preceded Rochelle into the room.

She had changed into a glaring, neon pink t-shirt with "HOT MAMA" across the bosom, denim cutoffs, and jewel-encrusted flip-flops. There was one scar across her face, from her left eyebrow to her jawline, and another scar from her jawline to the neckline of her shirt. The scar was purplish at the seam and puckered with stitches. Rochelle also had a belly on her, from the same man who drew the blade. She was surrounded by a haze of cigarette smoke.

"Rochelle, good to see you." Debra said, coughing discreetly.

"Sure, thanks. Who's this?" Rochelle asked, pointing at Linda Junior.

"This is your new housemate," Debra said. "Linda Junior."

"What's the junior for?" Rochelle asked, face crinkled in distaste.

"Ennis calls me that," Linda Junior said. She cleared her throat. "His first wife was also named Linda."

"That's really weird."

"I think it's kind of cute."

"Ok, fair enough." Rochelle pointed at the Bible tucked under Linda Junior's arm. "Are you some kind of preacher?"

"Oh heavens, no. But I am proud to be a Christian. Do you know Jesus as your personal savior?"

Rochelle turned to Debra. "She gonna be like this the whole time?"

"I think so, yes." Debra shrugged. Rochelle could use a little churching. Or perhaps an exorcism.

Rochelle's eyes narrowed as she inventoried Linda Junior. "Aren't you a little old to be here?"

"Aren't you a little pregnant to be smoking?" Tess said. They had not heard her coming up the stairs. "Go outside if you plan to court low birth weight."

"Lower birth weight is fine by me," Rochelle said, patting her stomach.

Tess held her keys aloft and jingled them. "Y'all ready to go?"

"Where we going now? Another minimum wage 'job opportunity'?"

"I thought it would be nice to send you ladies out for pizza, so you can get to know each other," Debra said.

"Hot damn!" Rochelle smirked, then leaned and stage-whispered in Linda Junior's ear, "Good luck with this one. She likes to be a hardass."

"Thank you, Rochelle," Tess said. "You never fail to remind me how rewarding this work is."

They made their way downstairs, where Tess's jeep idled at the curb. Rochelle plopped into the seat behind Tess, causing the vehicle to dip and shudder.

"Should I put her in four-wheel drive?" Tess asked, winking at Linda Junior in the rearview mirror. "Toting all this extra weight?"

"Go to hell," Rochelle said.

"Buy my ticket."

Debra shook her head at them. "You two."

Linda Junior appeared to be praying for all of them. Rochelle rummaged through her purse, emptying the contents on the bench seat, then triumphantly raised a fresh pack of cigarettes. "Score!"

"Hey, can I have one of those?" Tess asked.

Rochelle passed the pack to Tess, who opened it and poured the contents of her water bottle into the pack.

"Fuck you! Those are seven dollars now!"

"Please . . . language." Linda Junior cringed, covering her ears with her hands.

"You're welcome, sweetheart," Tess said. "Now let's go have some mandatory fun."

Debra waved to them from the curb, certain she had just sent Linda Junior as the proverbial Christian into the lion's den. Relieved as she was to be rid of Rochelle for an hour or two, Debra had no doubt that Rochelle would provide Linda Junior with the lowdown: that St. Francis was as bad as jail, that Debra was bitter and controlling and trying to turn all of them into nonsmoking man-haters. In truth, the only person Debra wanted to control was Celia. And Celia wasn't calling her back.

Debra held the table at Falino's, fuming between sips of strong black coffee. She texted Celia, waited fifteen minutes, and then tried again. The waiter returned and returned, his displeasure clear by the set of his eyebrows. To placate him, she ordered fettuccine alfredo with shrimp, Celia's favorite. Called again, and still no answer. It was getting on towards seven, and she'd have to head back to the shelter soon.

Debra knew Celia was on a downward spiral, and that this time it was worse than before. Celia's disappearances never boded well. Her daughter's trauma was compounded and blunted by addiction, and the one-two punch had transformed Debra's only child from a sweet, fragile little girl into a volatile young woman. Celia struggled with meth, heroin, Oxycontin, alcohol, and cocaine. Even worse than the drugs were the men who fed them to her, men with stupid nicknames, dirty hair, studded jeans, expensive jackets, and dented cars that shuttled the drugs up from Columbus and down through Cleveland. At twenty-six, Celia had been in and out of police custody, court-ordered rehab, homeless shelters, and group homes for a full decade.

Her daughter was coping, Debra reminded herself. Celia wasn't the only addict in Laurelton. Ten years ago, Debra—a fifty-year-old mother, nonprofit administrator, and devout churchgoer—wouldn't have had the foggiest idea where to buy street drugs. Now she could point out three houses within a stone's throw of St. Francis. Laurelton was vexed by its own location: the town's attempt to "save Laurelton's way of life" by refusing to allow the interstate to go through its resplendent Victorian downtown had backfired. I-71 was rerouted twenty miles west, leaving Laurelton isolated from large cities, airports, and centers of commerce. Laurelton's rural character may have been preserved, but contraband thrived: humans, drugs, guns, even exotic animals were occasionally rescued during the rural sheriff's traffic stops.

The influx of street drugs and the prescription painkiller epidemic transformed Laurelton and Debra's work at the shelter. In those early years, Debra's work was valued, even revered. She'd helped countless women desperate to escape violent relationships. Nowadays, Debra's clients at St. Francis were referred—or ordered—by the courts. Many of these clients were resentful, uncooperative in therapy, and resistant to ending contact with their abusers. Topping it all off, the women were arriving at St. Francis indifferent to Debra's appeals that a better life was possible for them.

Debra understood. She had dulled the pain of her own abusive marriage by self-medicating with sleeping pills, and she understood too well what it felt like to seek any port in a storm. That was one of the reasons that Celia had for hating her mother. The other reasons were well-documented in court filings and therapists' notes. Celia would never forgive Debra for rescuing her, and Debra would never stop attempting to rescue Celia again and again.

The last therapist Debra'd seen had all but begged her to give up on Celia. By then, Debra had second-mortgaged the house on Scott Road to pay for Celia's rehab and Celia had been doing well: working at the South County Mental Health Organization, attending NA meetings, staying clean, having dinner at Falino's with Debra every Tuesday. Then the money trouble started. Debra shook with anger recalling how the SCMHO Board went after Celia for embezzlement, failing to take her relapse into account.

By the time Debra's lawyer talked them out of pressing charges, Celia was back in Mansfield, living in one boarded-up hovel after another. Pregnant, then not. Bruised and battered and broke, Celia always made her way back to South County, to St. Francis, to Scott Road, the house where Debra had shot Celia's father for what he was doing to her little girl. Debra had done it to save Celia. Gone through all of it for Celia. And now, here sat this therapist scolding Debra that Celia was drowning, and if Debra kept trying to drag her to shore, they'd both go under.

Debra had listened politely, nodding and keeping her hands folded in her lap. When the session was over, Debra thanked her, wrote her a check, and never went back. As a trained counselor, she knew that the one overwhelming factor that no therapist or social worker or psychiatrist had yet been able to outmaneuver, was love. And she would always, always love Celia.

At 6:35, Debra asked the waiter to box up Celia's food and left two twenties on the table. Her hands shook on the drive back to St. Francis. She went directly to her bedroom, shut the door, and dialed Celia's number. When there was no answer, Debra left a message lecturing Celia for standing her up and told her authoritatively to call her mother, and do it *now*.

Debra shivered, despite the warm breeze wafting in from her bedroom window. She made it all of two minutes before her willpower broke, and she called Celia again. In the second message, she catalogued all the nonsense she had been putting up with from her daughter for years, shaming Celia for having put her through so much, begging her to call. Debra literally sat on her hands until 6:52, forcing herself to wait, breathing in through her nose and out through her mouth. Panic thundered in her chest and sent little shockwaves down her arms until Debra dialed again. This time, Debra lost it: she cursed Celia, unleashing a searing rant of hurt over Celia's callous disregard for her mother, her irresponsibility, her selfishness, her bullshit. Debra couldn't be sure how long she shouted into the phone before the timer cut her short, she just let the phone thud to the bed and sat still, watching the curtains flutter.

She leapt to her feet when she heard someone say, "Excuse me, Debra?"

Tess stood at her bedroom window, holding a sagging box of leftover pizza. Behind her were Linda Junior, Rochelle, and Marla—nearly everyone from the support group. Their faces bore the discomforted look of someone who had accidentally passed gas in public.

Debra broke into a clammy sweat and felt her face color with shame. "Hello?"

"Could you let us in? I forgot my key fob," Tess said.

"Oh sure, I'll be right there." Debra forced a singsong tone into her voice, a tone that would do little to hide her red, swollen nose and tear-streaked face. She hurried to open the door.

"I'm so sorry," Tess mumbled. "I rang the bell a couple times but no one answered."

Marla avoided Debra's gaze. Rochelle covered her mouth with her hand to stifle her laughter. Linda Junior's eyes were wide. Tess hung around the door, her expression clouded with worry. "Call me if you need me, ok?"

"Will do," Debra said, briskly. "Let's get started, shall we?"

Linda Junior read the Bible and Marla fidgeted with her purse while Debra plunked a plate of cookies on the table and got the coffee brewing. The coffeepot's gurgle and hiss was the only sound in the room, but for the ticking clock and the occasional squealing groan of a chair. Rochelle stared at Debra until Debra asked her to put the info packets on the table.

While they waited for the 7:00 hour, Debra asked the women to review the 'Power and Control Wheel,' an infographic that explained and categorized types of domestic violence. She suggested that the women take a look at it and write in their journals any behaviors they recognized in themselves and others. She reminded the women that abuse often straddled more than one category, admitting that "In my own experience, the power and control wheel turned so subtly that I didn't realize I'd been run over by it until I hit my breaking point."

They all jumped when Marla's phone blared "Carmen Ohio." Blushing, Marla silenced it, and glanced at the message. "Shelly can't make it, she's got to work."

Taking a deep breath, Debra said, "Then I guess this is everybody. Welcome to Healing Hearts. If you're here, you're already a survivor. Let's introduce ourselves, shall we?"

"Who is this 'we'?" Rochelle asked.

"You first, Rochelle, dear," Debra purred. Rochelle groused that she was there because her man was on the run. Marla was there because she wanted to do better in her second marriage, which was strained after her son drowned during a family outing.

Linda Junior's chin trembled when she introduced herself and said, "I was ordered here by the judge. I love my husband, and he loves me."

"Why'd the magistrate send you, then?" Rochelle asked.

"Ennis had me burn down the camper and I accidentally set the woods on fire. A big woods."

"Wait, that was you?" Rochelle sat up straight. "You didn't say nothing about it at dinner!"

"Well, he needed that insurance money."

"How'd you do it?" Marla asked. "Gasoline?"

"Kerosene. It was a little cheaper."

"That's true." Marla nodded sagely.

While Linda Junior told her story, Debra checked to see if she'd missed a call. A text? Nothing. Her heart felt like it was made of balled aluminum, tinny and collapsible and insufficient to the task of keeping her upright. She forced herself to focus on Linda Junior's story, on the buzzing of the fluorescent lights above the conference room table, the scent of fresh coffee wafting over from the sideboard.

". . . So they said it was coercion and arson by proxy," Linda Junior said. "That's what I don't understand. I wanted to help."

"I used to think the same thing, back when I was with Reggie," Marla said.

"Oh God, not him again," Rochelle muttered.

"He didn't hit me 'til he took up drinking," Marla said.

"Ennis doesn't hit me," Linda said.

"That's only 'cause he don't have to." Rochelle snorted. "You just fold your hands and pray and do whatever he says. Well, Miss Junior, I got my face cut for fighting, and I tell you what, if I had it to do all over again, I'd still punch that motherfucker. I'm not going to let no man tell me what to do."

Rochelle looked at each of them in turn, daring them to contradict her. Debra knew this was highly performative on Rochelle's part; she'd come to St. Francis just as weak and worried and terrified as anyone else. Nonetheless, Rochelle pursed her lips and shook her head. "I'm not weak like that. Can't nobody push me around."

"I'm not weak. The Lord is my strength." Linda Junior sat very, very still.

"Survival is a sign of strength," Debra added. "We're all strong in different ways."

"Is that so?" Rochelle asked. Her face was a mask of innocence. "You say that emotional abuse is just as bad as this?" Rochelle pulled down her shirt and turned towards the light, arching her back to show how the cut wound from her eyebrow to her jaw, down her neck, and curved around her breast. She let her bra snap back into place and adjusted her top. "Give me a break."

Debra cleared her throat but could not speak. The women looked at her, and she scanned their faces, by turns curious, worried, confused, and eager, waiting for Debra to continue. Debra always continued—she'd led group meetings when she was going through chemo and had to exit the room periodically to vomit. She'd held group by candlelight when the power went out. When Celia was in the hospital for a botched suicide, Debra only left her daughter's side for this hour, the hour when Debra felt she did the most good, bringing women together and assuring them that they were not alone in their suffering or in their recovery from it. For the first time in her history at St. Francis Shelter for Battered Women, Debra closed the curriculum book, and said, "I'm sorry, I can't do this tonight."

It was well after 11:00 p.m. when Debra stopped looking for Celia. She was not at her apartment in Stowe, not at any of her friends' houses, not in the parking lots of the bars in Buckton or Cavalle. Debra had even stopped by the ER to see if anyone by Celia's name or description had been admitted. Nothing. Debra pulled into the drive-through at AmVets, just before closing.

"What's up, Miss Scott?" Shelly asked. "Everything okay?"

"I guess so," Debra said. "Missed you at group."

Shelly leaned so far out the delivery window she had to put her hand on Debra's car door for balance. "Three more shifts and I can serve him with papers."

Debra's heart jumped. "That's such good news. You haven't seen Celia tonight, have you?"

"Not yet," Shelly said, shimmying back inside. "I'm real sorry."

"Thanks. Call me if you do?" Debra said. Shelly waited a moment, cleared her throat and asked if she could get Debra anything. "How about whiskey? A good bottle."

"Maker's all right?"

"Sure." Debra seldom drank now, and rarely allowed herself any kind of spirits. But this, this was necessary. It was the only way she'd sleep tonight. No shame in seeking rest.

As she pulled out of the parking lot, Debra's headlights caught a shadow in the vacant lot across the street, where the county kept a trio of recycling bins. A thin woman with long dark hair that reached to her waist. Celia. It was Celia, standing and talking through the window of a light-duty, rusted brown pickup truck with a cap on the back. Debra made a left into a parking space down the street and turned the ignition off, cut the lights, watching them through her rearview mirror.

As she talked, Celia swiveled her shoulders back and forth, overly animated and sly. The man's head edged closer and closer to her. The man said something. Celia threw back her head and laughed, twitching her tail like a cat, and sauntered away. Debra turned in her seat, and watched in the dim glow of the lone security light as Celia circled around to drop the truck's tailgate, beckoning with her free hand.

Debra choked back a cry. Celia climbed into the capped bed of the pickup on her hands and knees. The driver got out of the truck cab, looked around, then crawled in behind Celia, pulling the tailgate closed behind them. Debra laid her head on the steering wheel. She felt like she was choking, drowning, dying. When she looked up, the truck was jostling and jerking with the weight of Celia and the man who paid to have sex with her daughter, there, on the street. Debra opened her car door and vomited.

Debra remembered Celia's birth, how she'd stepped outside herself and howled as Celia crowned, her vision narrowing the brightly lit delivery room into blackness. Her daughter's bleating, strong cries were all she heard through the velvety curtain of pain. When the nurse put Celia to Debra's chest, her sight returned. Debra had fallen so deeply in love, love, love from the moment her crying baby shook her tiny fists, and Debra knew: Celia was the only truly good thing that had ever happened to her. She thought then, naively, that love was something no one, nothing, could ever take away from her and believed that nothing was stronger than that bond, that it was boundless as God's own love, as sacred as every heart.

Debra weighed her options: she could run over to the truck and pound on the windows, drag Celia out by her hair. She could pepper spray the john, take Celia's hand and hustle her off to safety. She could grab the tire iron from her trunk and bring it down on the man's head. She could. Oh, but she could.

But she would not.

Debra looked at her face in the rearview mirror: is this how she would live out her days, chasing after Celia? Being devastated in new ways by the breadth and depth of her daughter's years-long freefall? What else was there left for Debra to do?

She started the car. Debra drove away at a crawl, holding the horn down as she passed the pickup. Its windows were tinted and the glow of the security lights reflected off the glass, blocking Debra's view of the people in the back. Still, Debra imagined she saw Celia's head pop up, that the two figures froze as she passed. Debra drove back to Laurelton, back to the shelter, leaving Celia behind, gone from her sight.

All was quiet at St. Francis. Debra used the basement entry to sneak in. The paper bag rustled under her arm as she crept upstairs to the kitchen, closed the door, and turned on the light. The whiskey had a red wax seal on it that she could not break. Debra was rummaging around the utensil drawer for a serrated knife, when the door flew open, slamming against the refrigerator with a bang. Debra yelped, then clapped a hand over her mouth.

"Hey you!" Tess stood in the doorway, brandishing a baseball bat, Rochelle at her elbow with a rolling pin. Behind them, Linda Junior trembled, halfheartedly holding a rag mop. Tess lowered the bat to her side. "Sorry, boss."

"Thank God it's you," Linda Junior said. She let the mop fall to the floor.

"You scared us," Rochelle said. "We were just about to call the cops."

"Oh no, I'm sorry. It's just me." Debra shrugged.

"Oooh, what have we here? What's the occasion, party animal?" Rochelle asked.

"I'm quitting St. Francis," Debra said. She used the knife to pry the wax free and popped the cap open. "It's time I resign."

"What's happening?" Linda Junior asked.

"I bet it's her daughter." Rochelle's face was foxlike, eyes bright and alert.

"Good guess," Debra said. "Don't worry, though. Tess, you'll be running things . . . the Board's been making hints about my retirement since we hired you. You'll get the job, no problem."

"Um . . . what if I don't want it?"

"That'll make two of us." Debra winked at her, then took a swig from the bottle, not giving a tinker's damn that she was violating St. Francis policy. "What are you doing here, anyway? I thought you had the night off."

"They called me when you left," Tess gestured vaguely at the women.

"We was worried," Linda Junior said.

"*She* was worried," Rochelle said, pointing at Linda Junior.

Debra took another swig, enjoying the way the burn trickled down her throat and warmed her tongue. "That's nice of you."

"You cannot drink away your problems," Rochelle teased, imitating Debra's voice pretty well.

"Stop," Tess said, "She's upset."

Rochelle rolled her eyes. "I got problems, too."

Tess rested the baseball bat against the kitchen cupboard and took a step towards Debra. "Are you all right?"

"No," Debra said. "How about a nightcap?"

"Hell yeah."

"You're pregnant," Linda Junior said.

"I am?" Rochelle said, slapping a hand to her forehead. "Then I deserve a double."

Tess hesitated. "We could all get in trouble."

"Not if nobody tells," Rochelle said.

"I don't like this," Linda Junior said nervously. Her fingers wobbled at the lowest button on her sweater, pulling at a loose thread. She gestured towards Rochelle's belly. "Especially for you, drinking alcohol with a baby on the way."

Rochelle smiled sweetly, and turned to Tess. "Linda Junior used my phone earlier to call Ennis," she said, fishing the device out of her cleavage, scrolling it open and showing Debra the screen. "Look."

Linda Junior gasped. "You *promised*—"

"Never trust her," Tess said, shaking her head. "Snake, it'll bite you."

"I didn't even get to talk to him," Linda Junior groused. "She's got no minutes left."

"What? Why?" Tess asked. "I just refilled that phone for you—"

"None of your fuckin' business—"

"Don't swear, please," Linda Junior said, voice firm.

"Get off the cross, honey," Rochelle snapped, "Somebody needs the wood."

"Please, will you all shut up!" Debra said. "I've had a night. Everybody get a damn glass."

Rochelle whooped and danced a jig, while Tess went through the assortment of donated dishes. She chose an Audre Lorde coffee cup. Rochelle grabbed an OSU highball glass, and Linda Junior reluctantly accepted a child's plastic juice cup with cartoon tigers dancing on it. Debra filled a tumbler, dropped in two ice cubes and headed outside to the deck.

The night was warm, and peonies bobbed in its occasional breeze, filling the air with the sticky sweet scent of their blossoms. They sat at the patio table, Rochelle leaning her belly against the edge and propping her feet up on the spare chair.

"The heat has me swelling up something awful," Rochelle said, wiggling her toes in their flip-flops. "But mmm, that stuff is good."

Linda Junior barely sipped at the whiskey, complaining that it tasted like burnt cinnamon. Rochelle demanded two fingers more. Debra asked her to slow down. Then she told them about Celia.

"I thought you was the one with all the answers," Rochelle said.

"No," Debra said. Her voice was leathery with sorrow. "She's gone as far as anyone can go now."

"Sex work is still work," Tess said.

"Tell me that when it's your daughter," Debra snapped.

"Why don't you get her some help?" Linda Junior's face was soft with sorrow.

"She's been trying to for years now," Tess said, shaking her head.

"You can't help someone who doesn't want it," Rochelle rubbed her stomach. "That girl ain't ever going to get better."

"You don't know that for sure," Linda Junior said.

"You're never supposed to give up on a victim," Tess said. "Debra, you never gave up on any of us."

"Never gave us no second chances, either," Rochelle groused.

"That isn't true." Tess pointed at Rochelle. "We all got a lot of chances until we got better. You know that."

"I done some things," Rochelle acknowledged, sitting back in her chair. "I've done some fucked up shit, but I ain't never played with no heroin or been no whore."

"Maybe you never had to make those choices," Tess said. "Don't judge."

"Celia ain't coming back, " Rochelle said. "Once they turn to whoring, they're lost."

"Please don't say that," Debra said. She felt the color drain from her face, remembering that her own mother had cautioned Debra that once one traded one's body, one's spirit could surely follow. Debra thought that so old-fashioned, so condemnatory, and so overly harsh; but whose spirit was in trade now, she did not know.

Linda Junior said, "That's her daughter."

"Must run in the family. Her mother was one, now her daughter's one . . ."

"You don't know what you're talking about," Debra's pulse slowed, outrage roiling to a dull roar in her ears. "I've never discussed my mother with you." On another day, she would have patiently explained to Rochelle that sex workers deserved dignity like all other workers, and that her mother—not that it even mattered—had not been a comfort woman, but even if she had been, so what? She would not allow Rochelle to blame Celia for the generational trauma inflicted on her as a child.

"You know it's true," Rochelle smirked. "Guess you're no better than anybody else around here now are you, Debra?"

"Rochelle, stop," Tess said.

"I think that's enough," Debra said.

"A dancing whore mother—" Rochelle taunted.

"I said that's enough!"

"A drug whore daughter—"

Debra jerked the glass out of Rochelle's hand, and hurled it against the retaining wall. The glass broke, sending bright diamond shards of glass across the patio tiles, whiskey dripping down the ivy, but it was Rochelle who shattered. She shrieked, then dropped to the ground in a protective curl, arms around her belly, breathing heavy as a mare. Rochelle covered her face with her hands.

"Don't cut me, don't cut me, don't cut me, don't cut me," Rochelle said, teeth chattering wildly. "Don't!"

"Oh my God," Tess said, dropping down beside her. "It's okay, Rochelle . . . shhhhh . . . it's okay."

"I'm sorry," Debra said, "I'm so sorry."

Linda Junior threw up her hands and said, "No wonder this place is mandatory."

Debra hung her head and looked away. She had gone and lost control and reverted to violence. Rochelle was her charge, her responsibility. Rochelle and Linda Junior were the people she was obliged to help and save. How was it that they knew, long before Debra did, that she was incapable of either? The shame of it turned her blood to lead.

"Rochelle," Tess said, "Rochelle, you are safe." Tess repeated the words while rocking Rochelle back and forth, reminding her to breathe, shushing her and asking Rochelle to open her eyes when she was ready. Debra and Linda Junior waited in silence until Tess had Rochelle uncurled, and eased her over to a chair at the patio table.

"I better apologize," Debra said.

"Don't," Linda Junior turned to Debra, her face quivering. "Don't you dare."

"So what if you're sorry? I'm telling Father Michael," Rochelle said, her voice ragged as ripped cloth.

"Go ahead," Linda Junior said. "I'll tell him you had it coming."

"What?" Rochelle said.

"You," Linda Junior said, pointing at Rochelle. "You was out of line."

"It was my fault," Debra said. "I'm the one who is supposed to know better."

Linda Junior's voice was low, but leathery. "You're going to be a mother soon. What if someone says things like that about your daughter, to you?"

"She hit me!"

"She never laid a hand on you and you know it. It was a accident."

"She fucking assaulted me. I want to file a report."

"If that's what you want to do, we can do that," Tess said, avoiding Debra's gaze. Debra's fingertips tingled and her eyes welled with tears. She would be exposed and humiliated, fired, disciplined—and she would deserve it.

"We'll follow the letter of the law," Debra said to Rochelle. "I take responsibility."

"No you won't," Linda Junior said. Her eyes were wide, and her neck elongated in outrage, like a hen about to peck. She glared at Rochelle. "She won't quit, and you won't go running to Father Michael. You're the one started it all. She told you to stop and you didn't, and now you want to snitch to make yourself feel better!"

"I'm no snitch."

"Looks like you are," Linda Junior said, pressing her lips together and shaking her head. "Words hurt. What'd you tell me earlier about words?"

Rochelle froze up. "I don't remember."

"I think you do." Linda Junior imitated Rochelle. "Words ain't always enough. That's why there's fighting, and—and fucking."

From Linda Junior's lips, the adage sounded near holy. Linda Junior let the word hang in the air, then folded her hands and muttered, "Lord forgive me."

Rochelle smirked. "Such language."

Linda Junior said, "That's why I don't keep company with foul-mouthed people, it turns you into one."

"Funny, that's how I feel about Christians."

"Wouldn't hurt one bit for some of God's love to get ahold of you."

"Copy that," Tess said. Exasperated, Linda Junior sat down at the table and took a swig from her sippy cup. There was a short silence. Debra took a step forward.

"May I say something?" Debra asked. Rochelle stared ahead, but Linda Junior nodded. "Rochelle. I'm sorry I knocked the cup out of your hand. I'm sorry, and I won't be at St. Francis anymore and you can forget all about this. I was wrong."

"You can't quit," Linda Junior said. "You're a good woman. And you can't just give up. You help all sorts of people, and it's about time somebody helped you. Don't give up, Debra."

Debra sat blinking, the night air cool against her neck. She had given up. Given up everything for Celia, and tonight, she'd given up on Celia, too, and then given up on all the impossible things she loved: St. Francis, the women she tried to help, all her life's work.

Debra said, "It's not all up to me." And for the first time in years, she meant and understood it to be true.

Rochelle shifted her weight and rubbed her lower back. "I don't like you, Debra. You know that. But I don't blame you for what you done."

"It's ok if you do," Debra said. "I was wrong."

"Oh to hell with that," Rochelle said, throwing up her hands. "You mean well enough even when you're annoying. You ain't quitting, and I ain't going to be the one to get you fired."

Tess cleared her throat. "Technically, I think we are required to file a report . . ." Rochelle, Linda Junior, and Debra stared at her. Tess's voice trailed off, and she chewed at the inside of her lower lip. "Ok. Never mind."

"Yeah," Rochelle said. "Never mind is right."

The chapel bells chimed, and the women waited out the tones, listening to traffic on the street, the moths buzzing against the porch light, the low tones of wind chimes in the maple branches above them.

"Hey look—" Rochelle pointed at the fireflies glowing and fading in the yard. "I used to catch them in jars. Never realized how mean it was."

"Me too, and me either," Tess said. "They're better loose like that."

"Like all God's creatures." With that, Linda Junior rose up, smoothed her nightgown around her legs, and retrieved the whiskey.

"I'll take some," Tess said.

"Thank you," Debra said, when Linda Junior spilled the amber liquid into her cup.

"No more for me," Rochelle said. "I get indigestion this time of night."

Debra tried to take a drink, but it went down the wrong pipe. Spitting and coughing, she began to sob quietly, then louder, until her stomach cramped and her shoulders shook.

Linda Junior rubbed Debra's back. "Go on, go on . . . cry it out."

"My heart is just so broken," Debra sobbed. "My whole heart."

"Well," Rochelle said. "You've come to the right place."

She fished in her bra and handed Debra a wrinkled tissue. Debra cringed to think how, earlier that very afternoon, she would have used such an occasion to lecture Rochelle on hygiene, manners, decorum. She managed a half-smile and took it. "Thanks."

"I'm gonna have me a cigarette."

"Go ahead," Debra said.

Rochelle leaned back to one side and lifted her feet onto the chair next to her. She flicked the lighter, and drew the flame to the tip of the cigarette. Then she smiled at Debra, exhaling a plume of smoke. "I wasn't asking permission."

Lifeguards

Holding fast to the proverb that "whoever works his land will have bread, but he who follows worthless pursuits lacks sense," Jesse had quickly climbed to the rank of Snack Bar Manager at Laurelton Community Pool. A combination of faith and industry drove him to keep the fryer grate whistle-slick, shine the hot dog Ferris wheel spokes with baking soda, and reconcile his till to the penny every shift. Mr. Connor, the pool's absentee owner, was particularly pleased to discover Jesse didn't mind doling out neon colored carcinogenic Slurpees. Jesse was reliable as a Swiss watch and had never asked for Friday or Saturday nights off.

Until Jesse saw the new lifeguards clocking in that morning, he'd been looking forward to summer. Seth and Tyler graduated with Jesse, but they were part of the hipster-jock-achiever set, moving with ease amongst a crowd Jesse avoided in the hallways: running backs who called him "Chicken Choker" and "Jesse Jackoff," point guards and pitchers who pushed his books out of his hands. Jesse wasn't sure where he stood with Seth and Tyler now that they were coworkers, but he had little time to worry about it. Most of opening day passed him by in an expedited blur of cheese sticks, pizza burgers, and soft-serve cones. Then, Jesse saw the other new lifeguard: Amanda Hallinan.

Everyone knew Amanda because she was the sheriff's niece and one of the few black—or rather, half-black—kids at Laurelton High School. She excelled academically and earned letters for varsity track and volleyball. She played the piano at a church and served meals to homeless people on Wednesday nights. She was a passionate defender of animal rights, and the only vegetarian Jesse had ever heard of. She was, in other words, *awesome.*

Her awesomeness compounded because she was polite to Jesse while ordering a Coke and a garden burger. Jesse tried not to stare at the way her swimsuit gathered at the waist. He tried not to notice how dazzling her smile was. Love-struck, he slipped her two slices of cheddar cheese for health reasons, praying she did not register his attention to her food or her person. Amanda padded back over to the picnic tables, taking a seat on Tyler's lap while Seth sat across from them singing the chorus of "Summer Nights" from *Grease.*

While he sprayed cheese product on nachos, Jesse wondered what his mother would think of Amanda. Jesse knew his mother would approve of her "being churched," but Amanda also embodied all the dangers of immodest women—a definition that, in his mother's mind, included women who wore pants, called boys up on the telephone, or pierced their ears. His mother's fear of hellfire complicated everything.

That's why he was hoping that between the promotion and the overtime, he could get his own place in the fall. Maybe someday he could even go on a date with a girl like Amanda, a real date, not one during which he would be escorted by his mother under yet another of the onerous moral conditions of living at home. Jesse salted some French fries and dropped the basket into the oil, picturing himself in a tux and tie, arriving at Amanda's house on his bicycle . . . no, no—that wouldn't do. He would approach her house on foot like an old-fashioned suitor, offer his arm, and present her with a bouquet of wildflowers. They would stroll to church together, where Jesse would immediately propose and Amanda would accept, both of them blushing as they said their vows and plunged headlong into the holy sanction of conjugal bliss.

The microwave's bleating timer jolted Jesse from his reverie. He lifted the basket from the fryer, added jalapenos to the nachos, and called, "Order forty-two!"

A guy he recognized from school sauntered over, hat on backwards. His shoulders were meaty as a hogback. The guy smirked. "Hey, Chicken."

Jesse was used to this.

Twelve years had passed since Jesse found his brother Benjamin's body hanging in the barn, pants at his ankles. Whether Benjamin had been experimenting with autoerotic asphyxiation, sinning against God, or had been some kind of sick freak, depended on who was telling the story. Parents still whispered Benjamin's tale as a dire warning against the dangers of deviance. Teachers looked at Jesse with suspicion-tinged pity. The other kids just gave Jesse hell.

Jesse tried to blend in, but it didn't help that he wasn't allowed to take sex ed class, or read books assigned in English due to obscene situations. Blending in was impossible when he had to sit out gym class because his mother thought that changing in the locker room with the other boys was unwholesome. It definitely didn't help—no matter how often he begged her to stop—that his mother spent Fridays circling the town square playing the tambourine and wearing a sandwich board covered with hellfire Bible verses.

"Hey—I'm talking to you, Chicken."

Rudy. *That* was the guy's name. Jesse vaguely remembered taking a grade-school field trip to the llama farm Rudy's parents owned. Jesse slid the plastic tray across the counter.

"Nachos ready."

"Got a joke for you," Rudy sneered.

"Yes." Jesse knew better than to say it like a question.

"You hear about the retard they drowned in the river?"

"No," Jesse said. The baseball guys tittered, their laughter like rustling paper.

"The pervert was, uh, choking his chicken in front of the girls, so they tied him up and threw him in." Rudy ran his hand over the crotch of his swim trunks, cackling. The snack bar fell quiet.

"Wow," Jesse said, wiping the counter clean. "That's awful."

From the corner of his eye, Jesse saw Amanda stand up.

Rudy said, "You know how the story ends, right?"

"Gosh, no," Jesse said. He could feel Amanda's eyes on him. Before he could stop himself, he leaned in, looked Rudy right in the eyes and stage-whispered, "How'd you escape?"

There was a collective intake of breath, then a cacophony of laughter. Blood rushed to Rudy's face, ruddying the apples in his cheeks. Amanda got a round of applause going. Deft as a cat, Rudy sent Jesse's tip jar flying with a swat of his hand. "Come on out and say that to my face."

Jesse backed away, hands raised. Rudy lunged at him, then feinted. He laughed when Jesse stumbled back and burnt his hand on the grill. The searing flesh sent up a sickening hiss.

Rudy quit laughing when Tyler's arm tightened around his throat.

"Let me go, asshole—" Rudy said.

"You started it, he finished it. You're done," Tyler said as Rudy threw an elbow. Seth stepped in and twisted Rudy's free arm.

"Apologize," Tyler said.

"It's okay—" Jesse said. "It's all right—"

"Fuck you," Rudy growled.

"Whoopsie," Seth said, bringing his heel down on Rudy's bare foot. "Tell him you're sorry."

Rudy coughed a "No." Seth licked two fingers, stuck them up Rudy's nose, and plunged them up and down. The crowd hooted and groaned.

"You can either be sorry, or you can say sorry," Seth said, wiping his fingers clean on Rudy's shirt. "What's it gonna be, man?"

"Okay, okay." Rudy kept eyes fixed on the ground. "Sorry."

Tyler said, "I don't want to hear you—or anyone—giving him no more shit. Now get out." Rudy staggered against Tyler's final shove. Seth dispersed the crowd as Rudy strutted to the exit gate, a few friends trailing behind him, cawing.

By then, Amanda had slipped behind the counter. She scooped a few pieces of ice from the cooler and held it to Jesse's palm with a dishcloth while he tried hard not to stare at her perfect, blaze-orange pedicured toes. They matched her swimsuit. His ears roared.

"Are you okay?" she asked.

"Sure am," Jesse said. He straightened his shoulders and tried to look stoic, clenching his jaw the way men did in movies. It hurt his teeth.

"That," she said, "Was hilarious."

"Th-thanks." Jesse managed a thin smile, then back-nodded, shrugging.

"Any more problems, you come get me," Tyler said.

"Thanks." Jessie thought that was the last of it, but when he went to lock up that night, the lifeguards were waiting outside the gate.

"Seth's giving you a ride home," Tyler said.

"It's all right, I can walk."

Seth pointed to Rudy's pickup, idling in the parking lot. Jesse ducked into the back seat and thanked the lifeguards yet again, noting their side glances when he prayed for traveling mercies after buckling up.

"Amen," Amanda said.

"Amen," Seth added, making the sign of the cross.

"Amen," Tyler muttered. "Amen, sweet Jesus, all right . . . Amen."

The truck followed them closely for several blocks. On New River Road, Rudy overtook them, swerving so close that their side mirrors clicked. From then on, the lifeguards drove Jesse home, dropping him off at the end of the driveway where a giant cross glowed above the church, and his mother waited on the porch swing, Bible open in her lap.

How'd you escape? elevated Jesse to a certain notoriety, and suddenly, he had friends. When the lifeguards took their break, Tyler waved Jesse over to join them. If Jesse wasn't busy, he would take off his white apron and sit down with them while he read scriptures. He'd answer all of Tyler's questions about Old Testament law, lose debates with Amanda about the role of women in the ministry, and tease Seth that he should not necessarily take the Bible literally when it said, "whatever your hand finds to do, do it mightily."

During these breaks, Jesse learned that Seth was headed to State, the best school for the dollar according to his father, who wanted him to study accounting, business, or dentistry—anything but musical theater. Amanda won a full ride to Baron, but Tyler didn't have the grades for a selective university. She wanted him to go to the community college so they could stay together, but for Tyler, that meant four long years of delivering pizzas and taking classes part-time. To make matters worse, Tyler's parents hated Amanda. And while they claimed it was "definitely not because of her race. . ." they were pushing Tyler to join the military, get out of Laurelton, and see the world. They were bickering away one afternoon when Tyler tossed a piece of gravel at Jesse and said, "Hey, what about you?"

Jesse hesitated. "I signed up for plumbing and electric at the VoTech. Mr. Connor said he'd make me a business partner, so I have to learn pool maintenance."

"You?" Amanda said, laughing. "I've never even seen you in the water."

"I don't need to know how to swim. They'll teach me about chlorine and stuff—"

Amanda's mouth pursed into a teasing frown. "How are you going to jump with us at Class Bash if you can't swim?"

"I wasn't planning on going," Jesse stammered. He attempted nonchalance. "I'm not much of a partier."

"You *have* to jump off the trestle. It's a tradition," Seth said.

"Nah, I don't do risky stunts. It's not biblical."

"Coward," Tyler said.

"The gospel says you're not supposed to put God to the test."

The lifeguards looked at him blank-eyed.

Jesse sighed. "During his temptation, Jesus straight up told the devil you're not supposed to do stupid stuff so that God has to send down an angel and save your dumb ass."

"Wow," Tyler said. "Is that the King James version?"

Jesse went round and round with them, countering every argument with scripture, until an exasperated Amanda declared that, "Jesus may have walked on water, but the rest of us need to learn a basic breaststroke." Bested, that night found Jesse shivering in the pool after hours. He refused to get in the water without a shirt on and flailed so monstrously that even Seth declared him hopeless.

"I'm not giving up," Amanda said. She swam to the deep end, arms undulating like a dancer's while she treaded water. "There's nothing to be afraid of. Don't think, just do."

She held out her hands. Jesse gulped in a breath and swam toward her smile, surfacing in front of her. Amanda was so proud of him that she hugged him right there in the water, her body mortifyingly female and slick. Jesse nearly fainted.

The day after this triumph, Jesse astonished the lifeguards by showing up in a pair of brand-new tropical print swim trunks and a tank top that his mother declared immodest. Morning still found Jesse reading the Bible poolside and talking to them about things of the spirit. But when the lifeguards arrived, Jesse would strip down to his Hawaiians and take slow, tentative laps alongside them, learning to move through deep water, even if he did surface after every lap and murmur, "Praise Jesus!"

Rudy laid low for a while after the run-in. But by mid-June, he was back at the pool, and Jesse groaned when he spotted Rudy in line at the snack bar. Lower lip bulging with chaw, Rudy politely requested an empty to-go container. He even held up a dollar tip.

"No charge," Jesse said, waving it away. "Let bygones be bygones."

"Why thanks, Chicken," Rudy said, smiling. He pocketed the bill and left.

That night they found the Styrofoam box on the front seat of Amanda's car, a pile of shit coiled perfectly inside it. Amanda and Jesse sprayed the car down with Lysol pilfered from the supply closet, but Seth and Tyler plotted ways to get even. On the way home, Jesse chided them to remember that vengeance belonged to God and that Rudy would get his comeuppance.

"Probably sooner than you think," Tyler said, speeding past Jesse's driveway.

During the whole prank, Jesse's hands never stopped shaking. He fretted in the getaway car with Amanda while Seth and Tyler snuck into the barns at Good Shepherd Llama Farm, filled a paper bag with manure and set it afire. They rang Rudy's doorbell, then used Seth's camcorder to capture Rudy cursing while he stomped the flaming bag of shit. Seth and Tyler escaped through the woods, urging Amanda to drive fast while Jesse prayed for deliverance.

Afterward, Jesse and the lifeguards went to Lou's Diner where they ate fries and drank burnt coffee in the deserted restaurant. Despite himself, Jesse found their glee contagious and fell to laughing when Seth snarfed milk, and they were still snickering when they played rock-paper-scissors for the check. They giggled uncontrollably, hiccupping and gasping until Tyler reached in his back pocket and realized his wallet was missing.

One week later, Jesse and the lifeguards reported to Good Shepherd Llama Farm at seven a.m. They lucked out, in a way. None of them had been in trouble before, and Rudy's parents were less interested in pressing charges when they found out that their nearly-adult son had started the trouble by crapping in a Styrofoam box. There was porch damage to pay for, though—and Amanda's uncle was determined to make an example of the lifeguards and Jesse by ordering them to perform "restorative justice."

As they labored, Jesse tried to cheer up everyone by reminding them that, "The Lord disciplines those whom he loves," but the lifeguards were lousy workers. Amanda was distracted by the llamas and kept leaning on her rake to stare at the bucolic flock. Tyler and Seth amused themselves by frustrating Rudy with idiotic questions like, "Do I lift this wheelbarrow with both hands?", "Should I bend my knees while standing?", and "Which way is north?" By noon, they'd only mucked twelve pens, with twenty more to go. When Rudy called lunch, Tyler and Seth retreated to the shade of a huge tree to eat their sandwiches, but Amanda pestered Rudy into showing her one of the llamas. Jesse followed her.

"This is Fred," Rudy said, leading the animal to Amanda. Fred had a brown face, fuzzy white ears, and a mottled coat of knotted fur. The llama trotted, knelt, and leapt on command. Amanda clapped her hands as if Fred were the greatest llama ever, while Jesse's peanut butter sandwich turned to cement in his throat.

"So cute," Amanda said. "Can I pet him?"

"Sure," Rudy said. "But watch yourself. Fred's our stud—he kicks if he gets nervous."

"Be careful, Amanda," Jesse said, watching her long legs as she stepped through the fence. She ignored him, petting the llama's wig-like hairdo.

"Hi, Fred," Amanda cooed, scratching Fred's chin and giggling. Jesse felt a sharp pinch of jealousy when she wrapped her arms around the llama's neck.

"Your fur is so soft, Fred . . . awww . . . there's my sweet boy!"

"Oh, hey—never cuddle a guard llama," Rudy said. "Fred is trained to subdue any threat."

"Subdue, like, how?"

"If you order him after a coyote, he'll knock it down, sit on it, then smother it to death with his hindquarters."

"Butt smothering? You're kidding me."

"Nope," Rudy said, grinning. "That's how they do it. Kicking and butt smothering."

Amanda cowered when the llama bumped his nose against her chest.

"No, Fred." Rudy guided the animal back a few paces. "Stay."

Rudy stared at Fred until the llama lowered its gaze.

"Amanda, don't move out of the way for him . . . he'll think that he dominated you."

The llama nosed Amanda again. She put her hand against his chest. "No, Fred."

"Atta girl," Rudy said. Tyler and Seth headed back to work, but Amanda lingered. Jesse didn't like Amanda talking to Rudy, or petting Fred the butt-smothering llama.

"How long do llamas live?" Amanda asked.

"Depends." Rudy pointed to the pasture. "See that hill?"

Amanda nodded.

"A couple winters ago all these llamas got the flu. My dad had me treat them with the same antibiotic we give cattle. But he miscalculated about their muscle density."

Amanda tilted her head.

"I gave one an injection, then another, all the way down the line," Rudy said, pantomiming. "No sooner do I finish that the first llama collapses. Then the second, then another—all falling like dominoes. I had a stack of ten dead llamas—snow ass-deep, ground frozen solid."

Amanda grimaced, but Rudy continued, laughing. "There were dead llamas everywhere. We had to get Bobby Tanner over here with a backhoe to bury them."

Rudy's face shifted from amusement to bland confusion when met with Amanda's silence. She pursed her lips. Jesse remembered how the teacher looked at Rudy—with such pity—back in grade school because Rudy was slow in all subjects, and his lips moved when he read. Amanda was looking at Rudy like that now.

"That's terrible," Amanda said. "Did you get in trouble?"

The apples in Rudy's cheeks reddened. "A little, but my dad picked the medicine and so I didn't get in a lot of trouble."

"I feel badly for the llamas," she said. "Poor things."

"Why?" Rudy asked, unable to stifle his laughter. "At least they're dead."

After they got busted, Tyler showed up at the pool in tears because his parents reneged on paying tuition at the community college. A few nights later, he was on Seth's doorstep with a garbage bag full of clothes and a bruise on his jaw. Seth's parents took Tyler in, but it was no permanent solution. Jesse had a mind to ask Tyler if he wanted to go in on the apartment Mr. Connor offered to rent him, thinking it'd be fun to have a roommate. But Tyler had been so moody and preoccupied that Jesse hadn't broached the subject yet.

Jesse had his own worries. The night before, he'd broken the news to his mother that he was moving out the first of September. She'd fallen to her knees as if wounded, begging him not to abandon his Christian home. Jesse tried to be tender and patient with his mother, but she acted like he was taking off for Sodom or Gomorrah rather than moving a few miles across town—and when Jesse *said* that, his mother called him a "lost sheep." Her mortification was worse than any scolding or slap; Jesse cringed at the memory of her sagging shoulders when she turned her back on him and slammed the door.

Even the next day, he still suffered the starchy, muffled sound of her weeping. Work usually offered distraction, but the sky was overcast, the air was cold, and the pool was deserted. The lifeguards were hanging out on the lawn by the snack bar. Amanda rested her legs across Tyler's. He had his visor pulled low over his forehead and his hand on her stomach. Seth marked choreography in the grass as he sang, "Seasons of Love."

"Guys," Tyler said suddenly. He propped himself up on one elbow, "I joined the Marines."

Seth removed his earbuds, mouth hanging open.

Amanda sat up, slowly. "What?"

"I did it, babe." Tyler reached for Amanda's hand. "You're looking at a U.S. Marine."

"No, I'm not," Amanda said. She shook her head, slowly. "No, I'm looking at a lunatic. You're going to get yourself killed, you idiot!"

From there, things really went downhill.

The theater of breakup was astonishing. Tyler cashed in his sign-up bonus and immediately resigned from lifeguarding. Amanda returned all Tyler's gifts, cramming them into boxes she left atop the hood of his car. Jesse tried to avoid the fevered ramblings of the furious ex-lovers, each of them careening between distraught heartbreak, contrived nonchalance, and backhanded demands for loyalty. When Amanda found out that Tyler hooked up with Stefania—a notorious bartender five years their senior—Amanda spent the afternoon huddled in the snack bar, stabbing at the counter with a plastic fork and ranting that Tyler had found "the stupidest possible white girl."

"I don't think he likes her," Jesse said, blending extra M&Ms into a milkshake, hoping to soothe Amanda's ire.

"Looks like he does," Amanda snapped. "I hope he likes penicillin too. She's slept with like, three of my cousins and six barfly guys I know of."

"Maybe Tyler isn't part of God's plan for you." Jesse passed her the milkshake.

"I had plans of my own, you know," Amanda said. "And that motherfucker ruined them."

"You don't have to talk like that," he blushed. "Golly."

"God has bigger things to worry about than my cussing," Amanda said, slurping. She saw Jesse's downcast eyes and softened her voice. "Half our friends won't even talk to me anymore. I'm like a total pariah."

"When you're down, that's the best time to pray," Jesse said. "God will help you."

"Maybe you're right," Amanda said. She bowed her head. "Dear Jesus, please let Tyler contract every itchy STI then fall directly into a volcano . . ."

"Stop it," Jesse said, laughing.

"Okay, well if you won't pray with me," Amanda smiled, "Then I'll need a favor."

"Anything," he said, topping off her milkshake with more hot fudge. He saw the gleam in her eye and immediately regretted his words.

Jesse wrestled with the spirit and the flesh for a week before the favor that he feared would cause him to stumble. No matter how hard he petitioned, Jesse remained unsure it was God's will for him to escort Amanda to Class Bash. He fasted, meditating on a verse from Isaiah that promised, "You will hear a voice behind you, saying, *this is the way you should go*."

Usually, Jesse felt certain he heard that voice. This time it was elusive. Every step he took toward God seemed to darken his path. He'd gone to Amanda's church that Sunday, where he was amazed by its informality: the praise band that turned hymns into rock ballads, worshipers in blue jeans and shorts, the young minister with her spiked hair. Reverend Kate's preaching emphasized God's mercy and grace rather than a doctrine of damnation. Jesse left the service with his eyes opened to a truth he had long suspected, and that his mother fiercely denied: that there was more than one way to serve God.

Still, Jesse worried that going to a worldly party was taking things too far. He had a decision to make about what kind of Christian life he was going to live. How could he make that decision without knowing what living meant? Jesse prayed for direction as he made root beer floats at the snack bar. "Which way, God?" he nagged, scrubbing the stainless-steel sinks and bleaching the cutting boards. He even attempted informality, switching it up with, "Dear Heavenly Father, hey, what's good?"

Jesse was still seeking God with his whole heart by Friday night at closing. He dressed for the party, slipping on a new T-shirt that said, *Son Screen Prevents Sin Burn*. He implored God while he waited for Amanda in the parking lot, beseeching heaven one last time as they parked her car in the village of Stowe.

"Here goes," Jesse said, stashing her keys in the gas hatch. "Lord, lead us."

"Dude. Relax. Jesus loved parties so much he changed water to wine," Amanda deadpanned, slipping her elbow smoothly through his. She was in high spirits for the first time in ages. He shivered. She looked stunning—she had let out her braids, and her hair fell in little tantalizing curls against her forehead. He needed all the God he could get.

They headed downhill to the trestle. The cicadas were striking up their chorus and a light mist hung over the river. Music blasted from a laptop rigged to speakers rigged to an old car battery. He could hear shouts from a group of shirtless guys playing Frisbee in the shallows. The majorettes from the marching band passed around a concoction in a bright green bottle. Seth was joking around with a group of guys from the soccer team, along with Tyler and Stefania.

Amanda clasped Jesse's hand, tight. "I'm getting a beer."

"Get me one, too," Jesse said. A thrill ran through him when she smiled.

Jesse's first beer tasted alright, though more sour than he imagined. He drank it fast, then asked for another. It settled in his stomach and made him feel like things were moving quicker than before. He wanted to have a good time but wasn't sure how to be "in this world but not of it." He also wanted to keep an eye on Amanda. She was getting drunk. Very, very drunk. Jesse watched her hit a joint, something he had never known her to do. He wished he could assure Amanda of her own awesomeness, but the beer made his tongue feel like a roll of liverwurst and all the thoughts in his head popped like foamy bubbles.

"Let's go sit down," Jesse said. Amanda's balance was off, and she sat heavily on a fallen log. Jesse perched next to her, trying not to belch. Amanda waved at a group of friends, who nodded her way but went to hang with Tyler and Stefania, backs to her.

"You like this party?" Jesse asked her.

"Not really," she said. "I can't believe he was so mean all along. His friends, too."

"They're some rude sons of bitches," he said.

"Wow, look what a little beer does."

"Right back at you."

They clinked cans and she grinned and shook her head. Jesse felt a lump rising in his throat. He had to chance it. "Amanda."

His Adam's apple was made of frozen marbles. She stared at him, brown eyes darkening in the light from the bonfire.

"You look nice," he croaked.

"Thanks," she said with a sigh. "Thanks for being my friend-date."

"Of course," he said. "Do you know what they say in the Bible?"

"I bet you're going to tell me."

Jesse took a swig for courage. "In Song of Solomon, he compares the lady's teeth to, like, freshly shorn sheep and congratulates her that none of them are missing."

"No way."

"Yeah," Jesse said, "Then he tells her that her hair is puffy like a baby goat, and he calls her bosoms pomegranates and stuff."

"Wow," Amanda said, tracing a line in the sand with her foot. "What a smooth talker."

Jesse paused, lowering himself down to one knee before Amanda. He spoke earnestly, looking into her eyes. "Like a lily among thorns is my darling among the young women..."

He lumbered to his feet and put his hand on his heart. "That's verse 2. That's you."

Amanda threw back her head and laughed.

"Oh my God, sometimes you are so weird," she said. She ruffled his hair and excused herself to the bushes to pee. Jesse cracked open another one, heart throbbing. He drank it fast, reminding himself that it was all right to "let beer comfort the perishing."

The night was hot and sticky. People were coupling up, and the music got louder, raunchier. Amanda stopped to talk with some people on the way back to Jesse. He was just about to go join her when he saw Rudy wade through the river, leading Fred the llama.

Jesse watched Amanda reverse course and head toward Rudy, extending her hand to scratch Fred's chin. A small crowd gathered. Fred pranced and quivered from the attention. Rudy let Amanda give some commands to Fred, and the llama obliged. Her delighted giggle drifted across the evening air. Dread settled in Jesse's stomach as he realized Amanda was flirting.

Jesse could tell by the way she twisted her shoulders around and arched her back when she talked. Every now and then Amanda would sneak a glance at Tyler and Stefania. Tyler kept squeezing Stefania's butt and bragging that his dad gave him the thumbs-up on Stefania because "gentlemen prefer blondes."

Jesse saw Amanda's neck stiffen and her hand tug at her own loose, dark hair. She leaned over to Rudy, put her hand on his shoulder, and whispered in his ear.

They left, Rudy's elbow slightly brushing hers as they walked past Tyler, who grew quiet when he saw Amanda slide her hand into Rudy's. They walked along the riverbank,

Fred following dutifully on his lead. Rudy and Amanda detoured under the trestle, crossing through the shallows to the opposite bank. The jewelweed closed behind them like a curtain.

Jesse started to follow them, then stopped. He didn't want to deal with Rudy alone. He finally found Seth, just as he blew whistle and shouted, "Let's go, folks—time to jump!"

Jesse was swept up in a laughing, singing mass of bumping shoulders. There was no moon, so the revelers shone headlamps and flashlights. Jesse heard the rasping bark of someone throwing up into the weeds and paused. Tyler stood near Stefania, arms crossed.

"Hey," Jesse said. "You seen Amanda?"

"Why don't you ask that Rudy asshole?" Tyler said. "He'll know."

Seth's voice interrupted them. "Line up, Class Bash jumpers! Line up!"

"You jumping?" Tyler asked.

"I don't think I better—" Jesse said, eyeing the drop from the bridge to the water.

"Jesse," Seth yelled, beckoning. Jesse hesitated, but Tyler prodded him forward.

"I don't swim that good—"

"We're lifeguards," Tyler said, grabbing Stefania's hand. "We'll save you. C'mon!"

They swung themselves onto the bridge, hopping between railroad ties. Jesse peered down at the rushing water. It looked cold and mean.

"Amanda!" Jesse yelled. Where *was* she?

"Lights on the water," Seth said. Beams danced on the river, making the current glitter. Seth started his countdown. "Ready on the three . . . two . . ."

Scanning the jumpers, the beam of Seth's headlamp illuminated the brush alongside the river and stopped. Amanda was locked in a kiss with Rudy, reclining with her shirt off, her bikini top at her waist. Fred the llama grazed next to them.

"Oh my God," Seth said. Someone giggled, aiming another light onto the oblivious couple. Jesse felt a surge of nausea when Amanda closed her eyes against the glare and curled into Rudy's shoulder, limp as a possum. Rudy ground his hips against her.

"Holy shit," Tyler said. He gripped Jesse's arm hard. "What a whore."

"Wait," Jesse said. "Something's not right."

The crowd heckled Rudy and Amanda. Some were taking pictures. Rudy smiled and yelled, "Leave us alone, you dumb motherfuckers! Jump!"

Seth blew the whistle and tried to restore order. Jesse could see Rudy working to tug down Amanda's shorts. Over Rudy's shoulder, Amanda's eyes blinked open, then closed. Her head lolled to the side. A camera flash popped. Another.

"Lead me, God," Jesse whispered.

He ran and leapt.

The water knocked all the air out of his body. He bobbed to the surface and swam toward Amanda. His feet slipped on the pebbles and mud as he rushed from the shallows.

"Amanda!" Jesse shouted.

She pushed Rudy away and turned her head toward Jesse. Rudy scrambled to his feet, one hand on Amanda's shoulder. She leaned her head against his legs.

My heavens, she's drunk, Jesse thought.

Fred the llama stared at him, snorted, and spit.

"You ain't welcome here," Rudy said. He stepped in front of Amanda, blocking Jesse.

"Amanda." Jesse held his hand out and stepped forward. "Are you all right?"

"Hey," Amanda said, swaying. "What's up, Jesse?"

"It's time to go home," Jesse said. He could hear other jumpers plummeting into the water, one percussive splash after another broken by shrieks of laughter.

"My top is off," Amanda said. She covered her chest, struggling to right the straps of her bikini. "Oops. Sorry."

"Get out of here, Chicken."

"Let's go, Amanda."

"I was having fun—" she giggled. "What's the big deal?"

"You need to sober up—"

"Don't tell her what to do," Rudy said. "I know what she needs."

"I'm a big girl—" Amanda scolded Jesse. "I don't have a curfew—"

"I'm not leaving you with him." Jesse could hear the other jumpers frolicking in the water, getting closer. Rudy helped Amanda to her feet.

"Whoa. I am dizzy." Amanda blinked, steadying herself against Rudy's chest. "I . . . I better go home."

"You're staying with me," Rudy said, pulling her into a rough kiss.

"No, no." Amanda studied him. He kissed her again. "I don't like that."

"There is no *no*," Rudy said. He gripped her neck. She cringed.

"Let me go," she said. Rudy tightened his arm around her waist, cupping one hand around her breast.

"Wait," Amanda said. "Stop it."

Rudy wrestled Amanda, laughing as she tried to get away. Jesse stepped toward them.

"Come on, Rudy. You heard her."

"Fuck you."

"No. Fuck *you*, Rudy."

Jesse had never said it before. It felt good until Rudy ran at him and they locked arms, circling and shifting. The llama whined, straining at its lead. Jesse really didn't know how to punch or grapple, so he simply held on to Rudy's middle. Rudy overpowered him, taking hold of Jesse's hair. The next thing Jesse knew, he was upside down and Rudy was growling, "You want to drown, you fucking retard?" Rudy plunged Jesse's head underwater.

"Stop it!" Amanda said. Jesse heard voices and splashing. He punched dumbly at Rudy's face, but Rudy dunked him again and again. Amanda held Fred's halter. The llama's eyes were wild with fright, and he pranced, pulling at the lead.

"No!" Amanda said. "Let him go, Rudy!"

"Around here, we drown perverts like you." Rudy snickered.

"Let him go!" Amanda shrieked. Jesse saw her loosen Fred's lead. Jesse's lungs burned, and he started to black out. Rudy plunged him under.

"Coyote!" Amanda yelled, pointing. "Get him, Fred!"

Jesse saw the llama charge, nostrils flaring. Rudy loosened his grip. Jesse leapt aside. The llama's body made a hollow thumping sound when it pushed Rudy into the water, then laid its weight against Rudy. Rudy's legs thrashed. By then, jumpers were streaming over, dodging the llama's hooves, hitting it with their fists. Seth struck the llama with a stick. Finally, Tyler hit Fred on the head with a rock. The llama reared up, then retreated, bellowing as he zigzagged into the woods.

Seth and Tyler dragged Rudy from the river. Rudy's face was bleeding and his breath raspy as sandpaper.

"We're in deep fucking shit," Tyler said.

Jesse scrambled for the right words to pray. Amanda appeared next to him. She had her top back on and her towel around her shoulders. She was shivering. When she touched his arm, Jesse realized he was shivering too.

"Is the llama okay?" she asked.

"That's the least of our goddamn worries," Tyler snapped.

"I think a couple of his ribs are broken," Seth said, feeling around Rudy's torso. "Probably got a concussion, too."

Tyler ordered Stefania to call an ambulance, then gently pressed his hands to Rudy's chest. Rudy's eyes flickered open and he hissed, "That crazy bitch tried to kill me."

"You wouldn't stop," Amanda said. Her voice sounded plaintive, unreal. Amanda looked at the crowd gathered around them and squared her shoulders. "I told him no and he wouldn't stop."

"Didn't look like *no* to me," Tyler snorted. "You could have fucking killed him."

"You stupid, stupid whore," Rudy coughed. Some blood came up. Jesse could hear the crowd murmuring and felt his nerves tingle. Rudy's baseball friends stood cross-armed, shifting their weight. A coven of girls, eyes sharp as knives, whispered behind cupped palms.

Rudy spit a gob of phlegm at Amanda. "You fucking black bitch—I'll get you."

The air crackled. Jesse heard the slur first. Amanda's head snapped around at its echo. There was one murmur, then another, rising louder until they were in a swarm of riling hornets. Jesse's hands began to tingle. Amanda had a strange expression on her face, and Jesse realized it was fear.

Seth grabbed Jesse's arm. "Get her out of here. Now."

It wasn't even a half mile to Stowe, but they were winded and sore by the time they got to Amanda's car. They'd spoken little on the way uphill. Teeth rattling, Amanda asked Jesse to drive, but he had no idea where to go. She looked like a little kid, wrapped in her white towel stamped with a big red cross and the word *Lifeguard*.

"What should we do?"

"You feel like praying?" Amanda asked. "This is the time."

He did feel like it. But for the first time in his life, Jesse didn't think he *could*.

"I wouldn't even know where to start."

"Oh, yeah?" Amanda turned on him, eyes narrowed. "Go ahead and say it. Don't you have some Bible verse for me, or something like that? You think I learned my lesson?"

His stomach dropped. Jesse searched his mind for the right words, the scripture that would offer Amanda some hope instead of the dire verses circling his mind, verses about reaping what you sow and cutting off the hand that causes you to sin, eschewing drunken company.

"That's not what I was thinking." He looked out the window.

"Judge me all you want if you think it's my fault," she said, her voice cold. "Just like everyone else—"

"I think we're lost sheep," Jesse said, shaking his head. "Just lost sheep."

Amanda's eyes remained blank, dark pools in the glow of the dash light.

"God rejoices in finding the lost."

"Great," Amanda said. She put her hand to her forehead. "Shit."

"I think we better head home." He was so weary, but Amanda protested. Couldn't they just drive around for a while? She wasn't ready to face her uncle, this was no way to end his first night out—but Jesse just shook his head. He winced at the desperation in her voice when she wailed, "But we have to look for the llama."

"You know I can't."

His heart ached. Not an hour ago, Jesse had lain down his life for her, his friend. And she had done the same, saving him from Rudy. He wanted to tell Amanda that despite everything, he loved her and always would, and that God would too. Jesse knew in his soul that there was no greater love than this. He wished that he could be fearless, too, and so certain that the world would not disfigure his salvation. But Jesse saw clearly now that his own weakness and this all- consuming love that only promised him doom. Amanda moved faster than he did. He could stray no further.

"Man, you are really something else," Amanda said. She rested her head back against the seat, its gears chattering as she reclined and closed her eyes. "Whatever."

She fell asleep before they were out of Stowe. Hands shaking, Jesse thought about the meek inheriting the earth, and whether he even wanted it or not. At the last turnoff before Laurelton, Jesse steered away from New River Road and pointed them toward the hills, wheels churning as he followed the thin white line unfolding before them. Amanda snored, her body rocking when the car jostled at each break in the pavement. Jesse sighed. They didn't have to go straight home. He would find a place along the river, one of the canoe put-ins, and watch while Amanda slept, just this one time. Morning would come, and he would try to tell her goodbye then, if he could.

Love is Patient, Love is Kind

Charlene spent that Friday like any other, circling the park in the town square with a tambourine in one hand and a fistful of tracts in another. Her sandwich board declared *THE END IS NEAR* on the front and *CONFESS TO THY GOD, O SINNER* on the back. That particular day she found few to plead eternity with. There were only two pedestrians all afternoon, both of whom made a wide berth around her exhortations to repentance. Even the teenagers who routinely heckled her only half-heartedly tooted their horns and drove away. Charlene lifted the signs from her back well before rush hour and abandoned her mission, hoping that the Lord would forgive a little folding of the hands, a little laziness, a little despair of purpose.

She let up on the gas when she saw a man walking in the hot sun along New River Road. He wore a chambray shirt and khaki pants and listed slightly to the right from the weight of a duffel bag slung over his shoulder. Charlene passed him at a crawl, but then slowed to a stop.

They were but a few hundred yards from the parish house, where she lived. It sat tucked back from the road, at a short distance from Most Holy Yahweh Congregation, the church Charlene founded with her late husband. Twenty-five years ago, the bank considered it an "undesirable" property, but Charlene and Horace saw sacred potential in its abandoned swimming pool, weed-choked tennis court and bumpy golf course. The newlyweds labored feverishly to build the place up: rehabbing the former pro shop into a sanctuary, painting fieldstones white and arranging them in formations along the road frontage: a Star of David, a coiled snake with an apple in its mouth, the Christian fish. But the church's crown jewel was a fifty-foot-high wooden cross with a bas-relief stigmata of Jesus's crucified palm at its apex. The painter who rendered it spared no detail: a cruel gray nail spiked through its palm, bright vermillion blood pooled at the center, lit by a single red bulb. Charlene's car rested in the long shadow of the church's new sign, an LED display that declared *THIS IS GOD'S COUNTRY*, lest anyone driving by on the interstate attempt to forget.

The man leaned over the passenger door. His face had a gentleness to it that made Charlene suspect he had been anointed by the Holy Spirit, or soon would be. Always on the lookout for searching souls and sensitive to the keening timbre of the lost, Charlene handed him a bottle of water. She blushed when he smiled and said, "Thank you, ma'am."

"Do you need a ride somewhere, brother?"

"I believe I'm set to walk, ma'am."

"Suit yourself. It's awful hot out," Charlene said, digging into her pocketbook. She pressed a church tract into his hand.

"Well, God bless you," he said.

"We welcome everybody to worship." Charlene pointed at the church sign, then added, "And there's rooms to rent for sojourners."

The man nodded slowly, tucked the tract into his shirt pocket and snapped it closed. Charlene waved, said a quick prayer for both of them, and drove on.

TC waited in a rocker, checking his watch and letting the ice cubes melt in his glass of sun tea. Kim had called him but an hour ago to let him know their brother Gene was on the way home. The peonies Kim kept were in full bloom, their thick heads bobbing and sending up a sick-sweet perfume that always struck him as funereal; it soured the taste of his tea. He added another packet of sugar and caught a glimpse of Gene walking up the driveway.

The last time TC saw Gene was at his sentencing. In those days, TC was a slender young deputy with a reputation for kindness and a somber faith in lawful justice, faith that Gene's conviction sorely tested. Eighteen years had given TC a sizable paunch, one that strained against the buttons of his uniform shirt. It had also given him a breadth of experience—experience that he suspected his brother's parole would test again.

TC tried to smile when Gene gained the porch. His brother had the look of the just-released: hungry, slow, like a dog kicked into studied wariness. TC shook hands with him, invited him to sit. Gene sank into the plump floral cushions of the wicker couch, hands folded in his lap. In the distance, a mower droned, surly as a hornet.

"You want a cool drink?"

Gene nodded, mopping the sweat from his forehead.

"I got the car running good," TC said. "You could use it to go up and see the graves if you want to."

"I got that picture of Mama's headstone. It looks real nice."

Gene gulped down his ice tea, and TC refilled it. He watched his brother take in the neatly kept yard, the flowers Kim tended, the new coat of paint on the barn.

"Looks like you two are getting along all right out here," he said. "Roof new?"

"Hurricane blew it off year before last." TC glanced at his shoes. "Insurance paid for it."

TC's rocker squeaked against the porch floor. Gene cleared his throat. "I don't suppose you have the key to the work house."

Gene tilted his head in the direction of the small, wood-frame ranch that TC's father had deeded them. Gene had no doubt seen it standing empty when he passed by on the walk here. Still, TC had hoped his brother would not ask. For a moment, TC fumbled with a lie: it was rented, the pipes had froze and busted . . . but the truth would out. Now was as bad a time as any to tell it.

"Well, Gene . . . I do," TC began, "But—"

Gene's eyes narrowed as TC explained that, as an elected law enforcement officer, he could not associate with a convicted felon, let alone shelter one, not even if the felon was his own brother. After TC finished, Gene clasped and unclasped his hands as if kneading dough. The cawing cry of a hawk rose, crescendoed, fell away.

TC said, "I don't like it. But it's the law. We'll help you find a little place in town."

"No need. I got something in mind." Gene put his glass down, hard. The table rattled. "No skin off my nose."

TC did not care for the turn things were taking. He crossed his arms and stretched out his legs. "I set prisoners loose all day, every day, you know . . . most of them don't have a pot to piss in, but we got you in good shape."

"I'm not a prisoner no more." Gene stood up. "But thank you."

"What you make of yourself from here on out is up to you."

"I had a real bum deal done to me."

Here was Gene for you. A man more sinned against than sinning. TC handed Gene an envelope. "That's your portion of the farm rent. We been keeping it back for you." He watched Gene count the bills and added, "Kim put a paper in there showing your accounts, what we used for your share of the taxes and upkeep, plus all the money she put into your commissary."

"Thanks," Gene said. "I hear there's work for me out to Bobby Tanner's."

TC felt his eyebrows shoot upward, but pulled his face into a neutral expression. Bobby Tanner had a number of farm enterprises, not all of which, TC suspected, complied with the Ohio Revised Code. That did little to distinguish Bobby from half of the farmers in South County, but—Gene needed a job. "Well, that's great news, more than likely. Do you good to work."

He hated the words before they were halfway out of his mouth, but it was too late. TC added, "I hope you do well from here on out."

"I mean to stay out of trouble." Gene took a deep breath and asked, "Can I call you sometime?"

A season passed between them in the time it took TC to say, "Sure."

"I've changed."

Let's hope so hung in the air. They shook hands. TC told him again that he wished him well, that he'd just changed the oil and the car was full of hi-test. Gene thanked him, and headed out. TC listened to all the sounds of his brother's leaving: footsteps crunching on gravel, the buckle of metal when the door opened, the chime-tones when Gene placed the keys in the car's ignition. He waved when Gene started the engine of their mother's old Buick, the brakes keening as Gene turned towards New River Road. He kept one arm raised until Gene disappeared, the motor cleared its throat, and the sound faded away.

Gene found it exhilarating to drive again. He turned on the radio, startled to hear the voice of Bruce Masters still on KCRK's *Tradio*. Good old Bruce. Who else could tell you what most of South County already knew? That it was hot out, that somebody was willing to sell a Mustang cheap because the wife didn't want it up on blocks in the yard no more, that the city was cracking down on illegal flea markets.

As he drove, Gene thought about what his life was like before he went away. He worked his way up from one little car lot outside town, to a thriving business with four locations. Built a gorgeous home for himself and Mary Ann. He led Habitat for Humanity projects, hiring teams of Amish craftsmen to build homes for poor families. Sponsored Little League, attended church, and golfed at the new country club—until Hannah Glick.

Hannah Glick was supposed to keep quiet. Gene knew that. As a rule, the Amish did not use English courts. But when the church bishops declined to discipline Gene, Hannah Glick quit the sect rather than keep her silence—even after her husband had her teeth pulled to terrify her into staying. She fled to St. Francis Shelter for Battered Women, and they took Hannah to the Laurelton police. Hannah and her sons made startling allegations. After the Glick boys talked, another Amish boy came forward. Then another. More. Some as young as six, others old enough to be married, with wives of their own.

Gene's life teetered, and then toppled. He was arrested in the full light of day, cameras flashing while his own father's deputies handcuffed him in the dealership lobby. The bright, primary-colored plastic pennants that ringed the car lot flapped and snapped in the breeze, as if applauding his apprehension. His face was all over the local paper and the six o'clock evening news. At first, Mary Ann defended him, but she turned coat when they lost the house, ratted him out for cheating on their taxes, and filed for divorce. Gene's attorney stepped down, unwilling to defend Gene's puny insistence that he had merely been helping all those boys use the toilet.

After he was sentenced, Gene's own father told the papers that justice had barely been served. When Gene called home from prison, his mother spoke to him in a languid tone of deferential politeness, as if he were an acquaintance whose face she struggled to recall. His father refused to come to the phone at all. TC never once visited. Kim sent Hallmark cards on his birthday and money on the first of the month. Other than that, the world turned its back on him when he needed help the most.

Now he was free. Gene parked the car at the river and watched the locust blossoms fall and spread a blanket of petals across the water. He considered the conditions of his freedom: conditions that forbade him from residing within a thousand yards of a school or church, prohibited him from patronizing establishments that sold alcohol, and banned him from owning any images of children, including photographs of his own family members. The judge who set Gene's parole specifically barred him from any contact—verbal, online, or written—with any current or former member of the Amish sect.

"Don't even stop at the gas station and buy a fried pie," his parole officer told him.

Gene was offended by this. Things were different now. He didn't want what he used to want. How could he? Prison had given him time to remake himself, to reform his life. It was disappointing to find that the world hadn't bothered to reciprocate, still preferring justice to mercy.

He sat on the riverbank, hands tracing the long grass. A heron, gray as a pen stroke, swooped down to pluck a fish. Gene chucked a stone at the water, frightening the bird away. The heron's wings beat slowly, whooshing beneath its squall of protest. He felt the inside of his palms tickle with heat, nerves, and sweat. He leaned to rest his elbows on his knees, and the tract in his shirt pocket crumpled, its corner piercing through the fabric and poking him in the chest. He read it over, then drove towards Most Holy Yahweh Congregation's driveway, the pierced hand of Christ beckoning him and all sinners to repentance.

Gene didn't expect Charlene to show him in immediately, but she led him straight upstairs to a small dim bedroom with a lemon-colored chenille bedspread and religious pictures on the walls. Charlene laid out the rules: she would provide a hot breakfast and supper, dinner he was on his own. He was required to attend Sunday service at 10 a.m., but Wednesday night Bible study was optional. "One hundred dollars a week. Will that do, Mr. Hallinan?"

Gene nodded. He took a deep breath and confessed, "You should know that I just got out of prison. Here's my papers."

A shadow passed over Charlene's eyes. Gene braced himself. There was a moment between them in which he could feel her weighing him, ounce by ounce.

"Most of the saints and disciples were felons," she said.

"They were?"

"Indeed. The Lord himself has led you here," Charlene said. "I'll take you at your word if you'll open your heart to his."

Gene put the envelope from the parole officer back in his pocket and shook her hand, the warmth of her smile radiating up his veins and into his chest. He paid Charlene a month's rent from the cash TC had given him, and went to his room.

Prison had made Gene a creature of routine. He woke early, walking down to the kitchen in a long-sleeved work shirt despite keen heat, face bright from scrubbing with cold water. Charlene paused over her Bible study and smiled.

"Coffee's on, Mr. Hallinan," she trilled. "May the Lord richly bless your day."

He arrived at Bobby Tanner's by seven of the morning that first day. Bobby and Gene had known each other their whole lives; he'd graduated with Gene's sister Kim, and it was her who set up Gene's employment. Gene admired Bobby because he was the last of a breed still farming the old way, eschewing pesticides and synthetic manure for heirloom seeds and crop rotation. Most farmers like Bobby had long since gone broke, but Bobby kept the place going by taking advantage of the craze for whole foods, farm-to-table, and agro-tourism.

As Bobby showed Gene around, he boasted that, "Them city people can't get enough of us . . . you can't believe the high dollar they'll pay to do half our work—picking apples, running around the pumpkin patch, hell, they even come and do cut-your-own Christmas trees."

"Hope they don't work me out of a job," Gene said.

"Not a chance," Bobby said, clapping a hand on Gene's shoulder. "I want someone around here I can trust."

The only thing that worried him was that Bobby had an Amish man named Joseph Bontrager for a partner. From what Bobby said, Joseph was a bit of a ne'er-do-well, who kept a weedy farm and sired more children than a man ought to have. His wife was awful, faded to the pale greasy color of the dishtowels she hung on the clothesline, constantly complaining and threatening to have Joseph kicked out of the order for laziness.

"Joseph won't bother you none," Bobby assured him. "He keeps to himself, and you'll do the same." To keep him in compliance with parole, Bobby tightly delineated Gene's work area, forbidding Gene from the grain patch in the back forty where Joseph spent much of his time hand-tending the sweet corn crop and working the beehives. Gene readily agreed, and Bobby proceeded to show him the rest of his enterprise.

Gene was stunned to learn that Bobby and Joseph raked in enough with the Halloween Corn Maze to build the Party Barn free and clear. The Party Barn was rented out for birthdays, weddings, family reunions, bachelor and bachelorette parties, even a few company picnics and once, a New Age Solstice Festival through some hippies who all ran around naked for a solid week and camped out in the hay barn.

What Bobby didn't tell Gene, was that he always threw seed for the corn maze just a week or so later than the other farmers. That way, Bobby's corn sat lower and tasseled out purple and red a little later, matching the color of the ripe THC-laden blossoms of *cannabis sativa* that Bobby cultivated, cured, and smuggled off the farm in Joseph

Bontrager's horse-drawn hay wagon. Once Bobby harvested the dope, he'd run his tractor through the sweet corn in a pattern. His mazes allayed the suspicions of the law and baffled the directional sensibilities of fall revelers, who bit into Jonagold apples just yards away from one of the largest marijuana-growing operations in the state.

For Gene, laboring in innocence, the farm work proved fulfilling: power washing the tractors, mowing the road frontage, repairing the chainsaw, stacking bales of itchy, unforgiving straw. He trimmed and sprayed the apple trees, mowed endless acres of lawn and pasture and tended the nice, lush rows of geraniums and forget-me-nots that Bobby liked looking smart around the Party Barn. It surprised Gene to feel a neat rush of pride when Bobby paid him his first free and honest wages. He taped the first dollar bill he earned to the small mirror above his dresser. The second dollar, he tucked in his pocket and put in the collection plate at Holy Yahweh.

Work occupied his time and his mind, but it was in church that Gene found he felt best. He loved the austere white walls, Charlene's tinny soprano singing hymns, the whisper of onion skin paper when the congregants turned their Bible pages. At each meeting of the tiny congregation, there was spirited revival that lent Gene a sense of wild abandon in prayer, and impressed him to throw himself wholeheartedly before God. After three weeks of hand-clapping, tongue-speaking, tambourine-shaking and shouting to the hills of glory, Gene answered the altar call, tears wetting the front of his shirt. He made public profession of faith, accepted the Lord Jesus Christ as his savior and Yahweh as his one true God. The anointing of the Holy Spirit was on him after that, just like Charlene said. Gene could feel it. God's breath, coursing through his body. Entirely transformed, he was, at long last, finally free.

When it rained, Charlene's mind tended to chase its own tail, and it seemed that no matter what she did or how she tried to turn the stronghold of her grief over to the Lord, sorrow pursued her whenever her mind turned to her sons. Jesse had moved out and barely visited, living a life outside the church she had raised him in. And Benjamin, poor Benjamin, he waited in the grave for the resurrection. What, Charlene, never ceased to worry, would happen to Benjamin's soul then? Fridays on the square when the hurt was too much to bear, Charlene sang, jingling her tambourine with pleasingly chubby wrists, her eyes alight with the rapture of one who had been saved from a howling demon, long dark curls quivering down her ample back. The more she sang the more the demons were kept at bay. Most days it was enough, and the Holy Spirit would send rescue and the sweet balm of assured salvation. But on days when it rained, even the Holy Spirit was not enough, because the rain always brought Benjamin.

She went to the town square anyway that day, donning her signs declaring *THE LORD WILL DESTROY THE WICKED!* and *HE WILL PRESERVE THE RIGHTEOUS!* over a frail poncho that she bought at the 99-cent store. Its thin yellow skin was transparent and she felt sweaty as a turnip beneath it as cold drops of water ran down her neck. Her moccasins squished when she walked, and she took them off to wring them out, busting the seam along one side where she'd glued it twice already. Near tears, she whispered a prayer of forgiveness, and headed home.

She'd hoped for solitude, but Gene's car was in the drive when she arrived. The afternoon sky was so plum-colored it had the feel of evening. She greeted Gene, and fled to the kitchen to cook, but caught herself standing over the kitchen sink crying and staring out at the yard, black with rain. Gene led her to the front porch swing and patted her hand.

"It's all right," he told her, "It's all right, you just cry."

"It's this rain," Charlene said. "It's just this dreadful rain."

Charlene turned her eyes towards the remains of a barn at the edge of the property. The sheet-metal roof was peeling off in pieces, a lean-to collapsed entirely on one side. "How long was you in prison?"

"Eighteen years."

"So you don't know what happened here," Charlene said. "Best you hear it from me."

Back then, she explained, Horace was still alive. The house was all silence and structure, Bible study and somber reflection on sinfulness. The smallest upset—a fork dropped at dinner, shoes left in the hallway—made for stern reckoning. The boys played outside and in the barn where they could escape his shaming them for every natural primal instinct, be it hunger, thirst, or, in Benjamin's case, desire.

Her Benjamin was always a bit of a rebel, asking questions in Sunday school, listening to the radio. He was caught smiling at a girl in church, and Horace upbraided the boy for hours, scolding him about demon lust and sinning with your eyes. Charlene did not know that Benjamin's eyes also sinned in the barn, where he kept a stack of magazines stashed under an old water trough, full of blank-eyed naked women who stared at the camera in bored resignation.

The night he died, Benjamin slipped out of bed and little Jesse—only six years old at the time—followed his brother to the barn. Jesse hid in an old horse stall and watched his brother set up a chair, a rope, a bale of straw. Later, Jesse told the sheriff that Benjamin climbed on the chair and opened his pants, leaning his neck forward against the rope. When the chair slipped and fell over, the rope went taut, and Ben's neck made a strange, popping sound.

Jesse ran inside, calling for Charlene, soaked to the skin by the cold, pelting rain.

When Charlene opened the barn door, she fell to her knees and tore at her hair. Her mind's eye could never erase what she saw: Benjamin hanging, broken; Jesse, blinking, saying over and over again, *my brother. My brother, my brother. He fell off a chair.*

"That's how we found him," she sobbed, "And it rained all that night and for the next three days, nothing but rain. Rain just like this . . ."

"Shhhh, shhh . . ."

"It's all my fault," she said, shoulders quaking.

"You done the best you could."

"No, no," she said, "I didn't do good enough at all—"

Then, Charlene told him how Horace retreated into silence and fasting in his study. He let himself waste away with cancer of his pancreas, blaming Benjamin's sin for his declining strength. He refused to see the doctor, sending away to Florida for copper bracelets that he wore until they left green rings around his withering arms, and preaching from the pulpit each week on the restorative power of the Holy Spirit. The Holy Spirit declined to save Horace.

"Benjamin in March, Horace gone by Christmas," Charlene said, shaking her head. "And all I can think about is my poor baby, burning in hell forever."

"No," Gene said. "That ain't how the good Lord works."

"After what Ben did—" she sobbed, shaking her head. "There's no hope."

Gene handed her a handkerchief, and Charlene looked at him. She'd never told anyone, not another soul, the whole story like this. What would he think of her now?

"Let me ask you something."

Charlene trembled, but whispered, "What?"

"Do you remember Brother Allard talking about a God of mercy?" he asked.

She sniffled and wiped at her nose. "Do you believe in that? A God of mercy?"

"I have to," Gene said. "I used to wonder how anybody could believe in mercy, seeing as how I was done. But then . . . I started to know what I've been forgiven. If you believe that you been forgiven, then you have to believe in mercy."

Charlene put her face in her hands. "Where was Ben's mercy?"

She nearly jumped out of her skin when he clasped her hands and said, "Stop. Someone put a bad idea in your son's head. An idea that he didn't know what to do with, and . . . he didn't have age enough to know better than to try it. Your Ben didn't lose his life to sin. What took his life was his innocence."

Charlene slowly shook her head. This felt pure . . . it felt true . . . and for all the hours she'd spent praying, fasting, weeping . . . it had never, ever occurred to her. Could it be true, that she had this wrong all along, that her holiness was false, that Ben could be innocent? She gasped for air like she was drowning.

Gene continued, "If you believe in a merciful God, then you have to believe that your son is in the kingdom. What kind of loving God would punish an innocent child for a simple mistake?"

Charlene fell forward, burying her face in her hands.

"Love covers a multitude of sins, Miss Charlene." She shivered. He had never called her by her first name, before. He patted her on the back, and she rested her head in his shoulder, ever so lightly. As she leaned into him, something shifted, and she felt every beat of her heart. He kissed the top of her head as if she were a child and moved away a bit; but she drew him close to her. She leaned her face towards his, but he stopped her: cradling her chin, his calloused hand rough against her flesh.

"You don't know all the things I've done."

"If what you said about Ben is true," Charlene said, "Then they don't matter now."

His eyes filled, and a tear dribbled down his cheek. Charlene wiped it away. He leaned in and kissed her full on the lips, gently, then stopped. He tucked his arm around her, and drew her near. They sat like that well into the evening, watching the storm and the lightning make its way past, shifting only slightly when a tree fell across the driveway. The storm lingered for another hour until finally the sun sent streaks of brilliant magenta and pink across the horizon. They sat, waiting, until they heard a small buzz and click as the lights of the Holy Yahweh cross blinked on, and the blood-red wound at the center of the pierced palm began to glow.

From that day on, Gene and Charlene began playing house. She delighted in taking care of him, ironing his shirts and even his work jeans, fixing buttons and scrubbing at the coffee stains around his cuffs. They talked with his hand draped over hers, looking into each other's eyes and smiling for long spells. Charlene remained a faithful presence in the town square, her face shining above the foam sandwich board that proclaimed *LOVE THY NEIGHBOR AS THYSELF!* on one side, and *JESUS LOVES YOU! SO DO I!* on the other.

It was strange to feel someone, a woman, in his arms again. In prison, there were only men, men that Gene shuddered to remember. Before that had been the boys. Gene was determined *not* to remember that. Those sins of his former self were old things now passed away, and he was made new, new and clean by the grace of God. Falling in love with Charlene gave Gene a new sense of purpose, a spring in his step. At the last meeting with his parole officer, the man praised Gene's work ethic and his adherence to the terms of his freedom.

"I don't want what I used to want," Gene told him. "I been redeemed."

Gene considered telling the officer about Joseph Bontrager but decided against it. After all, Gene barely spoke to Joseph, and did his best to keep it that way. Sometimes Gene felt Joseph's eyes on him, and when he did, Gene busied himself and moved to another task, conscious of keeping the distance between them. He didn't have much choice. Gene knew better than to say anything to Bobby when the lug nuts were mysteriously loosened on the FarmAll. He simply tightened them again, even when the wrench he needed disappeared from his toolbox and he had to go hunting for another. Gene likewise kept quiet when he came into the tool room and found the battery charger unplugged from the wall or his new work gloves lying in a mud puddle. He kept his head down and worked: he needed gainful employ, steadiness, clearly delineated duties, and no trouble.

His life outside work was quiet. Gene took few outings other than the occasional late afternoon lunch at the restaurant where Kim worked, church services with Charlene, and a weekly trip to the Laurelton Wal-Mart. He preferred to go late in the evening, when the crowds thinned out and he was unlikely to run into old acquaintances from his previous life. But that night, a cohort of young rumspringa surprised him in the sporting goods section. The boys poured into the aisle, talking loudly in Low German and jostling each other with their elbows.

"Hello, excuse me please—" Gene said, trying to edge past the group of boys. They laughed and pointed at him, and his pulse began to race. He kept his eyes on the linoleum floor, tripping slightly on his own pant leg in his haste to get away.

"Mister, I have a question." A young, red-headed boy whose face was Appaloosa'd with freckles ran down the aisle, trailing behind Gene. He had a box of condoms in his hand, and Gene could hear the other boys laughing and tittering amongst themselves, no doubt watching this dare from behind the endcaps and eavesdropping in the next aisle over. The boy held up the box of condoms, his face twitching with the thrill of his own prank. Gene relaxed slightly; the kids were clearly just goofing off. Still, he glanced around.

"Are these the good ones?" the boy asked, holding up a box of Trojans, bright blue, ribbed. Then he held up another brand of prophylactics, bright neon. "Or are these better? With the tickler?"

"I can't help you, I don't work here." Gene said. "I have to go."

He fled, the boys' laughter ringing behind him as they slapped each other's backs and guffawed over their joke. Face aflame and hands shaking, Gene made a beeline for

Charlene. They were in line at the self-checkout when he heard the boys again, this time in line behind them.

"Hey mister, you never answered my question!" The red-haired kid called, cupping his hands around his mouth. A few people turned to stare, and Charlene looked confused.

"What's he want?"

"Oh nothing, they're just fooling around."

But the boy was determined to make sport, and having gained an audience, couldn't lose face by backing down. Suddenly, a voice growled, "That's enough, Eli."

Gene turned, midway through lifting a case of bottled water from the cart, and his eyes met Joseph Bontrager. Joseph glared at Gene, his eyes moving deliberately from the cart that Gene shared with Charlene, to the boys' eager faces. Joseph turned to his charges and barked, "Weitergehen! Er ist schmuddelig. Na."

The boys' glee collapsed, and he turned away. He heard their quiet voices fade into murmurs, as Joseph herded them to a checkout line several aisles over. Gene didn't dare to look.

"What was that?" Charlene asked. "I hope they didn't get in trouble."

"No, honey," Gene said, "I think he just wanted them to settle down."

He was sweating and nervous, unsure whether to hurry Charlene to the car or stall her to avoid Bontrager and all those young boys. From the corner of his eye, Gene saw Bontrager's broad shoulders as he led the boys out the entrance at the opposite end of the store. In the lobby, Gene played the fool for Charlene, buying her an enormous gumball from one of the shiny red vending machines. He ran quarter after quarter through every vending machine in the place, delighting her with prizes: temporary tattoos, little plastic soldiers, a tiny stuffed kitten, handfuls of glittering beads. Gene did not stop feeding coins until he heard the clop of hooves pass by outside. Then, he dared a glance and caught a glimpse of Bontrager driving away, the rumspringa boys carousing in the hay wagon behind him, headed towards Cavalle Road. Heaving a huge sigh of relief, Gene kissed Charlene on the lips.

"Honey," he said, "Let's get on home."

TC could hear Gene and Charlene at breakfast when he knocked at the door, a deputy standing behind him. He hadn't seen Charlene in years, not since the awful incident with her oldest boy. He hated to knock on her door again, and knew Charlene was frightened by the way she pulled her housecoat closed and stuttered, "What's wrong, Sheriff?"

"Just a routine matter," TC answered. He saw the look of disbelief on Gene's face. "Step out onto the porch for a minute, brother?"

Charlene hurried off to dress. The deputy was already counting off twenty-five-yard intervals, the soft smack of the tape measure and chalk line carrying across the lawn between the house and church.

"What's this?" Gene demanded, keeping his voice low.

"Just checking a couple things out," TC said. In the yard, the deputy paced, measured, and marked. "We had a call in to the office. You settled in good here?"

"I suppose," Gene said, buttoning his shirt. "What's it to you?"

The deputy reeled in the tape measure with a low whir and a click. "Hey boss," he called, shielding his eyes with his hand. "I'm already at a thousand."

TC tucked his pen into his shirt pocket. "That's good news for you, I guess. Brother, I hate to ask this but did you . . . inform the minister over there of your status?"

"I did," Gene lied.

"Ok," TC said. "We'll just confirm that—"

"Why are you hassling me here? I made a lot of changes."

"Hope so," TC said. You've got a fine woman in that house."

"Best I ever knew."

"You used to say the same thing about Mary Ann."

"Everybody's got a right to some happiness. Even me."

"I want you to be happy. And I have a job to do."

Gene said, "I never harmed any woman. I hope you don't, either."

TC froze. He looked at Gene, closed his eyes, and rubbed his eyelids. "You have got to be kidding me."

"Just a second, now—" Gene said, as TC walked towards the front door. He could not believe this shit. TC felt the rush of anger flood his veins, anger that turned to dread when he saw Charlene waiting behind the screen door, her face open as a child's frightened awake by a dream. Her eyes moved wildly from Gene, to TC, to Gene again.

"Miss Charlene," TC said, "We better have us a talk."

Later, Charlene would not remember everything TC said. Horrible, horrifying things, unnatural and ungodly. What she would remember was the hollow look in Gene's eyes when she asked him, "Is this true?"

"Look at me, Charlene . . ." he said.

Charlene felt bile rise in her throat. She stood, hands trembling. "No. No. No."

"Can't I even tell my side of the story?" Gene pleaded.

The clock ticked dully on the wall, the breeze made the front door sigh open, and closed again. TC's radio crackled static.

"No," she said. Her voice cracked. "No."

Then, she'd stumbled into her bedroom and sat on the floor, covering her mouth with her hands, rocking back and forth. Her nightdress lay folded neatly on a chair next to the bed. Just that morning, Gene had lain there with her, lifted that gown up, running his hands along her thighs. She recalled smiling at the quick intake of his breath, the keen thrill of holding a man again, the sharp scent of their hunger for each other.

She heard footfalls on the floorboards above her, as Gene packed his things to leave. *My God,* she thought, *what have I done?*

Charlene blushed at her own shame and foolishness. She wondered how she could have been so imprudently naive, and thanked the Lord that he hadn't hurt her any worse, that she was merely the victim of her own despicable weakness. She covered her ears with her hands and sat still on the floor until TC knocked gently at the door, and told her they were leaving, to which she gave no reply.

By evening, Gene had been turned away from every place he tried to find a bed. The hotels in Laurelton were full because of the Heritage Festival. The homeless shelter accepted minors, so that ruled Gene out. The campground in Stowe asked Gene for ID. When the man saw Gene's name, he said, "No vacancy." Door after door was closed against him, so Gene gave up and drove towards Bobby's, hoping to bed in the hayloft until he could find something suitable.

Gene didn't blame Charlene. It was his fault. He hadn't trusted, hadn't faith enough to be fully honest with her. He'd been afraid that extending grace to someone like him was too much to ask. He had been right.

When he saw the rows of cars parked in the field at Bobby's and the lights glowing from the Party Barn, Gene nearly turned back. He had forgotten all about the poker run Bobby hosted during the Heritage Festival. He wasn't supposed to be in any kind of place that served alcohol, and here he was, driving past hordes of partiers leaning on the seats of their motorcycles, lounging in lawn chairs, waiting for the bands to start playing.

Gene parked the Buick at the farthest end of the field and walked uphill towards the barn, hoping to slip by unnoticed. All he wanted to do was lay his head down somewhere. Night was falling, and he strained to see. When he rounded the corner to the hay barn, there sat Joseph Bontrager's horses hitched and waiting, a half-load of square bales stacked on the wagon. One horse stomped its foot. Another loosed a great gale of urine. Joseph had his back to him, smoking a cigarette and counting plastic-wrapped stacks on the heavy oak workbench. Gene tried to sneak past, but his foot caught on a stack of loose boards. Joseph whirled around, frozen like a spotlit deer.

"What are you doing here?"

"Bobby around?" Gene asked.

"No," Joseph said. He put his hands on his hips. "Best get you away from that wagon."

"I'm just looking for the boss—" Gene said.

"I said stay back," Joseph snapped, standing up. "You know you oughtn't be here."

"I got to talk to Bobby." The hair on the back of his neck was electric.

"I said leave." Joseph blew a plume of tobacco towards Gene and dropped his cigarette into the dirt. He began moving towards him.

"I don't want any trouble. Just need Bobby—"

"You are trouble. Nothing but trouble," Joseph growled. The Amish man's hot breath was in Gene's face, and Gene could smell the man's sweat, a pungent, meaty scent heavy with tobacco.

"Not anymore," Gene said. He put his hands up. "I done nothing to you. Let me leave, now . . ."

Bontrager kept advancing. Gene took a step back, and stumbled hard into the side of the hay wagon. Steadying himself, that's when he saw them, nestled in the ring of square bales: dozens of neatly vacuum-packed bricks of cannabis, veiny and full of green buds. In a rush of understanding, Gene gasped, "Oh my God."

He had to get out of there, fast. Gene scrambled to get away, stammering, "I'll leave, I'm sorry—just let me—"

But it was too late. The next thing he knew, Joseph's hands were on his shoulders, spinning him around. Gene brought his hands up, but Joseph punched him in the nose. Everything spun. Gene's head roared. "I'm sorry," Gene said, over and over again, thinking about the book of Matthew, about turning the other cheek. He covered his head with his hands while Joseph pummeled him, until they heard Bobby shouting, and he burst between them, demanding, "What the hell is going on here?"

Bobby pulled Joseph off Gene and pushed him aside. Gene stood dazed while Joseph and Bobby bellowed at each other, spit and sweat flying. Woozy and weak as he was, Gene still saw his chance: Bobby's minivan sat idling by Bontrager's horses. Joseph's cigarette lay smoldering in the dust.

Gene picked up the butt, and tossed it into Joseph's wagon. Red embers coiled the plastic and sank into the hay. A small pool of flame formed, sending up a thick plume of smoke. Gene ran.

He made it to Bobby's van, slipped into the driver's seat, and locked the doors, fumbling to roll up the windows. He slid the van into gear as the men ran towards him. He drove fast as he dared across the pasture, leaving Bobby and Joseph farther and farther behind, choking on the dust he stirred up. The throaty scrape of the van's undercarriage barked as Gene bounced along, shuddering out the back gate and onto New River Road. One quivering headlight illuminated his way back to Holy Yahweh, to Charlene.

It had already been a long day, and TC was working a double. Fulfilling his professional obligation to inform Charlene felt as cruel as it was necessary, and he'd been sick to his stomach since the scene with his brother this morning. What had Gene been thinking? There was no making a fresh start or leaving your sins behind in a town the size of Laurelton, and it was unfathomable to TC that Gene had been fool enough to try it. The longer he thought about all the hurt this mess had caused and the hurts that would keep coming, the worse he felt. What would become of Charlene, a woman already so crushed by sorrow? And what would Gene do, next? TC parked the cruiser in a speed trap on the East side of town towards Barron and holed up there until evening, neglecting duty for solitude and delegating all the Heritage Day crowd control to his deputies. He was half asleep when the radio crackled. “Sheriff Hallinan, come in please.”

“Go for TC.”

“We’ve got a ten-eight at location 3782 New River Road, probable ten-twenty-four. Fire and EMS en route. Over.”

“Is that Tanner’s?” TC asked.

“Affirmative.”

That was strange, TC thought; Bobby seldom ever had problems at the Party Barn. TC knew there was a little underage drinking that went on there, and possibly a few plants at the edge of the property. But Bobby had always been peaceable. TC left him alone and Bobby returned the favor by keeping his head down.

“Ok. I’m all the way over towards Barron. Be there in twenty?”

“Copy.”

TC had just turned on his lights and was preparing to pull into traffic when he noticed the message alert flashing on his cell phone. Four missed calls. The phone rang again, in his hand.

“I’m on the way, Bobby,” TC said. “Everything ok?”
“This isn’t Bobby,” Gene rasped. “It’s me. You better go out to Tanner’s hay barn, the one on the hill. Go look in the wagon. Joseph Bontrager’s wagon. They’ve got drugs—”

“Where are you, Gene?” TC asked. “What’s Bontrager got in this?”

“I had nothing to do with it, I swear,” Gene said, “It’s bad, TC, real bad.”

“Now hold on a second—Tell me what’s happened?”

“I can’t answer no more goddamned questions from you!” Gene shouted, leaving TC to stare at his phone, start the car, and head towards trouble.

Gene hung up the phone and threw it into the church parking lot, watching plastic shards chip and shatter as it skidded across the overgrown asphalt and came to rest in a patch of tiger lilies growing wild in the ditch. He looked up at the cross that towered above him and began to climb the ladder, like Jacob fleeing Esau. One hand over one bloody hand, aching knees pushing up each rung.

He took a seat on the small landing, the ground swaying beneath him. He threw his socks and shoes to the ground, and waited.

When TC crested the hill at Bobby's, he could see the hay barn burning, a red glow on the horizon.

"Holy shit," he muttered.

Two engines were pulling in ahead of him to battle the blaze. There were a couple hundred drunks from the poker run rubbernecking the scene, ignoring the fire department's attempts to disperse them. The partiers were neighbors and acquaintances and voters, not to mention a number of people TC considered friends and his own administrative assistant, Janelle. The crowd was rowdy as a pit-bull in a gunny sack, so TC called for backup. The stench of marijuana fogged up the crisp evening air. So, he squandered a half hour shouting into his bullhorn and watching the nightmare unfold before him: flames destroying all sorts of evidence that had been sitting under his nose for Lord knew how long.

TC had no idea where Gene was, but Bobby Tanner and Joseph Bontrager waited in his deputy's squad car, insisting that whatever had happened, the blame lay on Gene, a convicted felon and known pervert. It was Gene who had secreted all that weed, they said, and done it behind their backs. It was Gene who attacked Bontrager, stole Bobby's van, and set the barn on fire.

"Is that right?" TC asked. "It takes at least four months to get decent bud on a crop."

Bobby looked a little stunned, and snuck a glance at Joseph. TC stuck a toothpick in his mouth and continued. "Gene's only been out of jail for a little over a month, so . . . he must be one hell of a farmer."

TC radioed for Bobby and Joseph to be put in separate cars to prevent—he glanced at them when he said this—"Any further harebrained attempts at collusion," and turned his attention to the arrival of the State Police. An eager lieutenant requested jurisdiction over the scene, and TC gladly acquiesced. In truth, TC didn't want jurisdiction over anything at this point; he could just as easily have surrendered his badge and gun, filled out the paperwork for early retirement, and hopped on a flight to Florida. The crowd had started to disperse by then, but for a few malingerers standing gap-mawed at the roaring fire atop the hill. Occasionally, something inside the barn would explode, sending sparks up and making a thunderous popping sound.

Body and head aching, TC walked back to his cruiser. His radio bleated. Again.

"Go for Hallinan," TC sighed. "If you must."

Charlene was filling a glass of water when she noticed a green minivan sitting in the lot at Holy Yahweh, its front end mangled, grill hanging halfway off, one tire flat. Puzzled, she pulled back the curtain and gasped. There was Gene—she knew it was Gene—up on the catwalk. She dropped the glass in the sink, and hurried across the lawn, fresh-cut grass clinging to her slippers.

"Hello," Gene said. He was shirtless, his face bloody, feet bare, swinging his legs like he hadn't a care in the world, leaning his back against the pierced hand of Christ.

"Gene," Charlene said. "Come down. You're—you're trespassing."

"Will you forgive us our trespasses?" Gene said. His smile was made worse by the blood on his mouth.

"You want a cool drink of water?" Charlene offered.

"I thirst," Gene said, holding his arms out and hanging his head in imitation.

"You better stop it." She glared up at him. "I'll call the police."

"I beat you to it." The red glow from the sign gave him an aura, as if he were aflame. "Come up here with me."

"Please, Gene," she said, "Please climb down."

"Come up and pray with me or I'll jump." He stood and threw a leg over the railing.

"No. No—don't. Don't move." The ladder swayed underneath her first step, and she was terrified that the soft soles of her shoes were going to slip, but Gene helped her onto the platform. She sat next to him.

"Isn't it beautiful?" he asked. They could count the glow of houses ringing the top of Laurelton's seven hills, smell the exhaust from the paper factory, taste the sharp cold air of impending autumn. The wail of sirens interrupted them when a line of state troopers passed them by and turned onto New River Road.

"I feel better with you beside me," Gene said.

Well that makes one of us, Charlene thought.

Gene took her hand. She did not withdraw it, not yet.

"Don't jump."

"I won't," he said, "If you'll let me tell my side of things?"

Charlene thought she saw the flare of EMS lights on the horizon, and strained for the sound of a siren, but caught only the roar of a passing semi-trailer. If she could keep him talking, maybe he wouldn't do anything rash. It took every ounce of will for her to eke out a nod.

Gene began to talk. Charlene listened, one hand over her mouth. Sometimes she averted her eyes. Occasionally he heard her draw a long breath, as if her lungs would never fill. When he finished he said, "Now you know it all."

Charlene rocked back and forth, eyes closed.

"Do you think I'm forgiven?" he asked. "Do you really believe that God can love someone like me?"

Charlene fell still, but loosed his hand. "I do. I believe that."

"Then just stay with me a while," he said. "Please."

When TC arrived, he was relieved to see two shadowy figures seated on the catwalk of Holy Yahweh's cross, resting their backs against the painting of the pierced hand of Christ. The call had been about suicide jumpers, but these two—certainly Charlene and Gene—looked like they were sitting on a Ferris wheel. Hell, Gene was even swinging his legs. TC mopped the grit and sweat from his face with a couple tissues, pounded some water, and radioed the ambulance trailing him to fall back and cut off its lights. He couldn't go to Gene armed. The man was a threat to no one but himself, at least while he dangled in midair.

"To hell with regulations," TC muttered, then locked his weapon in the glovebox. He put his nightstick, mace, and handcuffs on the passenger seat, hefted himself out of the cruiser, and approached the foot of the giant cross, hat in hand.

He waved to them, and called up, "How you doing up there?"

Gene ignored him, but Charlene said she was fine, just a little tired. "You up there of your own free will, Mrs. Maddux?"

Charlene said that she supposed so. Gene put a protective hand in front of her and shouted, "Cut the crap, TC. I wouldn't hurt her."

"All right, then." TC leaned against Bobby's abandoned van. "I'd be happy if we could just talk."

"I bet you're happy now, brother," Gene said. "Happy to see me hanging on a cross."

"Why don't you come down here where we can help you?"

"Why don't you come up here and fetch me?" Gene's laughter echoed across the parking lot. "You're nothing but a damn coward . . . a coward and a hypocrite."

"Why's that?" TC asked.

"Because you don't want me to have forgiveness," Gene said. "You hate that."

"I want you to have peace."

"Then come up here," Gene said. "Sit with me."

"If I do that, will you let Charlene come down?"

"If she wants to."

Charlene opened her eyes, and nodded. TC put one hand on the cold, rickety ladder and felt goosebumps rise on his arms. "You know I hate heights, dammit."

Gene laughed. TC began to climb, knees groaning along with the suspension wires. TC eyed the platform and said, "I'm too much weight."

"Aww . . . it'll hold," Gene said. "There were three at Calvary."

"Yeah," TC said, "But they each had their own cross."

Next to Gene, Charlene folded her hands in an attitude of prayer, lips moving. TC hoped it would do some good. He lifted his foot to the last rung, and rested his elbows on the platform.

"You made it," Gene said.

"I believe I'd like to climb down now," Charlene said. Her voice had a tinny, plaintive quality to it, like an old phonograph record.

"Wait—" Gene said. "Will you let me come back home?"

Charlene took a gulp of air, glanced at TC.

"I don't know," she said. "I need to pray about that."

Heat lightning shuddered along the horizon.

"I was doing so good," Gene said. "So good. You loved me."

"I did," she admitted. "And nothing can separate you from the love of God."

"It ain't God leaving me behind." Gene snapped. "It's you."

Charlene breathed, "Yes."

"Do you know how that feels?" Gene demanded.

"I think so—"

The words were scarce out of Charlene's mouth when Gene sprang to his feet, and began to stomp on the wire platform. Charlene wobbled and fell to her knees, grasping at the railing. TC roared a warning, but Gene stomped harder and harder, making the cross and the bloody hand sway and the suspension wires wail. Finally, Charlene screamed, a long howling shriek. When she ran out of air, her voice thinned down to a low, milky cry, then a sob.

"Stop it!" she said, "Stop it!"

Gene stared at her, transfixed.

"You want to hurt yourself, go ahead," Charlene said, "But let me go! I been hurt enough."

"No," Gene said. "Please, no—"

She pushed past him. He tried to catch her hands, but she was already moving down the ladder, escaping.

"God loves you, Gene," Charlene snarled. "But I'm done."

She swung her weight down, forcing TC to tilt his body away from the ladder to let her pass. Hanging by one arm, he felt sick, even sicker when Gene knelt over the portal pleading, "Come back . . . please, come back . . ."

Charlene neither paused nor acknowledged him. When she reached the ground, she staggered a bit, as if stepping off a boat. Gene and TC watched her wave off the EMTs and stride across the yard to the house. A light came on in the kitchen, and then went dark.

"Well," TC said, "That backfired."

"Shut the fuck up, TC." Gene kept his face turned towards the hills. "You gonna arrest me?"

"Not yet." TC crawled into a sitting position. He reached into his pocket and found a handkerchief, then handed it to Gene. "One way or another, you got to come down from here, brother."

Gene drew the handkerchief across his forehead, wincing when it touched a raw patch on his temple. "I got no reason to. Not the way you want."

"Not sure how you know what I want. But you sure got a lot of things to think about."

Gene shrugged. "Wouldn't hurt you to do some thinking either."

"I suppose you might be right."

"You been hanging people from crosses for years."

"That ain't true and you know it."

Gene snorted. "You got no idea what it takes to survive what I been through—"

"What *you* been through?" TC paused. "What about the people you hurt?"

"If I told you about the love and grace of God, you wouldn't believe me, would you?"

"I'd rather you showed it to me."

"I bet you sure would. Don't you worry?"

"About what?"

"About mercy. Mercy!" The words came tumbling out of Gene like a waterfall. "You oughta worry, mister, because the mercy you'll get is the mercy you been given. You don't know nothing about real forgiveness, so you think I don't deserve it. That's why I feel sorry for you, you'll never know salvation. Not so long as you think yourself so righteous that you don't need it. I know better," Gene held TC's gaze. He admitted, "I go to the grave with a millstone on my neck. Every day I ask Jesus to throw it into the sea." Gene tossed the handkerchief down. It unfurled into a flag of soiled white on the grass below them. "Every day it's still there. My sin."

"So it ain't all someone else's fault then after all," TC said. "Well, good."

"You're a hand-washing son of a bitch sometimes, TC."

TC half-wanted to credit his brother the point. On the wind, TC could smell the faint acrid scent of smoke, burnt plastic, and paper wafting over from the fire at Bobby Tanner's. A raindrop landed on the metal, sending up a tiny pinging chime. Another drop splattered on the painting of the Savior's hand. TC only had one card left to play.

"Gene. If you want to jump, I won't stop you. I promise I won't." TC touched his brother's arm, and Gene drew it back. "You got every reason to give up now, don't you?"

"Who are you?" Gene's eyes were wide. His hands gripped the rail.

TC whispered, "Go ahead."

"That'd make it easy for you, wouldn't it?" Gene shook his head. "It's harder to admit I'm forgiven, whether you believe in the love and grace of God, or not."

"I believe."

Gene said, "I'm still redeemed. Even you can't take that from me."

"I never wanted to," TC said. "That's where you've got me all wrong."

The rain was picking up, droplets plopping against the metal platform, leaving quarter-sized splatters that darkened into splotches on the painted sign. TC stared at the painted hand of Christ, its cartoon-like, garish detail. When he looked back at his brother, Gene's face was contemplative, reflective.

"You've got me all wrong, too. But I'm trying. I'm trying to get right."

Acknowledgments

No artist works or creates in isolation, and I would not want to. This book owes a tremendous debt to the expertise and insight of the entire Cornerstone Press team. I owe special thanks to Dr. Ross Tangedal, Director and Publisher; Gavrielle McClung, Editor-in-Chief; and especially Kala Buttke, Managing Editor.

My world and my writing are far better for the love and support of so many people: Erin McGraw, who read draft after draft and whose comments guided and shaped these stories. Jody Kahn, my incredible and loyal literary agent; Lee Martin, who taught me so much about bringing this world to life on the page; David Lynn, who championed my work alongside the whole crew at *The Kenyon Review*, whose workshops and readings and friendships have been integral to my growth as a writer; my dear friends Barbara Kakiris, Erica Hardesty, Angelica de la Torre, and Claire Myree, whose encouragement, editing consultations, and manuscript comments were an invaluable part of making this book. I wish also to extend much gratitude to my gifted, spirited colleagues and compatriots at *BreakBread Literacy Project*: W. David Hall, Crystal AC Salas, and Cara Echols, who remind me again and again why community and friendship and faith are of such value to every artist.

I am ever humbled and grateful for the love and care of my family, ancestors, and creator; the God who has made my wandering, wild, weird life possible, and who let me write this book that I may sing with my spirit, and also sing with my mind. Most of all, thank you to my darling, my husband Brett Fletcher, for everything and for always.

Gratefully acknowledged are the following publications, where earlier versions of stories first appeared: "Nature Preserve" appeared in *The Kenyon Review,* June 2015; "Deprivation of Body, Generosity of Spirit" appeared in *American Literary Review*, Winter 2016; "A Line of Four Silver Maples" appeared in *The Boiler*, May 2016; "Lifeguards" appeared in *The Mississippi Review*, Summer 2018; "Search, Rescue, Recovery" appeared in *Sequestrum*, May 2019.

Jamie Lyn Smith is a writer, editor, and teacher. She earned her BA in English and Theatre from Kenyon College, her Masters in Education from Fordham University, and her MFA in Creative Writing from Ohio State University. Jamie Lyn is the Fiction Editor at *BreakBread Magazine* and a Consulting Editor for the *Kenyon Review*.

Her work has appeared in *The Pinch*, *Mississippi Review*, *Kenyon Review*, *American Literary Review*, *Yemassee*, *Bayou*, and other fine literary magazines. She is currently working on *Hometown*, a novel about millennial crises and the rise of white nationalism in the rural Midwest, for which she received a 2020 Ohio Arts Council Individual Excellence Award.